W9-AGV-868

A Bell *for*

A D A N O

⊓⊔⊓⊔⊓⊔⊓⊔⊓⊔⊓⊔⊓⊔⊓⊔⊓⊔⊓⊔⊓⊔⊓⊔⊓⊔

John Hersey

ALFRED A. KNOPF   *New York*   1944

THIS BOOK HAS NOT BEEN CONDENSED. ITS BULK
IS LESS BECAUSE GOVERNMENT REGULATIONS
PROHIBIT USE OF HEAVIER PAPER.

Copyright 1944 by John Hersey

Published simultaneously in Canada by The Ryerson Press

Foreword

MAJOR VICTOR JOPPOLO, U.S.A., WAS A GOOD MAN. YOU will see that. It is the whole reason why I want you to know his story.

He was the Amgot officer of a small Italian town called Adano. He was more or less the American mayor after our invasion.

Amgot, as you know, stood for Allied Military Government Occupied Territory. The authorities decided, shortly after the happenings of this story, that the word Amgot had an ugly Germanic sound, and they heard that the two syllables of the word, when taken separately, were the Turkish words for the male and female genital organs. So they decided to call it A.M.G. and forget about the Occupied Territory.

That was later, though. When I knew him, Major Joppolo was Amgot officer of Adano, and he was good.

There were probably not any really bad men in Amgot, but there were some stupid ones (and still are, even though the Turkish embarrassment has been taken care of). You see, the theories about administering occupied territories all turned out to be just theories, and in fact the thing which determined whether we Americans would be successful in that toughest of all jobs was nothing more or less than the quality of the men who did the administering.

That is why I think it is important for you to know about Major Joppolo. He was a good man, though weak in certain attractive, human ways, and what he did and what he was not able to do in Adano represented in miniature what America can and cannot do in Europe. Since he happened to be a good man, his works represented the best of the possibilities.

America is the international country. Major Joppolo was an Italian-American going to work in Italy. Our Army has Yugoslavs and Frenchmen and Austrians and Czechs and Norwegians in it, and everywhere our Army goes in Europe, a man can turn to the private beside him and say: "Hey, Mac, what's this furriner saying? How much does he want for that bunch of grapes?" And Mac will be able to translate.

That is where we are lucky. No other country has such a fund of men who speak the languages of the lands we must invade, who understand the ways and have listened to their parents sing the folk songs and have tasted the wine of the land on the palate of their memories. This is a lucky thing for America. We are very lucky to have our Joppolos. It is another reason why I think you should know the story of this particular Joppolo.

America is on its way into Europe. You can be as isolationist as you want to be, but there is a fact. Our armies are on their way in. Just as truly as Europe once invaded us, with wave after wave of immigrants, now we are invading Europe, with wave after wave of sons of immigrants.

Until there is a seeming stability in Europe, our armies and our after-armies will have to stay in Europe. Each American who stays may very well be extremely dependent on a Joppolo, not only for language, but for wisdom and justice and the other things we think we have to offer Europeans.

Therefore I beg you to get to know this man Joppolo well. We have need of him. He is our future in the world. Neither the eloquence of Churchill nor the humaneness of Roosevelt, no Charter, no four freedoms or fourteen points, no dreamer's diagram so symmetrical and so faultless on paper, no plan, no hope, no treaty—none of these things can guarantee anything. Only men can guarantee, only the behavior of men under pressure, only our Joppolos.

Chapter 1

INVASION had come to the town of Adano.

An American corporal ran tautly along the dirty Via Favemi and at the corner he threw himself down. He made certain arrangements with his light machine gun and then turned and beckoned to his friends to come forward.

In the Via Calabria, in another part of town, a party of three crept forward like cats. An explosion, possibly of a mortar shell, at some distance to the north but apparently inside the town, caused them to fall flat with a splash of dust. They waited on their bellies to see what would happen.

An entire platoon ducked from grave to grave in the Capucin Cemetery high on the hill overlooking town. The entire platoon was scared. They were out of touch with their unit. They did not know the situation. They were near their objective, which was the rocky crest not far off, but they wanted to find out what was going on in the town before they moved on.

All through the town of Adano, Americans were like this. They were not getting much resistance, but it was their first day of invasion, and they were tight in their muscles.

But at one of the sulphur loading jetties at the port a Major with a brief case under his arm stepped from the sliding gangway of LCI No. 9488, and he seemed to be wholly calm.

"Borth," he said to the sergeant who followed him onto the jetty, "this is like coming home, how often I have dreamed this." And he bent over and touched the palm of his hand to the jetty, then dusted his palm off on his woolen pants.

This man was Major Victor Joppolo, who had been named senior civil affairs officer of the town of Adano, representing Amgot. He was a man of medium height, with the dark skin of his parents, who were Italians from near Florence. He had a mustache. His face was round and his cheeks seemed cheerful but his eyes were intense and serious. He was about thirty-five.

The sergeant with him was Leonard Borth, an M.P., who was to be in charge of matters of security in Adano: he was to help weed out the bad Italians and make use of the good ones. Borth had volunteered to be the first to go into the town with the Major. Borth had no fear; he cared about nothing. He was of Hungarian parentage, and he had lived many places — in Budapest, where he had taken pre-medical studies, in Rome, where he had been a correspondent for *Pester Lloyd*, in Vienna, where he had worked in a travel agency, in Marseille, where he had been secretary to a rich exporter, in Boston, where he had been a reporter for the *Herald*, and in San Francisco, where he sold radios. Still he was less than thirty. He was an American citizen and an enlisted man by choice. To him the whole war was a cynical joke, and he considered his job in the war to make people take themselves less seriously.

When the Major touched Italian soil, Borth said: "You are too sentimental."

The Major said: "Maybe, but you will be the same when you get to Hungary."

"Never, not me."

The Major looked toward the town and said: "Do you think it's safe now?"

Borth said: "Why not?"

"Then how do we go?"

Borth unfolded a map case deliberately. He put a freckled finger on the celluloid cover and said: "Here, by the Via Barrino as far as the Via of October Twenty-eight, and the Piazza is at the top of the Via of October Twenty-eight."

"October Twenty-eight," the Major said, "what is that, October Twenty-eight?"

"That's the date of Mussolini's march on Rome, in 1922," Borth said. "It is the day when Mussolini thinks he began to be a big shot." Borth was very good at memory.

They started walking. The Major said: "I have lost all count, so what is today?"

"July tenth."

"We will call it the Via of July Ten."

"So you're renaming the streets already. Next you'll be raising monuments, Major Joppolo, first to an unknown soldier, then to yourself. I don't trust you men who are so sentimental and have too damn much conscience."

"Cut the kidding," the Major said. There was an echo in the way he said it, as if he were a boy having been called wop by others in school. In spite of the gold maple leaf of rank on the collar, there was an echo.

The two men walked up the Via Barrino. There was nobody in the street. All the people had either fled to the hills or were hiding in bomb shelters and cellars. The houses of this street were poor grey affairs, two-storey houses of grey brick, with grey shutters, all dusted over with grey dust which had been thrown up from bomb craters and shell holes. Here and there, where a house had been hit, grey bricks had cascaded into the grey street.

At the corner of the third alley running off the Via of October Twenty-eight, the two men came on a dead Italian woman. She had been dressed in black. Her right leg was blown off and the flies for some reason preferred the dark sticky pool of blood and dust to her stump.

"Awful," the Major said, for although the blood was

5

not yet dry, nevertheless there was already a beginning
of a sweet but vomitous odor. "It's a hell of a note," he
said, "that we had to do that to our friends."

"Friends," said Borth, "that's a laugh."

"It wasn't them, not the ones like her," the Major
said. "They weren't our enemies. My mother's mother
must have been like her. It wasn't the poor ones like her,
it was the bunch up there where we're going, those
crooks in the City Hall."

"Be careful," Borth said, and his face showed that he
was teasing the Major again. "You're going to have your
office in the City Hall. Be careful you don't get to be a
crook too."

"Lay off," the Major said.

Borth said: "I don't trust your conscience, sir, I'm ap-
pointing myself assistant conscience."

"Lay off," the Major said, and there was that echo.

They passed a house which had been crushed by a
naval shell. The Major said: "Too bad, look at that."

Borth said: "Maybe it was a crook's house, how can
you tell? Better forget the house and concern yourself
with that." He pointed into an alley at some horse dung
and goat dung and straw and melon seeds and old
chicken guts and flies. And Borth added: "No question
of guilty or not guilty there, Major. Just something to
get clean. You've got some business in that alley, not in
that house there."

"I know my business, I know what I want to do, I
know what it's like to be poor, Borth."

Borth was silent. He found the seriousness of this Major Joppolo something hard to penetrate.

They came in time to the town's main square, which
was called Piazza Progresso. And on that square they
saw the building they were looking for.

It was a building with a look of authority about it.
This was not one of those impermanent-looking, World's-

Fair-architecture Fascist headquarters which you see in so many Italian towns, buildings so up to the moment in design that, like airplanes, they were obsolete before they were ever finished. This was an old building, made of stone. At its second floor it had an old balcony, a place of many speeches. This building had served kings before Fascists and now was about to serve democracies after them. In case you couldn't recognize authority in the shape of the building, there stood, in embossed bronze letters across the front, the words *Palazzo di Città*.

There was a clock tower on the left hand front corner. On top of the tower there was a metal frame which must have been designed to hold a bell. It was baroque and looked very old. But there was no bell.

On the side of the clock tower big white letters said: *"Il Popolo Italiano ha creato col suo sangue l'Impero, lo feconderà col sua lavoro e lo difenderà contra chiunque colle sue armi."*

The Major pointed and said: "See, Borth, even after our invasion it says: 'The Italian people built the Empire with their blood, will make it fruitful with their work and will defend it against anyone with their arms.'"

Borth said: "I know you can read Italian. So can I. Don't translate for Borth."

The Major said: "I know, but think of how that sounds today."

Borth said: "It sounds silly, sure."

The Major said: "If they had seen any fruit of their work, they would have fought with their arms. I bet we could teach them to want to defend what they have. I want to do so much here, Borth."

Borth said: "That sounds silly too. Remember the alley, clean up the alleyway, sir, it is the alley that you ought to concentrate on."

The Major walked across the Piazza up to the big black door of the Palazzo, put his brief case down, took a piece of chalk out of his pocket, and wrote on a panel of the door: "Victor Joppolo, Major, U.S.A., AMGOT, Town of Adano."

Then both men went inside and up some marble stairs, looking all around them as they climbed. They took a turn and went through a door marked *Podestà*. The office on the other side of that door took Victor Joppolo's breath away.

In the first place, it was so very big. It must have been seventy feet long and thirty feet wide. The ceiling was high, and the floor was marble.

After all the poverty which had shouted and begged in the streets, this room was stiflingly rich. The furniture was of a heavy black Italian style which seemed to be bursting with some kind of creatures half man and half fruit. The curtains were of rich brocade, and the walls were lined with a silken stuff.

The door where the men came in was near the southwest corner of the room. To the right of it a huge table stood, with some maps and aerial photos on it which had been left behind by the officers of an American regiment, who had used the room as a command post early in the morning. There was an incongruous bundle of Italian brooms in the corner. The south wall had a double white door in the middle, and on either side a huge sofa bound in black leather. Then on the opposite side, facing the street and giving onto the place of speeches, there were two big French doors.

Scattered along the wall and pressed against it, as if frightened, were a heavy table, several throne-like chairs of various sizes, another couch and, in the far corner, a white stone statue of a saint. She, besides being decently swathed in a marble scarf, had a piece of American signal corps telephone wire wound around her neck on its way from the nearest French door to the desk, where a field phone had evidently been set up. To the left of the door there was a tremendous bookcase with a glass front, beyond it an enamel washstand with a big stone pitcher beside it, and then a weirdly ornate upright piano.

Up to the right, over the two sofas, there were huge pictures of Italy's King Victor Emmanuel and his Queen, facing each other in sympathetic misery. On the outside wall there was a picture of Crown Prince Umberto, smiling at everything that happened in the room. Over the Saint of the Telephone there was a photograph of Princess Marie José of Belgium, Umberto's wife, dressed as a Red Cross nurse. Above the bookcase there was a great dustless square where a picture had been but was not now.

All this, both the heavy furniture and the ironic pictures, seemed placed there merely to press the eye toward the opposite end of the room, toward the biggest picture in the room, a romantic oil of a group of men pointing into the distance, and especially toward the desk.

The scale of everything in that room was so big that hugeness in the desk did not seem unnatural. It was of wood. On either end there were wooden bas-reliefs of fasces and of the phrase Anno XV, for the fifteenth year of Fascism, or 1937, when the desk was presumably made. Under the desk there was a wooden scrollwork footstool.

"Say," said Major Joppolo, "this is okay."

"Looks like that office of Mussolini's," Borth said. "Come to think of it, you look quite a lot like Mussolini, sir, except the mustache. Will it be okay with you to be a Mussolini?"

"Cut the kidding," the Major said. "Let's look around."

They went out through the white door at the end of the room and walked through several offices, all of which were crowded with desks and files and bookcases.

The files had not been emptied or even disturbed. "Good," said Borth, "lists of names, every one registered and all their records. It'll be easy for us here."

The Major said: "What a difference between my office and these others. It is shameful."

All Borth said was: "Your office?"

When the two went back into the big office there was an Italian there. He had evidently been hiding in the building. He was a small man, with a shiny linen office coat on, with his collar buttoned but no tie.

The small Italian gave the Fascist salute and with an eager face said in Italian: "Welcome to the Americans! Live Roosevelt! How glad I am that you have arrived. For many years I have hated the Fascists."

The Major said in Italian: "Who are you?"

The little man said: "Zito Giovanni. I have been well known as anti-Fascist."

Major Joppolo said: "What do you do?"

Zito said: "I greet the Americans."

Borth said in an Italian which was heavily accented: "Idiot, what was your job before the disembarkation?"

Zito said: "Zito Giovanni, usher in the *Palazzo di Città*, native of Adano."

Major Joppolo said: "You were the usher here?"

"Every day from eight to eight."

"Why did you work for the Fascists if you hated them?"

"I have hated them many years, I am well known as anti-Fascist, I have lived under a great suspicion."

The Major said: "Usher, I love the truth, you will find that out. If you lie to me, you will be in very serious trouble. Do not lie to me. If you were a Fascist, you were a Fascist. There is no need to lie."

Zito said: "One had to eat, one had to earn a living. I have six children."

10

Major Joppolo said: "So you were a Fascist. Now you will have to learn to live in a democracy. You will be my usher."

The little Zito was delighted.

The Major said: "Do not salute me that way."

Zito bowed and said: "The fascist salute, no sir."

Major Joppolo said: "Do not bow. There is no need to grovel here. I am only a Major. Borth here is a Sergeant. Are you a man?"

Little Zito was getting very mixed up. "No sir," he said cautiously. Then he saw by the Major's expression that he should have said yes, and he did.

The Major said: "You may greet me by shaking my hand. You will greet Sergeant Borth in the same way."

Borth said, and his expression showed that he was teasing the Italian: "First I will find out if he's a dangerous Fascist."

Little Zito did not know whether to laugh or cry. He was frightened but he was also flattered by these men. He said: "I will never lie to you, Mister Major. I am anti-Fascist, Mister Sergeant. I will be usher here."

Major Joppolo said: "Be here at seven o'clock each morning."

"Seven o'clock," said Zito.

A brief burst of machine gun and rifle fire echoed from distant streets. Zito cringed.

Borth said: "You are perhaps a man but you are also frightened."

Major Joppolo said: "Has it been bad here?"

Zito started jabbering about the bombardments and the air raids. "We are very hungry," he said when he had cooled down a little. "For three days we have not had bread. All the important ones ran away and left me here to guard the Palazzo. The stink of dead is very bad, especially in the Piazza San Angelo. Some people are sick

11

because the drivers of the water carts have not had the courage to get water for several days, because of the planes along the roads. We do not believe in victory. And our bell is gone."

Major Joppolo said: "Your bell?"

Zito said: "Our bell which was seven hundred years old. Mussolini took it. It rang with a good tone each quarter hour. Mussolini took it to make rifle barrels or something. The town was very angry. Everyone begged the Monsignor, who is the uncle of the Mayor, to offer some church bells instead. But the Monsignor is uncle of the Mayor, he is not the sort to desecrate churches, he says. It meant we lost our bell. And only two weeks before you came. Why did you not come sooner?"

"Where was this bell?"

"Right here." Zito pointed over his head. "The whole building tingled when it rang."

Major Joppolo said to Borth: "I saw the framework for the bell up on the tower, did you?" Then he added to Zito: "That is your reason for wanting us to have come sooner, is it?"

Zito was careful. "Partly," he said.

Borth said: "Usher, if you were a good Fascist you would be able to tell me why there is a big blank space up there on the wall over which there used to hang a picture. It is easy to see by the square of dust that there was a rather large picture there."

Zito smiled and said: "The picture does not exist. It has been destroyed."

Borth said: "You are not hiding it in the basement? You are not afraid that the Americans will be driven out by your German allies and that your leader will return some day and see the square of dust on the wall and ask questions?"

Zito said: "It is destroyed, I swear it. I cannot lie before the Mister Major."

12

Major Joppolo said: "Usher, what is that big picture over my desk?"

This was where the little Zito told a beautiful lie. The picture was of a group of men in antique costume. One of them, by expression of face, position in the picture and by the accident of being the only one in the sunlight of all the men, was obviously their leader, and he was pointing out the side of the picture to the left.

Zito thought quickly and said: "That, Mister Major, is Columbus discovering America."

Zito smiled because it was a beautiful lie. Major Joppolo did not discover for three weeks that the picture was really a scene from the Sicilian Vespers, that bloody revolt which the Sicilians mounted against a previous invader.

Now Major Joppolo said in English more or less to himself: "It's a nice picture, I wonder how old it is, maybe it's by somebody famous."

The Major went to the desk, pulled out the high-backed chair and sat in it, carefully putting his feet on the scrollwork footstool.

Borth said: "How does it feel, Duce?"

The Major said: "There is so much to do, I hardly know where to begin."

Borth said: "I know what I must do. I've got to find the offices of the Fascist Party, to see if I can find more records. May I take the Mister Usher and look for the Fascio?"

"Go ahead, Borth," the Major said.

When the two had left, Major Joppolo opened his brief case and took out some papers. He put them in a neat pile on the desk in front of him and began to read:

"INSTRUCTIONS TO CIVIL AFFAIRS OFFI-CERS. *First day:* Enter the city with the first column. Cooperate with C.I.C. in placing guards and seizing records. Place all food warehouses, enemy food dumps, wholesale food concerns, and other major food stocks under guard. Secure an estimate from local food distributors of the number of days of food supplies which are on hand or available. Make a report through channels on food situation in your area. See that the following establishments are placed under guard or protection: foundries, machine shops, electrical works, chemical plants, flour mills, breweries, cement plants, refrigeration plants, ice plants, warehouses, olive oil refineries, sulphur refineries, tunny oil mills, soap manufacturing plants, and any other important establishments. Locate and make available to port authorities all known local pilots. . . ."

And the list went on and on. When he had read three pages, Major Joppolo looked at his wrist watch. It was eleven thirty. Almost half of this first day was gone. He took the sheets of instructions up from the desk and tore them in half, and tore the halves in quarters, and crumpled up the quarters and threw them into a cane wastebasket under the desk.

Then he sat and stared out the nearest French door into the empty street for a long time. He looked tired and defeated.

He stirred and reached into his brief case again and took out a small black loose leaf notebook. The pages were filled with notes on his Amgot school lectures: notes on civilian supply, on public safety, on public health, on finance, on agriculture, industry, utilities, transportation, and all the businesses of an invading authority. But he passed all these pages by, and turned to the page marked: *Notes to Joppolo from Joppolo.*

And he read: "Don't make yourself cheap. Always be accessible to the public. Don't play favorites. Speak Italian whenever possible. Don't lose your temper. When plans fall down, improvise. . . ."

That was the one he wanted. When plans fall down, improvise.

Plans for this first day were in the wastebasket. They were absurd. Enough was set forth in those plans to keep a regiment busy for a week.

Now Victor Joppolo felt on his own, and he no longer looker tired. He got up briskly, went out onto the balcony and saw that there were two flagpoles there. He went back in, reached in his brief case and pulled out two flags, one American, the other British.

He tucked the Union Jack under his arm as he walked out again, felt for the toggles on the American flag, mounted them on the halyard on the left-hand flagpole, and raised the flag.

Before the flag reached the top of the pole there were five Italians in the Piazza. Before he had the British flag attached to the halyard on the right-hand pole, there were twenty. By the time he had both flags up, forty people were shouting: *"Buon giorno, buon giorno, Americano."*

He waved to them and went back into his office. Now he was happy and quick.

He took up his brief case again, reached in and pulled out a pile of proclamations. He took them over to the table by the door, set the leftover maps and photos aside, and arranged the proclamations in order on the table. While he was on his way back to his desk, there was a knock on the door.

"Come in," he said in Italian.

The door opened. A man came in whose appearance was vaguely familiar to Major Joppolo. The Major realized later that he had seen, not this man, but several who looked just like him, in bad American movies. He was the type of the second-rate Italian gangster, the small fellow in the gang who always stood behind the boss and who always took the rap. He had the bald head, the weak mouth. He had a scar across his cheek. His eye was furtive and he had the appearance of being willing but in need of instructions.

He said in English: "You pull up a flag. War's a finish here in Adano, huh?"

The Major said: "Yes, who are you?"

The Italian said: "I'm from a Cleveland, Ohio. I been here a three year. You got a work for me?"

Major Joppolo said: "What's your name?"

The Italian said: "Ribaudo Giuseppe. In a Cleveland, call a me Joe."

Major Joppolo said: "What can you do?"

Ribaudo said: "I'm a good American. I'm a hate these Fascisti. I could do a good a job for you."

Major Joppolo said: "If you're such a good American, why did you leave the States?"

Ribaudo said: "I'm a kick out."

"Why?"

"I'm a no passport."

"How'd you get in, then?"

"I got a plenty friends in a Cleveland and a Buffalo."

"What did you do in the States?"

"Oh, I work a here, work a there."

Major Joppolo was pleased with Ribaudo for not trying to lie about his illegal entry and repatriation. He said: "Okay, I'll hire you. You will be my interpreter."

"You don't a speak Italian?"

"Yes, but there'll be other Americans here who don't, and I may need you for other things, too. Do you know these people well, do you know who's for us Americans and who's against us?"

"Sure, a boss, I help a you plenty."

"All right, what did you say your name was?"

"Ribaudo Giuseppe, just a Joe for you."

"No, we're in Italy, I'll call you Giuseppe here. Just two things now, Giuseppe. You've got to be honest with

16

me; if you're not, you'll be in bad trouble. The other is, don't expect me to do you any favors I wouldn't do for anyone else, see?"

"Oh sure, a boss. You don't a worry."

"Now tell me, what does this town need the most?"

"I could a go for a movie house, a boss."

"No, Giuseppe, I mean right now."

"Food, a boss. Food is a bad now in Adano. Three days a lot a people no eat a nothing."

"Why is that, because of a shortage of flour?"

"No, everyone been a scared. Baker don't a work, nobody sell a pasta, water don't a come in a carts. That's all, a boss."

"How many bakers are there in town?"

But before Giuseppe could answer this question, there were two simultaneous knocks on the door, one strong, and one weak.

"I open 'em up, a boss?" Giuseppe was at least eager.

"Please, Giuseppe."

Giuseppe hurried down the long room and opened the door. Two men almost tumbled in. Both were well dressed, and had neckties on. One of them was quite old. The other was very fat and looked forty. They hurried down the room, and each seemed anxious not to let the other get ahead of him.

The old one said in English, with a careful British accent: "My name is Cacopardo, at your service, Major. I am eighty-two. I own most of the sulphurs in this place. Here Cacopardo is sulphur and sulphur is Cacopardo. I wish to give you advices whenever you need of it."

The fat one, who seemed annoyed with Cacopardo for speaking first, said in English: "Craxi, my name. I have a telegram."

Major Joppolo said: "What can I do for vou gentlemen?"

17

Cacopardo said: "Advices."

Craxi said: "Telegram."

Cacopardo said: "The Americans coming to Italian countryside need some advices." The old man looked straight at Giuseppe the interpreter and added: "I wish to advise you to be careful, in Adano are many men who were illegal in America, some men too who were condemned to the electrical chair in Brooklyn of New York."

Major Joppolo, seeing Giuseppe's embarrassment, said: "Giuseppe, I want to speak to the priest of the town. Will you get him for me?"

Giuseppe said: "Which priest, a boss?"

Cacopardo said: "In Adano are thirteen churches, Major, and in some, like Sant' Angelo and San Sebastiano, are two or three priests."

Major Joppolo said: "Which church is best?"

Cacopardo said: "In churches ought not to be good and bad, but Sant' Angelo is best, because Father Pensovecchio is best of all."

Major Joppolo said to Giuseppe: "Get him for me, will you?"

"Yes, a boss," Giuseppe said, and left.

When he had left, Major Joppolo said to Cacopardo: "Is this Giuseppe fellow not to be trusted?"

Cacopardo bowed and said: "I mention only the electrical chair, I am not one to name the names."

Major Joppolo spoke sharply: "You said you came to advise me. I must know about this Giuseppe. Is he to be trusted or not?"

The old man bowed again and said: "Giuseppe is a harmless one."

The fat Craxi was growing very annoyed that Cacopardo was getting all the attention. He said: "I have a telegram. Please to deliver."

Major Joppolo said: "This isn't a telegraph office.

There's a war going on. Do you think we have nothing better to do than deliver telegrams?"

Craxi was apologetic. "I am anti-Fascist. I have a telegram. You are the one who can deliver it." And he pulled out from his pocket a piece of ruled paper, folded four ways and pinned shut with a safety pin. He handed the paper to the Major, who put it down on his desk, to the disappointment of Craxi.

The Major said: "You say you've come to advise me. Then tell me, what does this town need the most right now?"

This time the fat Craxi got there first: "To eat," he said, "much to eat."

Cacopardo said: "It needs a bell more than anything."

Craxi said: "Foolishness, a bell. More than anything, to eat is necessary."

Cacopardo said: "The town needs its bell back. You can always eat."

Craxi, who had been rather slighted in the conversation anyhow, now became quite angry. "*You* can always eat, you Cacopardo," he said. "You have a million lira, you sulphur. You can eat, but not all the people here can eat." And he turned to the Major: "To eat here is most necessary, more necessary than any bell."

Cacopardo broke into furious Italian: "Fat one, you think only of your stomach. The spirit is more important than the stomach. The bell was of our spirit. It was of our history. It was hung on the tower by Pietro of Aragona. It was designed by the sculptor Lucio de Anj of Modica."

Craxi said in Italian: "People who are very hungry have a ringing in their ears. They have no need of bells."

Cacopardo said: "By this bell the people were warned of the invasion of Roberto King of Naples, and he was driven back."

Craxi said: "People with malaria also have a ringing in their ears."

Cacopardo said: "The bell warned the people when Admiral Targout brought his French and his Turks to this place in 1553 and burned many homes and churches, and all that was left in the Church of Our Mother was the little silver crucifix which you will see now in the Church of San Angelo."

The Major said in Italian: "We have no time for this recital. I wish to know what things are pressing and must be taken care of at once."

Craxi said: "I have spoken. Food is the first thing."

Cacopardo said: "The bell must be taken care of at once. The bell did not warn us of *this* invasion, or we would have been in the streets with flowers to welcome you."

Craxi said: "I needed no bell. I was on the beach to welcome the Americans. My woman was with me, the formidable Margherita, and my seven children. We were on the beach in spite of the shooting, to greet the Americans. But what did my children shout? They did not shout: 'We miss the tinkling of the bell.' They shouted: '*Caramelle! Caramelle!*' They were hungry. They wanted candy. I myself, who had had enough to eat as it happens, shouted for cigarets, not for the pealing of a bell."

Borth and the usher Zito came back. Borth said: "It's nifty, Major. All the records are intact. They tell everything. There are lists of anti-Fascists and lists of those who were enthusiastic and the others who were lukewarm. There's a dossier on each important person. It's perfect. Who are these guys?"

Cacopardo said: "Cacopardo is my name, at your service, sir. Cacopardo is sulphur and sulphur is Cacopardo."

Borth said: "I remember that name. In the records it says Cacopardo's crazy."

Craxi said: "That is true. He thinks that bells are more important than food."

Borth turned on Craxi in mock anger: "And who is this?"

Craxi was apologetic again: "I am anti-Fascist. Craxi. I believe in food for the moment."

Major Joppolo said: "They are arguing which is more important, food or restoring the bell. Since we obviously can't do anything about the bell just now, food is our concern."

Craxi looked very proud of himself, but Cacopardo turned to Zito and said: "We will leave this matter to the son of Rosa who was the wife of Zito. What do you say, small Zito, do you consider the food or the bell more important?"

Surprisingly Zito said: "I think the bell."

Major Joppolo was interested by this. He leaned forward and said: "Why, Zito?"

Zito said: "Because the tone of the bell was so satisfactory."

"No," said Cacopardo, "it is because of the history of the bell. When the bell spoke, our fathers and their fathers far back spoke to us."

Even Craxi was swept into this argument. "No," he said, "it was because the bell rang the times of day. It told us when to do things, such as eating. It told us when to have the morning egg and when to have pasta and rabbit and when to drink wine. in the evening."

Zito said: "I thing it was the tone which mattered. It soothed all the people of this town. It chided those who were angry, it cheered the unhappy ones, it even laughed with those who were drunk. It was a tone for everybody."

21

Giuseppe came in bringing the priest. Father Penso-vecchio was grey-haired and cheerful, and as he approached the group around the Major's desk he made a motion with his right hand which might have been interpreted either as a blessing or as a Fascist salute.

After the introductions, Major Joppolo said to the priest: "Father, we are speaking of the old bell which was taken away."

Father Pensovecchio said: "That is the disgrace of this town. I have in my church a bell which is just as loud as the one which was taken away, though not so sweet and much younger and altogether meaningless as a bell. Any other bell would have done as well in my belfry. I wanted to send my bell. But the Monsignor would not permit it. The Monsignor is the uncle of the Mayor. He has reasons for doing the things he does — " Father Pensovecchio crossed himself, indicating that the things which the Monsignor did were somewhat ugly; " — but in this case I believe he was wrong."

Major Joppolo said: "Why was this bell important, then?"

The priest said: "This bell was the center of the town. All life revolved around it. The farmers in the country were wakened by it in the morning, the drivers of the carts knew when to start by it, the bakers baked by it, even we in the churches depended on that bell more than our own bells. At noon on the Sabbath, when all the bells in town rang at once, this bell rose above all the others and that was the one you listened to."

Cacopardo, who was old enough not to have reverence for anything, said: "I think that even the Monsignor regrets the sending away of the bell, because he used to regulate his fornication by it."

Craxi said: "I am certain too that he regulated his eating by it, as everyone else did."

Major Joppolo said to Borth in English: "We'll have

to try to do something about getting another bell."

Borth said: "It's ridiculous. There are lots of things more important than this bell. Get them some food and don't forget that alleyway."

Major Joppolo said: "All the same, the bell is important to them." And he said then in Italian: "Thank you for telling me about the bell. I promise you that I will do all I can to get another bell which will have some meaning as a bell and will have a good tone and its history will be that it was given to you by the Americans to take the place of the one which was taken away by the Fascists to make gun barrels."

Cacopardo said: "You are kind."

Craxi said: "I thank you, Mister Major, and I kiss your hand."

Major Joppolo said: "You what?"

Cacopardo the historian said: "He meant no offense. It is an old custom here. Once the important people make us kiss their hands, and later when the actual kissing became too much of a bother, it became the habit merely to mention the kissing, as if it had been done."

Craxi said: "I meant no offense, Mister Major. I am anti-Fascist."

Major Joppolo said: "It appears that everyone in this town is anti-Fascist. Well, we will see about the bell. Now I wish to speak alone with the priest. Zito, you may stay. You are my usher. Giuseppe, you may stay. You are my interpreter."

Craxi said: "Mister Major, the telegram."

Major Joppolo said: "I will try to send it."

Craxi mentioned the kissing again, and turned to go.

When the others had gone, Major Joppolo said to Father Pensovecchio: "Father, I wish to tell you that the Americans want to bring only good to this town. As in every nation, there are some bad men in America.

23

It is possible that some Americans who come here will do bad things. If they do, I can assure you that most of the Americans will be just as ashamed of those things as you are annoyed by them."

Father Pensovecchio said: "I think we will understand weakness in your men just as we try to understand it in our own."

Major Joppolo said: "Thank you. Father, I have been told that you are the best priest in Adano."

The priest said with quite honest modesty: "I am here to do my duty."

Major Joppolo said: "Therefore I should like to ask a favor of you. You must feel perfectly free to refuse me if you wish. I should like to ask you to say a few words before your mass tomorrow morning about the Americans. I shall leave it to you to say what you wish, if you will merely add that there are certain proclamations which the Americans have posted which ought to be read."

Father Pensovecchio said: "That I can easily do."

Major Joppolo said: "I myself am a Catholic. If you will have me, I should like to attend your mass."

The priest said: "It will be a pleasure to have you." Major Joppolo was glad that he did not say it would be an honor.

Major Joppolo said: "I shall see you tomorrow then."

Father Pensovecchio said, just to make sure: "At the Church of Sant' Angelo. It is by the Piazza of that name. At seven in the morning. Until then, son."

When the priest had left, Giuseppe said in his brand of English: "You doing okay, a boss. All you got a do now is fix a food."

"Yes," said Major Joppolo, "food. We'll go to the bakeries. But first, do you have a crier here?"

Giuseppe said to Zito in Italian: "What is the name of the crier? Did he run into the hills with the others?"

Zito said: "No, he is here. Mercurio Salvatore. He is here. Only, Mister Major, he does not always say exactly what you tell him to say. He will say the general meaning of what you wish, but he will change it some. Even if you write it down, he will change it some."

Major Joppolo said: "Will you get him, please, Zito? I want to send him out to tell the people to read the proclamations."

Zito went. Major Joppolo said to Giuseppe: "We will go to the bakeries, then we will post the proclamations."

Giuseppe said: "Okay, a boss."

Major Joppolo looked down at his desk and saw Craxi's telegram. He undid the safety pin and unfolded the paper and read:

"To Franklin D. Roosevelt, Capitol Building, Washington D.C. *Fremente di gioia per la libertà da molto tempo attesa che i vostri valorosi soldati anno dato alla città d'Adano stop vi prego accettare i sentimenti sinceri della mia gratitudine e riconoscenza.* Antifascista Giovanni Craxi fu Pietro."

"Giuseppe," the Major said, "let's see how good you are as an interpreter. Now, this is for President Roosevelt. You must make it as eloquent as you can. What does it say?"

"To Franklin D. Roosevelt and a so forth," said Giuseppe. "Crazy with joy because of a liberty so long time awaited which your brave a soldier have a give to a town of Adano. What's a *stop?*"

"That's just the end of a sentence, Giuseppe."

"End a sentence. I beg a you accept a sincere sentiments of my gratitude and a recognition. Signed a this Craxi. You going to deliver it, a boss?"

"Sure," the Major said, "the President will be glad to hear."

Chapter 2

MERCURIO SALVATORE, crier of the town of Adano, took a little time to show up, because he had to get into his uniform. His face was happy when he did arrive, because he had thought that his crying days were over. Having been a voice of Fascism for seventeen years, he thought that the newcomers would not want his loud shouts. He had taken his uniform off and hidden it in the house of Carmelina the wife of Fatta. He had then awkwardly paraded himself in civilian clothes and the people, having seen him in uniform for seventeen years, laughed at him.

"Where is the crier?" they asked each other in his presence.

"He has disappeared into the clothes of Fatta which do not fit him," they shouted, and laughed.

Therefore Mercurio Salvatore was happy and grateful when he presented himself to Major Joppolo. "I am glad to be able to serve you and I kiss your hand," he said in his husky voice. Indoors he had learned to speak in a kind of whisper, because he knew the strength of his throat.

Mercurio Salvatore stood before Major Joppolo in tawdry splendor. He wore a uniform of the eighteenth century, and looked as if he had been wearing it ever since that time. The tights had once been blue, but now they were a light and spotted grey. The turn-back coat had once been lined with red silk, but the silk had long since fallen apart, and Carmelina the wife of Fatta had replaced it with sacking from the sulphur refinery which she had dyed purple with grape juice, but the purple had washed out in the first few rains, so that now Mer-

curio Salvatore was a walking advertisement of Cacopardo Sulphur.

If Major Joppolo had been any other American officer, he would have laughed outright at Mercurio Salvatore. But Major Joppolo was so intent on what he
wanted to say that he scarcely noticed the uniform.

He said: "Crier, I have a job for you. I must explain
this to you: the Americans are different from the Fascists. They are different in many ways. For this reason
there will be quite a few changes in Adano. I hope that
they will be changes for the better."

Mercurio Salvatore said: "Yes, Mister Major," to show
that he would remember every word of it.

The Major said: "In order to explain some of these
changes, I am going to post at various prominent places
around the town a number of proclamations, which will
make everything clear. All I want you to do is to tell the
people to read these proclamations. Impress on them
that the penalties for not obeying the proclamations will
be severe. That is all."

Mercurio Salvatore looked disappointed. "That is not
much to shout," he said.

Major Joppolo said: "Shall I name a new crier?"

Mercurio Salvatore said quickly: "Oh no, Mister
Major, I will make something beautiful of what you
have said."

Major Joppolo said: "The proclamations will be
posted before five o'clock this afternoon."

Mercurio Salvatore said: "Yes, Mister Major," and
left.

He picked up his drum where he had left it outside
the Major's office. Ordinarily he had made his first cry
in the Piazza Progresso, right in front of the Palazzo,
but this time he was self-conscious, and wanted to have
a few tries before crying within earshot of the Major.

Therefore he went first to the park opposite the Cathedral.

He rolled his drum long and sharply.

He saw Italian heads pop out of windows and several people sauntered out of their doors and leaned against the walls. Because of the number who had run to the hills, he could see that he would not have so good an audience this time as he had often had in the past. But at least he had an audience, and that was more than he had expected an hour before.

He took a deep breath. Blood and wind rushed into his throat, and his throat roared: "Well, you laughed. But you can see that Mercurio Salvatore is still your crier. The Americans are friends of Mercurio Salvatore. The Americans wish to be your friends, too. You have been expecting the Americans for some time, but did you expect the changes which would come after the Americans? Did you know that they were going to change many things after they came? Did you know that they were going to change practically everything except the crier? Well, your crier is here to tell you this."

Mercurio Salvatore, who had not had any shouting to do for nearly six weeks, was somewhat winded. He rested a moment, took another deep breath, and roared: "Your crier has not time to enumerate all these changes. They will be listed for you in certain proclamations which the crier's friends, the Americans, will post around the town later today, at about five o'clock. Read these proclamations, people! Obey them, or your new friends will be angry and will behave like the Fascists who are now, thank Jesus, hiding in the hills. Choose, people: friendliness or Fascist punishments! Read the proclamations and choose. I have cried."

And Mercurio Salvatore hitched his drum around back and marched off to the high ground in front of the ruins of the Castello San Giovanni. There he gave the drum another sharp roll and waited for people to get their ears outdoors.

Now Mercurio Salvatore filled his lungs and bellowed: "Opposite me I see Carmelina the wife of Fatta in front of her house. I also see the lazy Fatta leaning against the wall of his wife's house. The crier wishes to thank Carmelina for storage of his uniform during the difficult time of the invasion. He wishes also to address a few words to her lazy husband. It is unfortuate, lazy Fatta, that you never learned to read. It is too bad that you were too slothful to memorize the letters of the alphabet. This afternoon you would have had a chance to read of the changes which our friends the Americans intend to bring about here in Adano.

"You could have read the proclamations which our friends will post, Fatta. You would not have had anything to lean against while reading because the proclamations will be posted on the walls upon which you depend. The hour of the reading, that is to say about five o'clock, would have been bad for you, because it is the hour when you are overcome with energy and are able to lift a bottle of wine to your lips.

"But the others will read, Fatta. They will learn that the Americans are our friends. They will learn of the changes. They will know what to do. They will avoid the punishments. For them, Adano will be a new town, and life will be different. For you, it will be the same. You will do wrong, and you will be punished. Adano will still be a place of fear.

"Look at the lazy Fatta, people! Do not be like him. Read the proclamations. Acquaint yourself with the new Adano! I have cried."

And Mercurio Salvatore moved the drum around behind him and marched off to the several other places convenient for shouting, and in his own way he told the people about the changes which were to come.

Chapter 3

FATHER PENSOVECCHIO could not remember when so
many people had come to the Church of Sant' Angelo.

Perhaps he had not been without guile when he had
mentioned to ten or twelve people, quite casually, that
the American Major would be in Church in the morning,
and that he himself had something to say about the
Americans. What priest does not like to have many listeners? What priest is not proud of the jingle of many
coins in the box, coins for the Mother Church?

Father Pensovecchio, in the wildest hopes of his cas-
ual remarks, had not expected a crowd to equal this.

The priest knew that he would repent later of his
pleasure in drawing so many people away from the
twelve other churches of the town, but for the moment
he let his pleasure have rein. He stood in the front and
nodded to the ones he had not seen in his church for
years. There was Margherita the wife of Craxi, from
the Church of San Sebastiano. There was old Bellanca
the Notary, from the Church of the Orphanage. There
was Afronti the loud-voiced cartman and Basile the fat
cartman, both from the Church of the Benedettini.
There were people standing up in the side aisles. There
was even the lazy Fatta, who had not gone to any church
since the baptism of his last baby in 1935, leaning
against one of the pillars.

It was a pleasure, certainly it was a pleasure, to have
so many come to the Church of Sant' Angelo.

But now Father Pensovecchio had a thought which
made him very uneasy. What if the Mister Major should
not come? Think of the shame. Think of how the other
priests would laugh. Think how this vanity, this large

crowd, would complain. Think of how his own-faithful would flock on later Sundays to the other churches. Think of preaching to empty pews.

It was already five minutes past seven. The senior acolyte had already whispered in his ear that it was time to begin the mass. And the Mister Major had not come.

The Mister Major, at that moment, was sitting in his office having a breakfast of fruit and discussing with Borth and with the usher Zito, who never went to church, the matter of the bell. Major Joppolo sat with his feet on the huge desk eating fruit, Borth sat on the end of the desk also eating, and the little Zito stood at attention in front of it, not eating but wishing he were.

Borth said: "As usual, Major, you're letting your heart run your head. Forget the bell and clean up the alleyway. This is too sentimental, this bell business."

The Major said to Zito in Italian: "Zito, exactly when was the bell taken away?"

Zito said promptly, without having to think it over: "June the fourteenth. It was the day when Mayor Nasta fined me three thousand lira for leaving my Atlas open at the page of North America. I used to read my Atlas in dull hours outside the door there, and that day I left it open at North America. Like everyone else, Mayor Nasta knew the Americans were coming here. It made him nervous. He thought I was mocking him. He fined me six months' pay."

The Major said: "June fourteenth, almost exactly a month."

Zito said: "It took them two days to take the bell down. They used six sets of block and tackle. Then it took another day to crate it. They started taking it down on the eleventh and finally carted it away on the fourteenth."

31

The Major said: "The fourteenth," but he was thinking. He was thinking so hard that he had forgotten all about going to church.

In the Church of Sant' Angelo, meanwhile, Father Pensovecchio was growing frantic. Most of the heads in his crowd, his lovely crowd, kept turning toward the door instead of facing the silver crucifix which survived the fire of 1553.

He could see that he was about to lose their attention altogether. They would all get up and go out in the streets looking for the Mister Major in a few minutes. There was nothing to do but begin.

It was most irregular, but Father Pensovecchio knew that much was at stake for his Church, so he did not begin with the beginning of the mass, but instead began to recite the war litany, hoping in this way to kill time until the Major appeared.

His voice began to drone: *"Regina pacis ora pro nobis . . ."*

In his office Major Joppolo was saying his thoughts out loud — in Italian, because he wanted to test them out on Zito: "We could get another. But we could not just get any bell. It would have to be a bell with meaning. Zito, what would you think if we got you a Liberty Bell?"

Zito said: "What is this Liberty Bell?"

Major Joppolo said: "It is the bell the Americans rang when they declared themselves free from the English."

Zito said: "The idea is good. But would America be willing to part with this bell for Adano?"

Major Joppolo said: "We would have to get a replica, Zito."

Zito said: "Describe this bell."

Major Joppolo said: "Well, it hangs in a tower in Philadelphia, I think. It is of bronze, I think. It has a large crack near the bottom from its age. You can see it on postage stamps, and many companies use it for their trade mark."

Zito said: "How is the tone?"

The Major said: "That would depend on the replica, Zito. We could get one with good tone, I think."

Zito said: "I do not like that about the crack. A bell should not crack just because it is old. Our bell was seven hundred years old, but it had no crack. I doubt if America is that old, to say nothing of your bell."

Major Joppolo said: "Perhaps it cracked because we rang it so hard to announce our liberty."

Zito said: "I do not think the people of Adano want any liberty that has a crack in it. No, they would not like that business of the crack. Maybe you could get us a Liberty Bell without a crack."

The Major said: "But without a crack it wouldn't be a Liberty Bell. That is the way the real Liberty Bell is, Zito."

Zito said: "Then Adano will not want your Liberty Bell. Adano would not like to have a crack, I am sure."

Major Joppolo said: "Then that's out." And he thought some more.

In this time Father Pensovecchio finished the war litany and looked nervously at the door, but the Mister Major still did not come. He beckoned to the senior acolyte and whispered in his ear. "Send out the little Ludovico and tell him to look for the American Major and bring him here. Do this for Sant' Angelo and tell him to hurry."

The Priest then began the supplication: *"Propitius esto, parce nobis, Domine. Propitius esto, exaudi nos, Domine."* Father Pensovecchio mentioned the sins, nervously watching the door, and the people chanted the responses, turning their heads between responses.

"Ab ira tua," said the priest.

"Libera nos, Domine," said the people.

"*A subitanea et improvisa morte,*" said the priest, fearing the non-appearance of Major Joppolo much more than sudden and unexpected death.

"*Libera nos, Domine,*" said the people, twisting and turning.

"*A spiritu fornicationis,*" said the priest, not even thinking of the Monsignor, as he usually did at this point.

"*Libera nos, Domine,*" said the people, peeking at the door.

The senior acolyte drew the small acolyte named Ludovico aside and took him out into the vestry and told him to do what the priest had said. Little Ludovico, not having been outside the Church at seventeen minutes past seven on a Sunday morning for most of the years he could remember, rushed out into the sunlight without thinking to ask where the American Major would be found, or, for that matter, who the American Major was, and why there was an American Major in the town, and whether there was any connection between the loud bangs one had heard for several days and the presence of the American Major.

So little Ludovico sat down on the steps of the Church of Sant' Angelo in the sun and wondered about these things.

In his office Major Joppolo said: "They took the bell away on the fourteenth of June. That is a month less two days. That is not so much time. Considering how things are done in our Army, perhaps not much has been done with the bell. Where was it sent, Zito?"

Zito said: "To the provincial government at the town of Vicinamare."

Major Joppolo said: "Perhaps it got no farther. Perhaps the bell is still sitting in its crate in Vicinamare."

Zito grew exicted: "Do you think that is possible?" he asked.

The Major said: "It is possible. We must find out."

And he took a piece of foolscap from his brief case and began a letter:

"To: Lt. Col. R. N. Sartorius, C.A.O., Vicinamare. Prov. of Vicinamare.

"From: Major V. Joppolo, C.A.O., Adano, Prov. of Vicinamare.

"Re: Bell belonging to town of Adano.

"Undersigned would very much appreciate your initiating investigation of records of provincial government of Vicinamare to see if you can trace. . . ."

The service in the Church of Sant' Angelo was taking a most unusual course. Having completed the supplication, Father Pensovecchio started reciting the Litany of Saint Joseph. It was the longest litany he could think of offhand, and he repeated the words without any sense of their meaning.

"Joseph, most valiant, Joseph, most obedient, Joseph, most faithful, mirror of patience, lover of poverty, model of workmen, ornament of the domestic life, guardian of virgins, safeguard of families. . . ."

Suddenly Father Pensovecchio broke off. He had had an idea. He beckoned again to the senior acolyte and whispered in his ear: "Have old Guzzo ring the bell."

"*Now*, father?"

"Do as I say. Hurry."

And then the priest resumed in his hollow voice: ". . . consolation of the poor, hope of the sick, patron of the dying, terror of the demons."

And the people responded: "Pray for us."

The priest said: "Protector of the Holy Church."

The people were just in the middle of responding: "Pray for us," when they heard a stroke of the bell over their heads. Worship had to stop while the bell rang, for its vibrations shook the whole church.

In his office Major Joppolo blotted the letter and folded it.

Borth said: "What time is it?"

The Major looked at his wrist watch. "Seven twenty-six," he said.

Borth said in Italian: "Zito, if you are such an expert on bells, what is that one ringing for at seven twenty-six in the morning, and all alone?"

Zito said: "It is strange. That is a church bell. From the tone I would say it was the bell of Sant' Angelo."

"Sant' Angelo!" The Major jumped up. "My God," he said, "I promised the priest I would come, I got thinking about the old bell. Zito, show me the way. Run, Zito, this is terrible."

Zito darted out of the door, and the Major ran after him.

Three or four idlers, sitting in the morning sun, thought it was undignified of the new American Major to chase little Zito through the streets. If he wanted to punish Zito, why did he not send some of his military police after him? It did not suit his office to chase Zito himself, especially since it was unlikely that he would catch him.

The acolyte Ludovico, sitting on the steps of the Church, looked up in amazement at the little Italian being chased by the American officer. He wondered why the American was chasing the Italian. The pair had run right past Ludovico up the steps of the Church before it occurred to him that perhaps this was the American Major. He got up quickly and ran up the steps after the two of them, but he was too late; they were already inside the door.

The entire congregation stood up. The lazy Fatta even stopped leaning against the pillar. There was a considerable amount of murmuring, and as the Major walked up the aisle, puffing and wiping the sweat from his face, many people whispered: "Kiss your hand, kiss your hand."

36

In spite of the fact that he never went to church, Zito was impressed by the huge crowd and decided to stay. He followed the Major forward.

Father Pensovecchio, whose face was also covered with perspiration, as if he too had run a great distance, smiled and turned from ashen white back to his normal pink.

As soon as he saw a pew that was not too crowded, Major Joppolo genuflected and slid into it. Zito imitated him and squeezed into the same pew, which was too crowded then.

The congregation seated itself. Father Pensovecchio cleared his throat. His confidence, which had very nearly left him, was now very much in evidence. He had his crowd and he had his Major.

The priest stepped forward, outside the communion rail. "I have a word to say to all of you on this occasion," he said.

Then he paused, waiting for quiet. The Church fell into absolute silence, except for the hard breathing of Major Joppolo and Zito.

"My children," said Father Pensovecchio, "everything that is done in this world is done by God. God gave us wheat, and God gave us the sun. God also sent us these liberators after all our prayers. Our prayers are now answered, and the men we feared are now in the hills, which God in his infinite forgiveness gave them to hide in."

Major Joppolo couldn't help noticing two heads in the pew right in front of him. One was the head of a man, and it was bald. The other was the head of a woman, and it was blonde.

"But as you all know," Father Pensovecchio said, "no matter who you have as the authorities, you must obey the law. If a child does something wrong, he is punished by his father. If you do something wrong, you'll be pun-

37

A BELL FOR ADANO

ished by your new governors. When you go out from
mass, read the proclamations which your new governors
have posted, and spread the word that all must obey
them exactly as they are written."

By tilting his head a very little bit, Major Joppolo was
able to find out that the bald head belonged to his interpreter, Giuseppe. He was not able, by tilting, to see the
face of the blonde head, but he could see that the hair
was arranged fastidiously, with no loose strands.

"If you remember," said the priest, "we were told
that Americans attacked priests and attacked and killed
women, and were all Protestants. But right here now
is an American of Italian descent who is attending
mass, and is just as reverent as you are toward the
Church of Sant' Angelo. He is a very busy man. He is so
busy that he had to run all the way to church, and even
then was somewhat late. But we are very glad to have
him here." Father Pensovecchio spoke with feeling.
"We are glad that he is one of us. Because of this man, I
believe that the Americans are my friends. You must believe the same thing, my children."

Major Joppolo noticed that the skin of the neck be-
low the blonde hair, though clean, was quite dark, and
he wondered whether the hair was naturally blonde. He
wondered about this off and on during the mass which
followed.

After mass he left quickly, to avoid the embarrassment he knew would result from mingling too much
with the crowd. He took time only to tell Giuseppe that
he had a little interpreting for him to do that afternoon,
and to look into the face of the blonde.

Chapter 4

On the fifth day of the invasion a babel stood in line in front of the shop of the baker Zapulla. There were many women, mostly dressed in black, and a few men. They talked in loud voices, each clamoring for an audience.

"He has a furious energy," said Maria Carolina the wife of the noisy cartman Afronti. "He told small Zito to report for work at seven each morning. Zito thought that no official would be up that early. Zito went to work at seven and a half, and the Mister Major told him that there would be a new usher unless the old usher could wake up on time in the morning."

Carmelina the wife of the lazy Fatta, who was at the head of the line, said loudly: "It would be pleasing if Zapulla the baker got up on time in the morning so that the bread would be ready."

Zapulla the baker, black with the wood coke of his oven, came out to the front of the shop and roared: "Zapulla the baker has been up since four in the morning. If Zapulla the baker hears remarks, he is liable to go back to bed and let the bread burn up."

"Do you remember," said Margherita the fat Craxi's formidable wife, "do you remember how the Mayor Nasta used to hold office hours from noon until one, each day, the hour when we were all busy with our children? And how we had to apply in writing to see him? And how we had to wait ten days? And how he would treat us when we did see him? Now it is different. You can walk in any time all day." She paused. "He stands up when you enter," she said impressively.

"Is that so?" said Laura Sofia, who was not the wife of anyone and at her age was not likely to be ever. "I think I shall go and see him."

"On what pretext?" jibed Maria Carolina, wife of the noisy cartman Afronti. "To make eyes at him?"

"Oh," said Laura Sofia, "I have my complaints, just like the rest of you — even if I haven't litters of children grunting like pigs on my floor."

Carmelina, wife of the lazy Fatta, said: "My children are hungry. It would be nice if they could get their bread on time."

From the depths of his shop Zapulla the baker shouted: "The children of certain people may stay hungry if certain people do not hold their tongues."

Mercurio Salvatore, crier of the town of Adano, was near the end of the line, but even though he toned his voice down to his conversational whisper, the whole line could hear him when he said: "I wish to tell you something. I asked him if I could listen to my radio.

"He said: 'Why not, crier?'

"I asked him what station I would be permitted to listen to. I asked: 'Should it be the Radio of Algiers, or should it be the Radio of London which is called B.B.C.?'

"He said: 'Reception here is best for Radio Roma. Why don't you listen to the one you can hear the best?'

"I said: 'Can you mean it? Radio Roma is anti-American. It has nothing but slander for the Americans.'

"And he said to me: 'Crier, I love the truth, and I want you to love it too. You listen to Radio Roma. You will hear that it is three fourths lies. I want you to judge for yourself and to want the truth. Then perhaps you will want to listen to the other broadcasts which you cannot hear quite so clearly.'"

Margherita, the formidable wife of Craxi, said: "Have you listened, crier?"

Mercurio Salvatore said: "I have listened. I could detect only one lie yesterday, but it was a big one. Radio Roma said that Italian forces in the city of Vicinamare threw back three vicious Allied attacks. We all knew that Vicinamare was in the hands of the Americans late on the first day of the disembarkation."

Carmelina the wife of the lazy Fatta said: "It will be late on the fifth day before we get bread from this baker Zapulla."

Zapulla was impolite to Carmelina because of what she said. He came forward and threw a piece of woodcoke at her head and roared: "Silence, whore!"

The woodcoke missed Carmelina's head, but hit the stomach of the formidable Margherita. She advanced, shaking her large fists. Zapulla went back to his ovens, as if he had not noticed where his woodcoke went.

At this angry moment, Gargano, Chief of the Carabinieri, came up to the line. This man was called by the people The Man With Two Hands, because of his continuous and dramatic gesturing. He was, he seemed to think, an actor, and he could not say two words without gesturing with both hands. He possessed and exercised all the essentially Italian gestures: the two forefingers laid side by side, the circle of thumb and forefinger, the hands up in stop position, the sign of the cuckold and of the genitals, the salute to the forehead with palm forward, the fingertips of the two hands placed tip to tip, the fingers linked, the hands flat and downward as if patting sand, the hands up heel to heel and pulled toward the chest, the attitude of prayer, the pointing forefinger of accusation, the V as if for victory or smoking cigarets, the forefinger on the chin, the rolling of the hands. All, he used them all.

When he approached the line, everyone thought that he was coming to restore order. There was a question in some people's minds whether he still had authority, but they did not feel that this was a good time to flout the question. It would be better to see first whether he made any arrests.

He did not make any arrests. He merely went up to

41

Carmelina, wife of the lazy Fatta, and squeezed between her and the door of Zapulla's shop, and stood there. The people could see that he was merely taking his place at the head of the line to wait for bread.

Carmelina, who was annoyed by having had wood-coke thrown at her, said truculently: "Mister Gargano, you were Chief of the Carabinieri under the old regime, and that entitled you to stand at the head of the line. I am not sure that you are still Chief of the Carabinieri."

Gargano said: "I am the Chief," and he made a kind of Fascist salute with both hands.

Carmelina said: "I doubt it. Where is the proof?"

Gargano said: "See my uniform," and he ran his two forefingers from his shoulders to his knees.

Carmelina said: "That is no proof. The Americans do not care how we dress. I could dress as a rabbit and the Americans would not arrest me."

Gargano said: "Woman, stop your shouting, or I will arrest you," and he gripped his own left wrist with his own right hand, signifying arrest.

Carmelina said: "Where is your authority?"

Margherita the formidable wife of Craxi said: "I believe that this man is still Chief, since the Mister Major is keeping many Fascist scoundrels in office until they prove themselves bad. But I do not believe that under American law he has the right to go to the head of the line. That is where I think you are right, Carmelina."

Gargano said: "I have always come to the head of the line. I shall continue to do so," and he ran his forefinger along the length of the line until he came to the head, where he stood, then he pointed the finger at the ground.

Maria Carolina, the wife of the noisy cartman Afronti, who had once been arrested by Gargano, shouted: "You have no right, Two-Hands. The Americans would not permit it." This was the first time Gargano had ever been called Two-Hands to his face. He did not understand the reference.

Gargano stepped out of the line. "Who questions my right?" he roared, and he pounded one clenched fist on the other clenched fist.

Carmelina, wife of the lazy Fatta, standing right beside him, startled him by whispering in his ear: "I question it, Two-Hands."

Up to this time Zapulla the baker, standing in the front of his shop, had been torn between the two authorities, the old and the new. But he was so annoyed with Carmelina for having prodded him that he now said: "Arrest her, Mister Chief, if you have any courage."

Up to this time Gargano the Chief, somewhat unsure of his ground, had been trying to think of a way of retiring gracefully. But now his manhood, as well as his authority, was challenged. He moved toward Carmelina and said: "Woman, you are under arrest."

Carmelina shouted: "Keep your two active hands off me, Gargano."

Zapulla said: "Will you let this woman shriek down your courage?"

Gargano clapped his hands on Carmelina. She screamed. All up and down the line women shouted: "Out with the Fascist Chief of Carabinieri. Out with Two-Hands. Out with men who push themselves to the head of a line ahead of women who have been waiting three hours."

Gargano dragged Carmelina off screaming and kicking, and the anti-Gargano, anti-Fascist screams in the line grew louder and louder. Even Mercurio Salvatore, although as crier he was more or less an official and should have remained neutral or even taken the side of Gargano, raised his huge voice in a careful shout: "Down with injustice!"

When Gargano pulled Carmelina into Major Joppolo's office, she was still screaming. But the Major jumped to his feet and said sharply: "Silence, shrew," and she fell quiet at once.

"What is this all about?" the Major asked.

Gargano said: "This woman questioned my authority," and he pointed at her with both forefingers.

Carmelina said: "There is more to it than that."

Major Joppolo said: "Your authority to do what, Gargano?"

Carmelina shouted: "To push his way to the head of the line in front of Zapulla's bread shop."

Gargano said: "It is a privilege the officials of the town have always enjoyed."

Major Joppolo said: "Is that so?"

Gargano said: "I charge this women with disturbing the peace and questioning authority." Gargano was shrewd in saying this, for he saw that things were going against him, and now he had put the matter on an official rather than a personal basis. The Major would have to decide the case officially.

The Major decided with a speed which dazzled Gargano. He decided that the woman was right but that he could not say so, because if he did the Chief would never regain his authority, and the Major wanted to keep him in office. Therefore he said: "I sentence this woman to one day in jail, suspended sentence. Let her go, Gargano, and gather all the officials of Adano for me at once."

When Carmelina got outside, she ran straight back to the bread shop. The bread was not ready yet, and the people gave her back her place at the head of the line and shouted to her: "What happened, Carmelina? What did they do to you?"

Carmelina told what had happened and she said: "Did you ever hear of such a light sentence in Adano? I

44

believe in my heart that the Mister Major thought I was right. And what was the meaning of assembling the officials? I believe that he was for me."

In the Major's office, the officials gradually assembled. Some were held-over Fascists, some were new appointments to take the place of Fascists who had fled to the hills. In whispers, and with ample gestures, Gargano described to them the humiliation he had suffered, until Major Joppolo said: "Silence, please."

The officials drew up in a circle around the Major's desk. The Major stood up.

"I want you to be my friends," he said. "As my friends, I will consider it my duty to tell you everything I think, for we do not want Adano to be a town of mysteries and a place of suspicion.

"Adano has been a Fascist town. That is natural, because the country was Fascist, therefore the town was also. But now that the Americans have come, we are going to run the town as a democracy.

"Perhaps you do not know what a democracy is. I will tell you.

"Democracy is this: democracy is that the men of the government are no longer the masters of the people. They are the servants of the people. What makes a man master of another man? It is that he pays him for his work. Who pays the men in the government? The people do, for they pay the taxes out of which you are paid.

"Therefore you are now the servants of the people of Adano. I too am their servant. When I go to buy bread, I shall take my place at the end of the line, and I will wait my turn. You too must behave now as servants, not as masters. You must behave as the servant of the man without shoes just as much as of the baron. If I find that any of you are not giving the type of service that I desire, I shall have to remove you from office.

"Remember: you are servants now. You are servants

of the people of Adano. And watch: this thing will make you happier than you have ever been in your lives."

Chapter 5

AT last, one afternoon a day or two later, the Major found himself alone with Giuseppe, the interpreter.

"Giuseppe," he said, "do you have natural blondes in this part of the country?"

Giuseppe winked understandingly: "Oh, so you got a pair a eyes after all, eh, boss?"

Major Joppolo said coolly: "Do you have natural blondes in this part, Giuseppe?"

Giuseppe said: "I guess a you seen the blonde in a church last Sunday, next a me, eh, boss?"

"Answer my question, interpreter," the Major said severely.

"Okay, a boss," Giuseppe said. "Blondes is natural in a north. Down here not so natural, a boss."

"I thought not."

The Major went back to his work. Giuseppe puttered around a bit and then said: "Boss."

Major Joppolo answered with some temper. "What is it, Giuseppe?" he said.

"If a boss is a lonely, Giuseppe could fix a good date, maybe my friend a blonde."

Major Joppolo said: "Who said I was lonely?"

Giuseppe said: "Boss, I been in a Cleveland, Ohio, I can tell what's a like to be a long way from a home. Fellow gets a lonely."

The Major said: "I haven't got time to be lonely. I'm busy now, Giuseppe."

"Yes, a boss."

46

After he had worked a while, Major Joppolo said: "Giuseppe."

"Yes, a boss."

"Who was this blonde you were with last Sunday?"

This time Giuseppe was very careful to keep his face grave, and to answer the Major's question precisely. "Name's a Tina. She's a daughter a Tomasino. He's a fisherman."

"A fisherman? Is he a good fisherman?"

"Best a one, a boss."

"Do the other fishermen respect him?"

"Sure, he's a best a one."

"Good, I want to see him, Giuseppe."

This time Giuseppe couldn't resist winking. "Sure, a boss, I get it."

Major Joppolo said: "Bring him in to see me early next week, Giuseppe. I want to start the fishermen going out again. It'll supplement the food supply. By the first of next week, I'm sure I can get permission from the Navy."

Chapter 6

I DON'T know how much you know about General Marvin. Probably you just know what has been in the Sunday supplements.

Probably you think of him as one of the heroes of the invasion; the genial, pipe-smoking history-quoting, snappy-looking, map-carrying, adjective-defying divisional commander; the man who still wears spurs even though he rides everywhere in an armored car; the man who fires twelve rounds from his captured Luger pistol every morning before breakfast; the man who can name you the hero and date of every invasion of Italy from the beginning of time; the father of his division and the beloved deliverer of Italian soil.

You couldn't be blamed for having this picture. You can't get the truth except from the boys who come home and finally limp out of the hospitals and even then the truth is bent by their anger.

But I can tell you perfectly calmly that General Marvin showed himself during the invasion to be a bad man, something worse than what our troops were trying to throw out.

By the time it was nine days old, the invasion was developing very successfully. The American beachheads were secure. One heavy counterattack had been thrown back, and our troops began to go ahead all along the line.

On the ninth morning, General Marvin was driving along the road toward Vicinamare and came to the town of Adano. From time to time along the road his driver had had to slow down behind the little Italian two-wheeled carts of the countryside until traffic from the opposite direction had gone by. Then he passed the carts.

As they passed each cart, General Marvin waved his riding crop in such a way as to indicate that the cart should move over. Since there was nothing to move over into except the ditch, which at intervals along the road expanded into tank traps, the carts never did move over. The General grew angrier and angrier.

Now it happened that just as he came to the Fiume Rosso, or Red River, just before Adano, the General's armored car was obliged to slow down for a cart which meandered along right in the center of the road.

The General stood up in his car and shouted in his deep bass voice (you've read about that voice in the supplements; it's famous; one writer said it was like "a foghorn gone articulate"): "Goddam you goddam cart get off the road!"

Unfortunately the driver of the cart was one Errante Gaetano, who earlier that morning had sold three dozen eggs to American soldiers at fourteen times the proper price, had immediately sunk most of his profits in the wine of his friend Mattaliano, and was now sleeping a deep and happy sleep on the seat of his cart. At this particular moment, he was dreaming about eating the nicer parts of a fish nine feet long. Naturally he did not pay much attention to the voice of General Marvin, no matter how famous the voice, because he could not hear it.

General Marvin roared at his driver: "Blow your horn. Blow that bastard off the road."

The driver, a nice boy from Massachusetts, put the heel of his hand on the horn button against his own wish. He was in no hurry, and knew that no matter how fast they went, he would only have to wait when they got wherever they were going.

The mind of Errante did not react to the horn, even though the horn was something urgent called a klaxon. The cart kept right down the middle of the road, inasmuch as Errante's mule was a cautious creature, just as wary of ditches on the right as of ditches on the left. This was a quality in his mule of which Errante Gaetano often boasted to his friends. "Give me none of your lopsided mules," he would say, "give me a mule with a sense of the middle."

This sense was going to be the undoing of his mule just now, because General Marvin's face was beginning to grow dark, and some veins which have never been described in the supplements began to wriggle and pound on his forehead.

"I've had enough of these goddam carts," the General shouted. He was standing up in the car, waving his riding crop around. "Do they think they're going to stop the goddam invasion with goddam carts?"

Errante slept beautifully. He was coming to the grey part of the fish just under the ribs. It melted in the mouth of his dream. There was, however, a sound of thunder in the distance which made him think perhaps he had better cover the fish and finish eating the nice parts after the rain.

General Marvin roared: "Do these goddam Italians think they're going to stop a bunch of goddam tanks with a bunch of goddam wooden carts?"

Colonel Middleton, the General's Chief of Staff, and Lieutenant Byrd, his aide, could see the violence coming. Lieutenant Byrd looked back along the road, but he couldn't see any bunch of goddam tanks. The only thing he could see that was being held up besides the General's armored car was one seep, or amphibious jeep, which did not seem to be in a hurry.

Here it came. General Marvin shouted: "Throw that goddam cart off the road."

Colonel Middleton, Lieutenant Byrd and the nice boy from Massachusetts ached all over with regret, but there was nothing they could do but obey. The driver stopped the car. The three got out. They held up the seep and enlisted the puzzled aid of three sergeants who were riding in it.

The six men walked forward on the road with the bass aria of General Marvin's anger ringing in their ears. They did not have to run to catch up with the cart. That was another thing about the mule of Errante Gaetano which he liked. The mule was good and slow. "It is a mule," he would say, "which lives in the present and is not always trotting into the future."

Errante stirred in his sleep. The thunder of his dream was the most beautiful and most continuous thunder he had ever heard.

The six men surrounded the cart. Colonel Middleton reached up to waken Errante, but the General's roars grew louder. "What are you doing?" he bellowed. "I told you to throw the goddam thing off the road."

"We were just going to wake this fellow up and get him off first," Colonel Middleton shouted back, but the shout was weak because he knew what the answer would be.

"Serve him goddam right. Throw him too. Just turn the whole goddam thing over."

There was no protest from any of the six men. The only thing which was said was muttered by Lieutenant Byrd: "The old man hasn't been getting enough sleep lately."

Colonel Middleton went to the head of the mule and guided it to the side of the road. He directed the other five men to take positions on the left side of the cart and to lift together when he gave the signal.

General Marvin roared: "Come on, get it over with. What a bunch of goddam softies. Get it over with."

Colonel Middleton gave the signal. The five men lifted.

In his dream, Errante rose up above the nine-foot fish and soared off into space. The sensation was extremely pleasant.

The cart groaned. The right wheel crumbled around the axle. The whole weight of the thing rolled slowly over into the ditch, and the shafts twisted and upset the mule, and the mule, which had always feared ditches on the right, screamed to find itself falling into what it had feared.

Errante hit the earth hard. He woke up, but what with his dazedness, his drunkenness, his surprise and his natural stupidity, he was unable to do anything except roar wordlessly.

General Marvin was still roaring too. "Serve the sonofabitch right," he shouted. "Holding up traffic. Trying to stop the goddam invasion."

A new fury rushed up the General's cheeks. "Middle-ton," he shouted, "shoot that goddam mule."

Colonel Middleton's blood froze. He shouted back: "Do you think it's wise, sir?"

The General shouted: "What's that? Goddamit, what's that?"

Colonel Middleton knew it was hopeless but he shouted again: "I said, do you think it is wise, sir?" Try-ing to reason with any man, and especially with this man, at two hundred feet and the top of one's lungs was not rewarding work.

The General shouted: "Goddamit, Middleton, you trying to stop the goddam invasion too? Do what I say."

So Colonel Middleton pulled out his Colt and fired three shots into the head of the screaming mule.

All this was accomplished before Errante Gaetano was able to shape his roaring into words. He stood there in absolute amazement at the shooting.

General Marvin shouted: "Let's go, goddamit, can't spend all day here."

The men got back into the armored car and the seep. As they started up, General Marvin said: "Got to teach these people a lesson. Take me to the mayor of this goddam town, what is this town anyhow?"

And they drove off, leaving Errante sobbing on the flank of his mule, lying with his arms around the neck of the mule which had had a sense of the middle but no sense of urgency.

The General's armored car pulled up in front of the Palazzo di Città. Lieutenant Byrd ran across the wide sidewalk and up the marble stairs and burst into Major Joppolo's office. He interrupted the Major in the middle of a conversation with Gargano, the Chief of the Cara-binieri.

"General Marvin's downstairs and wants to see you,"

the Lieutenant said. "He's mad as hell, so you better hurry."

"General Marvin," said Major Joppolo, and the tone of his voice was not of delight. Though he had never met the General, he had heard much about him. "I'll be right down."

Lieutenant Byrd turned and ran downstairs. Major Joppolo absent-mindedly arranged the papers on his desk in neat piles. Then he stood up and walked out of his office. Half way down the marble stairs he realized that he was out of uniform. He had heard stories of General Marvin's insistence on correct uniform. Here he was in pink pants and khaki shirt, when he was supposed to be in woolens. He was suddenly very frightened, and he turned and began walking up the stairs again, trying to figure out what to do, how to get into proper uniform.

Colonel Middleton ran to the foot of the marble stairs and shouted up: "Hey, you, what do you mean by keeping the General waiting?"

"Yes, sir," Major Joppolo said. "Be right down."

There was nothing to do. He ran down the stairs.

When Major Joppolo reached the armored car, the General was sitting with his left arm raised in front of him, glaring at his wrist watch.

Major Joppolo saluted. General Marvin roared: "One minute and twenty seconds. You've been keeping me waiting one minute and twenty seconds. Goddamit, do you think I have all day to wait for you? Who are you, anyway?"

"Major Joppolo, sir, senior civil affairs officer, town of Adano, sir."

General Marvin remembered the cart and was apparently too angry even to notice Major Joppolo's uniform. "Goddamit, Major, these Italian carts are holding up our whole goddam invasion. Keep them out of this town. Don't you let another cart come across that bridge back there into this town. What the hell is this town, anyway?"

"Adano, sir, town of Adano."

"Adano. Keep the goddam carts out of this town, you hear me?"

"Yes, sir, I'll take care of that right away."

The General shouted: "Right away? That's not soon enough for me."

"Sir, I'll go right up and call the M.P.'s and tell them about it."

"That's not soon enough. Goddamit, I want action. No more carts. Adano's the name of this town, remember that, Middleton, Adano. No more carts at all, Major, do you understand? Goddamit, what are you standing there gawking about? Action, goddamit. Let's get going, let's get out of here, do you think I have all day?"

And before Major Joppolo could even salute, the armored car had roared away.

By the time he reached his desk again, Major Joppolo realized what the consequences of keeping the carts out of town would be. He knew very well how essential they were to the life of the place.

With a heavy heart he cranked his field telephone, asked for Rowboat Blue Forward, got the ear of Captain Purvis, head of the M.P.'s in Adano, and ordered him in the name of General Marvin, to keep all carts out of Adano, to stop them at the bridge on the east and at the sulphur refinery on the west.

Then he called for Zito, his usher, and asked him to assemble all the officials of the town in his office.

Gargano, the police chief, was already there. Of the others old Bellanca, the honest notary whom Major Joppolo had chosen to be his mayor, came in first. He had sad eyes, the eyes of a man who had suffered for his honesty through several years of corruption. He wore a black coat and black tie, as always. Behind Bellanca the others trooped in: D'Arpa, the weasel-like vice mayor; Tagliavia, the maresciallo of finance; the bull-voiced Mercurio Salvatore, crier; Major Joppolo's unctuous little municipal secretary, Panteleone; the pear-shaped Signora Carmelina Spinnato, volunteer health officer; Rotondo, lieutenant of Carabinieri; and the man who was charged with keeping the streets clean, the cleanest man in town, Saitta, in a white suit.

When they were all in, Major Joppolo stood at his desk and said: "I have promised to tell you every important thing which the American authorities decide to do in this town. I do not want this to be a town of mysteries. In a democracy one of the most important things is for everyone to know as much as possible about what is going on.

"The American authorities have decided that because of military necessities it will no longer be possible for mule carts to come into the streets of town."

Major Joppolo could see his audience suck in its collective breath. He said: "I am not happy to have to announce this decision. It is because of military necessities. I am sorry. That is all."

The officials of Adano, a comic-looking collection, turned sadly to go. They did not protest. They had learned during the years of Fascism how to swallow their protests. But Major Joppolo could tell that they were not with him, that for the first time in nine days they were against him.

Before the first of them reached the door, Major Joppolo said: "I wish to tell you that I will do all that is in my power to have this unjust order revoked."

And when the comic-looking officials of Adano went out of the door of the Major's office, they were still sad but they were for him.

The Major worried all day about the order and wondered what he could do about it. He slept very badly during the night, because of his worry.

Early in the morning, Zito, the little usher, came up to his desk and said: "Mister Major, there are three men to see you about the carts."

Because it worried him, the Major snapped back angrily at Zito: "What do they want about the carts?"

"That is something they wish to tell you, Mister Major," Zito said. "It is something they did not tell me."

"Well, show them in."

The three Italians were evidently poor but respected men. There was a kind of democracy in their coming to see the Major: they were the chosen delegates of all the cartmen, to argue this thing out.

They all had old, clean coats on, and they all clutched cloth caps in their hands. Zito brought three chairs forward, and they sat in a half circle opposite the Major.

The Major pointed with a fountain pen at one of the men and said in Italian: "You. What is your name?"

The man was about sixty. His hair was pure white but the skin of his forehead, though furrowed, was the skin of a tough young man. He jumped to his feet, twisting his cap in his strong hands, and he shouted: "Afronti Pietro, Mister Major." Then he gave the Major a Fascist salute.

"Speak softly here," the Major said. "I am not deaf." He leaned and spoke to the other two men. "Are you deaf?"

"No, Mister Major," they both said.

"Then speak softly," he said to the strong-voiced man. "What do you desire?"

"I desire," the old man said, trying to keep his voice quiet, "to raise the question of the carts coming into the town of Adano. I desire to tell you, Mister Major, that these carts are most dear to us. I wish to tell you about my cart. It has two wooden wheels, Mister Major — "

56

"I have seen these carts. It is not necessary to describe the carts."

Old Afronti gave the Major another salute. "But have you heard the music which is made by the wheels, Mister Major? The two wooden wheels of my cart sing to me. They do not sing Fascist songs, Mister Major, they do not sing *Giovinezza* or anything to do with marching. You may think this is squeaking, this music, but I can hear what the wheels are trying to sing."

The Major said: "We are concerned here with the question of whether these carts should or should not come across the bridge into Adano. When you waste time with this talk, you are wasting the time of your friends who are waiting outside that door."

Afronti gave another Fascist salute. "One day last summer," he said in a louder voice, "I drove my cart all the way to Gioia di Monti, and all the way the wheels sang a song which was also a prophecy. At the time none of my friends would believe this song, would you, my friends?" And he turned to the other two.

The two nodded their heads, but the expression of their faces was blank because they were thinking of the speeches they were about to make.

Afronti's voice grew louder and louder, as if he were outdoors. "Do you wish to hear this song, Mister Major?"

Major Joppolo said: "No, please come to the point."

Afronti stepped back. He unbuttoned his coat. He held his cap out at arm's length and he sang. It was not exactly a tune he sang, but his voice went up and down, very loud. This is what he sang:

> *"The Americans are coming here, Signor Afronti,*
> *The Americans are very just men,*
> *Especially with regard to carts."*

Major Joppolo said: "Do not joke with me, old man. We have no time for humor this morning. I want to help you if you have something reasonable to ask of me. Come to the point."

Afronti shouted: "The music has stopped. There is no more music."

The Major said: "Please do not shout here. You seem to think that Americans are deaf men. We are not deaf. Do not shout."

Afronti said very softly: "The music has stopped, there is no more music, Mister Major. Thank you, Mister Major." And he sat down abruptly.

The Major lifted his pen and pointed it at the next man. "And you," he said, "your name."

This was a man who seemed a little backward. He was timid in the way he stood up and he did not twist his cap with any enthusiasm, as the others did. His voice was slow and he had to think a long time before he could say his own name. Finally it came out: "Erba Carlo, Mister Major."

"And you desire?"

Erba stopped and thought. His eyes wandered. He looked at the Saint of the Telephone. He looked at the Red Cross badge on the breast of Princess Marie José. He thought and thought, but he could not think what it was he desired. He had forgotten his speech entirely.

After an embarrassing pause, the other two left off thinking about their own speeches and came to the assistance of Erba.

"Tell him," one of them said, "about the water carts."

A look of vast relief came over the face of Erba. "It is about the water carts, Mister Major."

"Yes?"

Erba looked at the huge painting over the Major's head. He studied many details of the painting. But he could not remember exactly what it was about the water carts that he wished to say.

The other of his friends said: "Describe your cart, Erba."

Erba said: "It is big. Outside it is dirty but inside it is clean. It holds water. My friends drink the water."

After this sustained effort, Erba's face was covered with perspiration. At first he looked proud and triumphant, but then he could see another hurdle coming. This time he looked frankly and directly at his friends for prompting.

Major Joppolo was frantic with impatience, but he said: "Yes, my friend, tell me some more about the water cart." This was a quality in the Major that came out time and again: he was always gentle with those who evoked impatience, and he was always impatient with those who begged for gentleness.

"The thirst," said one of Erba's friends, "the great thirst."

Erba turned to the Major with an expression of delight which belied the seriousness of what he was to say. He was delighted because it was all coming back to him now. He said: "You will not let my cart across the bridge. There is no water in Adano without my cart and the other water carts. There is a thirst in Adano. Since yesterday morning at eleven o'clock there is a great thirst. Carmelina who is the wife of the lazy Fatta says that her daughter will die of the thirst. It is all because of the bridge . . . and the carts . . . and the —"

Erba, like the town, had run dry. He turned to his friends. One of them said: "Erba, the proclamation, the matter of being clean."

Erba said: "Oh yes, the proclamation. In one proclamation, Mister Major, I forget the number of the proclamation, there are so many, does the number matter, Mister Major?"

"No, Erba. I am sorry, there are too many proclamations." And the Major turned to Erba's friends, who were a little more intelligent and would understand. "That is the fault of the authorities. I did not wish to post so many proclamations. That is not my fault. I am sorry. The number does not matter, Erba."

Erba said: "The number does not matter. The proclamation says it is necessary to be clean. It says the people must be clean with water, and even the streets must be clean. Our streets, which have been the same since the time of — who was it the time of, Afronti?"

Afronti roared: "Since the time of Pietro of Aragona and of Roberto King of Naples."

Erba said: "The streets have been the same. Now the proclamation speaks of being clean with water. There is much sameness which has accumulated on the streets since the time of those men of whom Afronti speaks. This being clean takes much water. My cart is on the other side of the bridge, Mister Major."

Major Joppolo said: "The cleanliness is very important, Erba. Let us make Adano the cleanest town in the whole province of Vicinamare."

Erba caught the challenge. His eye brightened. "We will do this thing, even if the sameness has piled up since the time of Jesus, Mister Major." Then his eye went dull again. "But my cart is on the other side of the bridge. You have said it may not pass."

The Major said: "Let the next one speak. You. Your name." And he pointed at the third man with his pen.

Erba said: "Thank you, Mister Major."

The third man jumped up. He was quite fat but comparatively handsome. His hair was plastered down with something off the axle of his cart, and his black coat was the newest looking of the four. "Basile Giovanni, Mister Major," he said.

"You wish?"

Basile spoke gravely and slowly. "Mister Major," he said, "the worst of all the things about the carts is the

60

food. You can see, Mister Major" — and he ran his hands down over the size of his belly — "that I am a man who can speak of food with understanding. This matter of the carts does not hurt me. I am like a man with money in the bank, I have something to draw on in hard times. But there are others in Adano who are not so lucky. Galioto Bartolomeo is so thin that you can count the several teeth of his mouth even when his lips are closed. The nine children of Raffaela who is the wife of Manetto have big bellies, but their bellies are big only with the gas of hunger. Shall I name others who are very thin?"

The Major said: "No, go on."

Basile said: "I am the one to tell you about the food and the carts. You have not seen my cart, have you, Mister Major?"

"I may have. I have seen many of them."

Basile said: "I think you would remember my cart. You know how all the carts have pictures painted on the panels of the sides? Scenes of the Saints, scenes of the history of Adano, scenes of the fine accidents we have had in the province of Vicinamare —"

The Major said: "I tell you it is not necessary to describe these carts. I have seen many of them. I am getting sick of the carts."

Basile said: "But Mister Major, you have not seen my cart. On my cart there are four scenes. They are all from the Holy Word, and they are all concerned with eating. There is the miracle of the loaves and fishes. There is the last supper. There is the widow's jar which never emptied no matter how much food she took out. There is the wedding at Cana where the water turned to wine. Now, all the people in all these pictures are fat people. I do not believe that this is sacrilege, even though Jesus himself is fat on my cart. It is simply that I told Lojacono Arturo, who painted the cart, to make all the people fat, like me and my Elisabetta, because

61

mine was a cart for food, to make other people fat and jovial, though they might have a certain amount of hard breathing."

The Major said: "This is a waste of time." But Basile could see, and the other two could see, that the Major was nearly persuaded by this time-wasting talk.

Basile pressed on: "How can I drive my cart now, even in the country? How can I put my fat horse, whose name is General Eisenhower in honor of our deliverer, between the shafts, and put my fat self on the seat, and drive around with my pictures of fat and holy people — when the people of Adano are starving, Mister Major? This fills me with shame, even though I cannot bring the cart into town."

And then, with great craft, Basile said: "There is nothing in all the proclamations, even though it takes you a week to read them, which says that the Americans came to Adano in order to make people die of hunger. And there is nothing in all the proclamations which refers to such things as the dead mule of Errante Gaetano. Why then do we have this thing of the carts?"

The Major said to himself in English: "Damn."

He reached for the field telephone, cranked the handle and said: "Give me Rowboat Blue Forward."

While he waited for an answer, the Major said to Basile gruffly: "Sit down.

"Hello. This Rowboat Blue Forward? Captain Purvis, please. . . .

"Purvis? Joppolo. Listen. . . .

"No, now this is serious, Purvis. This thing about the carts. I've made up my mind. By one sentence General Marvin destroyed the work of nine days in this town. I know it may mean a court martial, but I've decided to countermand his order. What? . . .

"I know I'm taking a hell of a chance, but I've got to do it. We can't let these people starve. . . .

"I have to do it, Purvis. This town is dying. No food can get into the town if the carts don't come. The town depends on the carts for water: there isn't any running water here, you know that. The people can't go out into the fields to work in the morning. Taking carts away from this town is like taking automobiles away from a country town in the States. You just can't do it all at once. People will die. I'm not here to kill people."

Captain Purvis evidently put up an argument.

Finally the Major said: "Purvis, I order you, on my authority, to start letting carts back into the town, beginning now. I take absolute and complete responsibility for countermanding General Marvin's order. . . .

"Listen friend, if we never took chances around here, this place would go right on being a Fascism. All right, the hell with you, it's on my responsibility."

The three cartmen sat through the telephone conversation not comprehending. To judge by their faces they seemed to think that Major Joppolo was devising some punishment for them. They had the habit of fear, and they thought that this man of authority would of course be exactly like the men of authority they had known for so long.

Major Joppolo hung up. He turned to the three cartmen and said: "You may bring your carts into the town."

For a long moment they did not understand. Then they stood up and began shouting and waving their caps.

"We thank you, we thank you and we kiss your hand," they roared.

"Oh, Mister Major, there has never been a thing like this," the fat one named Basile shouted, "that the poor should come to the Palazzo di Città, and that their request should be granted."

"Especially," shouted the loud one named Afronti, "especially without a wait of two to three weeks."

"It was not necessary to write you a letter," Basile shouted.

"The police did not even examine us," roared Afronti.

The slow one named Erba finally got out a sentence. It was one of the few beautiful sentences he ever managed to say, and one of the longest. He said: "When the people come and take water from my cart to drink for their thirst, I shall say to them: 'Thank the Mister Major, my friends.'"

Major Joppolo said: "Get out of here. You are wasting my time and the time of all the people who are waiting outside that door." And he gestured impatiently at the men.

The cartmen went out, shouting and congratulating America.

Chapter 7

THE COMMAND post of the M.P.'s was housed in the Fascio, the one-storey building which had been the headquarters of the Fascist Party. It was simply a string of rooms facing on the Via Dogana, just off the Piazza. The walls of the rooms were covered with pictures of various Fascist heroisms. Each room had a couple of desks, a filing cabinet, three or four uncomfortable chairs, and that was all. The building made a very convenient headquarters for both the M.P.'s and especially for Sergeant Borth's security detail, because the filing cabinets contained complete records on practically everyone in town, both party members and anti-Fascists.

On the morning when Major Joppolo called about the carts, there were three men in the main office of the M.P.'s. Besides Captain Purvis, there were Technical

Sergeant Frank Trapani, who kept Captain Purvis's records and was more or less his secretary, and Corporal Chuck Schultz, who was the M.P. on guard.

Captain Purvis put down the telephone and said: "That Joppolo, I think he's nuts."

Sergeant Trapani said: "What's he done now, sir?"

"Oh, hell," the Captain said, "he's always talking about democracy like it was his mother. He ought to relax and have a little fun. Bet he's never been drunk in his life."

Corporal Schultz said: "He can have this Dago wine." He put his hands over his belly and made a face. "Jesus, last night."

The Captain said: "Besides, he's going to get us all in trouble."

Sergeant Trapani said: "What's he done, sir?"

An Italian stuck his head in the door just out of curiosity.

"Get out of here, damn it, Trapani, tell that wop to get out of here and stay out." Captain Purvis did not speak a word of Italian, and it made him feel frustrated. Trapani told the curious one to move along.

"The carts," Captain Purvis said. "Joppolo has the nerve to tell General Marvin he knows where he can stick the carts, *he* wants them to come back into town."

Sergeant Trapani said: "It wasn't a very wise order in the first place, I think maybe the Major's right."

"Right?" Captain Purvis put his palm against his cheek in a gesture of amazement. "Why hell, man, General Marvin'll shoot him and us too. What do you think this man's army would be like if everybody just did what he wanted and went around countermanding orders every day? We got little enough discipline in our army anyhow without going around ignoring orders, especially from generals." Captain Purvis had been commissioned just eight months. He was very military.

"Yes, sir," Sergeant Trapani said. He knew what to say

65

when his Captain started lecturing on discipline.

"Well, I got my orders," the Captain said. "I got to go out and take the guards off the road by the bridge and the sulphur works. But listen, I'm not going to burn for this guy Joppolo. He's all right, but he's just too serious. Damn it, I'd sure like to see him high just once."

Corporal Schultz said: "Last night, Jesus, I'll never drink that stuff again."

"Listen," the Captain said. "I don't want to get in trouble and you don't either. We got to carry out this order and let the carts back in, but if General Marvin should drive back through this town, we'd all get hung for it. Just to cover ourselves, we'll make out a report saying just what happened, that General Marvin ordered us to keep the carts out, that Major Joppolo countermanded the order. You make it out, Trapani, and send it to G-one of the division."

"Yes, sir." Captain Purvis left.

Sergeant Trapani said to Schultz: "That's a hell of a note, General Marvin's liable never to came back here, and if he did he'd probably never notice the carts. But once you get the thing on paper, it's just a sure way to ruin the Major. And he's so right about these carts anyway."

Corporal Schultz said: "Don't bother me, I got a headache of my own this morning."

Sergeant Trapani rolled a slip of purple paper, off a Fascist pad, into his typewriter. He wrote:

For *Lieutenant Colonel W. W. Norris, G-1, 49th Division.*
From *Captain N. Purvis, 123rd M.P. Company, Adano.*
Subject: *Mule Carts, town of Adano.*
1. *On July 19, orders were received from General Marvin, 49th Division, to keep all mule carts out of the town of Adano. Guards were posted at bridge over*

*Rosso River and at Cacopardo Sulphur Refinery. Or-
der carried out.*

2. *On July 20, guards were removed on order of Major
Victor Joppolo, Civil Affairs Officer, town of Adano,
because carts were essential to town and town was in
bad shape without same.*

Sergeant Trapani read over what he had written.

Then he said: "Schultz, listen to this, do you think
this'll get the Major in trouble?" And he read the report
out loud. "I thought that part about the town needing
the carts might make it okay for the Major."

"What's this Major to you?" Schultz said. "If he can't
have any fun, what's he to you?"

Sergeant Trapani said: "Oh, nothing, I just hate to
see a guy get in trouble when he's trying to do right."

Schultz said: "Well, then, why don't you let the order
get lost in Captain Purvis's papers? Don't bother me,
God, I feel awful."

Sergeant Trapani looked hard at Corporal Schultz.
Then he stood up and went over to Captain Purvis's
desk and put the purple slip in the middle of a disorderly
pile of papers which Captain Purvis touched only in add-
ing to it.

"Good idea," Trapani said.

"You're Eyetalian," Schultz said, "what do these Eye-
talians put in their booze, for godsake?"

Chapter 8

EARLY the next week, Giuseppe the interpreter came to
Major Joppolo in some embarrassment.

"I'm a sorry, boss," he said.

"About what?" the Major said.

"Boss, you say you want a go out with a blonde a Tina. I'm a sorry, boss."

"I never said any such thing, Giuseppe. What's got into you?"

"Boss, you tell a me other day you want a see Tina's old a man."

"Yes, I do want to see him."

"I'm a sorry, boss."

"Well, what's that go to do with going out with the blonde?"

Giuseppe winked. When Giuseppe winked, his scar wrinkled up and his whole face looked weaker than ever. "Don't a kid Giuseppe, boss."

"Don't kid your boss, Giuseppe," Major Joppolo said sharply. "Now tell me, what's this all about?"

Giuseppe said: "You want a see Tina's old a man. Okay. Don't you want a go out with a blonde a Tina?"

"Giuseppe," the Major said, "I want to see Tina's father because you said he was the most respected of all the fishermen. I want to start the fishermen going out again, so that Adano will have something besides pasta and tomatoes and eggplant to eat. That's all there is to it."

"Boss, you're a kid Giuseppe."

"Giuseppe, do you want me to get another interpreter?"

"Okay, a boss, you're not a kid Giuseppe."

"I do want to see the old man. Will you fix that for me?"

"That's what I'm a sorry, boss."

"What do you mean?"

"Tina's old a man Tomasino no want a see you, a boss."

"Why not? Did you say something about my wanting to go out with his daughter?"

"Oh no, a boss. Old a man Tomasino say he never been in a Palazzo di Citta in a life. He hate a Fascist a crooks. He don't know you're a different. He won't a come a here."

"That's easy, Giuseppe. We'll go see him." The Major looked at a pad of appointments he had begun to keep on his desk. "Be ready to go at three this afternoon, Giuseppe."

And so it happened that another precedent was broken in Adano. Never in the memory of anyone in the town had an official gone calling on a citizen on business. Either the citizen had come willingly to the Palazzo, or else the citizen had been arrested, and had come against his will.

Between the time of this conversation and three o'clock, Giuseppe told several people about this amazing flexibility on the part of the Major. And therefore when it came time for them to go down to the port looking for old Tomasino, quite a large crowd had gathered in front of the Palazzo, and the crowd followed the Major and Giuseppe as they walked.

"Where do these people think they're going?" the Major asked Giuseppe.

"Just a bunch a busybody," Giuseppe said.

The Major turned around. "Go home, you people," he said in Italian. "Don't you have anything better to do at three in the afternoon?"

But the people kept right on following Giuseppe and the Major.

At the corner of the Via Dogana and the Via Barrino, the Major turned again. "If you people have nothing better to do in the middle of the afternoon than this, I have something better for you to do. I am looking for laborers at very low wages. I will put you all to work."

But the people kept right on following. In fact the

crowd grew as the Major and Giuseppe moved forward. Whenever a head popped out of a window or a person stepped curiously out of a door, the crowd shouted invitations.

"Come along," they shouted. "The Mister Major's going to hold office hours down at the port."

"You'd better come, he's going to call on old Tomasino, who hates authority," they shouted.

"The mountain is going to Mohammed," they shouted. And the crowd grew.

Giuseppe led the Major, and therefore the crowd, down to the harbor and past the stone pier, past the sulphur loading jetties, past the patent slips, past the Molo Martino to the Molo di Ponente, where the fishing boats were tied up.

The Major sensed that he was going to have a tough time with old Tomasino, so he said to Giuseppe: "Interpreter, unless you keep this crowd well back, you will lose your job."

It was therefore with considerable enthusiasm that Giuseppe ran back to the crowd, holding up his hands and shouting: "Stop, do not move forward, you are ordered to stop!"

"By whom?" people in the crowd shouted. "By the man who is favored just because he can speak two languages?" The crowd had come quite a distance for its show, and it was not to be denied now.

"Please stop," Giuseppe said. "If you do not stop, Ribaudo Giuseppe will lose his job."

"What is an interpreter to us," people said, "when we have a chance to see something new in Adano? . . . This has never happened before . . . What is the unemployment of one man?" And they kept moving forward.

Giuseppe shouted: "The Major will be very angry if you do not stop right here." And then he added softly:

"Let us make a deal. If you stop, I will listen to the conversation, and I will tell you what is said."

On this basis the crowd was willing to stop.

By this time, Major Joppolo had come to the boat of old Tomasino. He recognized the boat not only by the fact that there was a morose-looking man sitting on the after-deck, but also by the illuminated inscription, with its letters trailing off into leaves and fruits, just under the eye-piece of the bow: *Tina.*

The Major jumped up onto the bow.

"All right, man of authority," said the morose man, "arrest me."

"I haven't come to arrest you, Tomasino," the Major said.

Giuseppe came running up to listen. He stayed on the mole, so that he could commute easily between actors and audience.

"Why are you wearing your pistol?" the morose man said. "Shoot me, go ahead, shoot me."

"I always wear my pistol, Tomasino," the Major said.

"You have come to arrest me because I refused to go and see the American Major," the morose man said.

"That is not true," the Major said.

"Then why have you brought this informer, Ribaudo Giuseppe, who asked me to go see the American Major, and to whom I refused?"

"I am the American Major, Tomasino."

Tomasino did not bat an eye. "Why have you brought this crowd, if you were not planning to arrest me?"

"I didn't bring it, Tomasino, it just came. I don't want the crowd any more than you do. I just want to talk with you about fishing."

"I do not believe it," the morose man said. "All men of authority are alike. You came to arrest me, or perhaps to shoot me."

"I beg you to believe me," the Major said.

Giuseppe whistled to himself and ran back to the crowd. "It is amazing," he said impressively. "The Major said to Tomasino: 'I beg you to believe me.'"

"'*Beg*,'" said the people in the front of the crowd. "Amazing."

"There has never been such a begging," others said. "The Mister Major is willing to be a beggar to this Tomasino."

"What did he say?" shouted people in the back of the crowd.

"He said: 'I beg you, Tomasino,'" shouted people in the front of the crowd.

"Amazing," shouted the ones in back.

Giuseppe ran back out onto the mole.

The Major was saying: "It is this, Tomasino: I want you and the others to start fishing again."

"Why?" said the morose Tomasino. "So we can line the pockets of the authorities?"

"No, Tomasino, so that you can line the stomachs of the people of Adano."

"Hah," said Tomasino bitterly, "a benevolent man of authority."

"Tomasino, you don't understand. The Americans are different from the Fascists."

"Hah," said Tomasino. "I have heard that before. The Mayor Crapa said he was going to be different from the Mayor Martoglio, and the Mayor Nasta after him said he was going to be different from the Mayor Crapa. The only difference was that the tribute and the protection money and the taxes got higher each time. How much protection money do you want, American?"

"You have the wrong idea, Tomasino."

"Hah," said the morose Tomasino. "I am an old man, American. I have seen men of authority come and go. I don't believe that you are any different from all the others."

Here Major Joppolo got angry. "Old fisherman," he said, "you will have to understand something. The people of Adano are hungry. They must have fish. Do you get that through your thick skull?"

Giuseppe ran back to the crowd. "It is wonderful," he said. "The Mister Major said: 'The people of Adano are hungry. They must have fish.'"

The people in front repeated this and then shouted at the top of their voices: "Live the Mister Major! Live the Mister Major!"

The people in back shouted: "What did he say?"

The people in front shouted: "He thinks we ought to have fish for our hunger."

The whole crowd shouted then: "Live the Mister Major!"

Tomasino on the boat heard this, and it made him suspicious. "Why have you hired these people to come and jeer at me? No, I will not go fishing."

Major Joppolo shouted to Giuseppe in English: "Make the people go away! They are ruining everything."

Giuseppe passed on the Major's request, but the people just laughed at him. "Now?" they said. "You are crazy, interpreter. Speaking two languages has made you crazy."

Giuseppe shouted to the Major: "I'm a can't a do nothing, a boss."

So the Major said to Tomasino: "Wait for me, Tomasino, I will show you that I mean well toward you." And he jumped down on the mole and went to the crowd.

"Do you want fish?" he asked the crowd.

"Yes!" the people shouted.

"Then you must go home," the Major said. "It is not easy to persuade Tomasino to go fishing. You must choose between this stupid gaping and having fish."

The crowd chose. Watching this unprecedented conversation and getting bulletins on it from Giuseppe was

73

immediate, it was now. Eating fish was future and uncertain at best. The crowd chose staying to watch.

When he saw that he could not argue them into going home, Major Joppolo said to Giuseppe: "Where is the nearest telephone?"

Giuseppe said: "I guess she's in a Port a Captain's office, I show a you."

A thrill of curiosity ran through the crowd as the Major and Giuseppe went off. What had previously been the Italian Port Captain's office was now the office of the American Naval Lieutenant in charge of harbor facilities at Adano. This was Lieutenant Livingston, who had gone into the Navy's V-7 program early in the war, and had entered on his application blank as one of his main qualifications to be an officer and a gentleman: "Have had experience with small boats." This experience, as a matter of fact, consisted of rowing on the crew at Kent School and at Yale. At Yale, Crofts Livingston was known as a fellow who would do anything for you if he liked you, but he was rather choosy in his friends.

Lieutenant Livingston had not yet decided to like Major Joppolo. The Major had not gone to either Kent or Yale. There was a rumor around that he had once been some kind of clerk in the New York City government under Walker and O'Brien. Lieutenant Livingston was inclined to the opinion that it was too bad the Army had sent such a meatball to be administrator of a town like Adano. And besides, when the Major saw a Navy officer wearing two bars, which anyone ought to know stood for Lieutenant Senior Grade, Major Joppolo would address him as Captain.

"Hello, Captain," the Major said when he walked into Lieutenant Livingston's office, "can I use your phone?"

"Good morning," the Lieutenant said, "what are you doing down here?" The tone of the Lieutenant's Kent-Yale voice indicated that he thought the Army ought to stay on Army ground, and let the Navy stay on Navy shore.

"Can I use your phone?" the Major said. The Major was a single-minded man.

"Sure, help yourself."

The Major called Rowboat Blue Forward.

While he was waiting, he said to the Lieutenant: "I'm trying to get these fishermen organized, got to get rid of a mob first."

The Lieutenant did not look particularly pleased with this summary of the Major's activities.

"Hello, this the M.P.'s? Purvis? Listen, I want you to come down here. I got a mob to break up. Bring your Colt along. I think if you fire six into the air, that's all we'll need to send 'em home. . . . We're down at the port, over by the breakwater on the western side. Okay, hurry down."

The Major thanked Lieutenant Livingston for the use of the phone.

Lieutenant Livingston said: "Uh, Major, seems to me this fishing racket is more or less a Navy deal, isn't it?"

The Major said: "Yeah, I'll be back to see you, I'm in a hurry now. Thanks for the phone, Captain. See you later."

As the Major and Giuseppe passed the crowd on the way back to the *Tina,* Giuseppe said to the crowd: "As a friend, I advise you to go home."

People in the crowd, delighted with the mystery of the Major's hurried visit to the Port Captain's office, mocked Giuseppe. "Poor Ribaudo Giuseppe," they said, "speaking two languages has weakened his head."

"All right," Giuseppe said, "I have advised you as a friend."

At the *Tina,* Tomasino was sullen again. "I see you gave your hired crowd their instructions," he said. "Go ahead, take me, what have I to lose?"

Major Joppolo said: "They will all go home soon, Tomasino. I have given instructions for them to be sent home. Now, about the fishing. Do you think you could get together crews for five or six boats?"

Tomasino said: "Who is to be the protector of these crews? What criminal?"

"Protector?"

"To whom do the fishermen have to pay tribute this time?"

"Don't mock me, fisherman. What are you talking about?"

"Hah," said Tomasino, a man who could be amused with the most gruesomely sad face. "Hah, does the man of authority pretend he doesn't understand the system of protection?"

Major Joppolo spoke harshly: "What are you talking about, fisherman?"

Tomasino was shaken. "Protection," he said. "Before you came we had to pay protection money to Enea, the Supervisor of the Fisheries, an evil man. In return he 'protected' us. Hah, Fiorentino said one time that he did not feel the need of protection, and the next week his boat, the pretty *Mattina,* burned up as it lay at its mooring."

The Major said: "There will be no such thing under the Americans, Tomasino. That's the kind of thing we want to eliminate."

Tomasino said: "You are lying to me. There is a trick."

At this moment Captain Purvis swung into the port area in his jeep. He jumped out and ran into the delighted crowd, shouting as he ran: "Scram, you bastards. Get the hell out of here."

He pulled out his automatic and fired six shots into the air.

The crowd broke instantly. "The Germans, the Germans," one shouted.

"The Fascists have come back," someone else shouted.
"It's all over," a woman screamed.

"I've been wounded," a man moaned. Of course he had not been. All of Captain Purvis's shots went into the air.

Within twenty seconds the entire crowd had disappeared into the streets of Adano, and there was nothing left at the head of the Molo di Ponente except the smoke from Captain Purvis's Colt. The Captain got into his jeep and drove off.

Tomasino was alarmed by the shots. "You have come to shoot me," he shouted, springing to his feet. "I knew there was a trick. You want to kill me."

But Major Joppolo calmed him. "That was just to get rid of the crowd. I don't want anything except to send you out fishing, Tomasino."

Tomasino said: "There is a trick," but he sat down again.

The Major said: "Tomasino, we will need about half a dozen boats. Can you help arrange this?"

"To whom will the tribute be paid? How much will it be?"

"You won't have to pay any tribute to the Americans, Tomasino."

"No protection. No tribute. I do not believe it. And how much tax must we pay on the gross weight of our catch?"

"There will not be any tax on your catch, Tomasino. You will only have to pay the regular taxes. It is true that your profit will be limited to fifteen per cent of what you take in. The rest you must spend in wages to your fishermen and upkeep on your boats."

"No protection, no tribute, no special tax. You are making fun of me, American."

"Why should I make fun of you, fisherman? It is my job to run this town. I consider it my job to keep the people of this town alive. They haven't enough to eat. I want fish for them. I want you to go fishing. Why in the name of God should I make fun of you?"

Tomasino stood up. "American," he said, "I begin to think you are different from the others."

The Major ignored this concession and said: "Tomasino, I want you to be the head of the fishermen of Adano. There will no longer be a criminal like — what was his name?"

"Enea."

"There will no longer be an Enea over the fishermen. I want a fisherman to be in charge of the fishermen."

Tomasino's sad face almost broke into a smile. "There would be justice in that, and we fishermen aren't very well acquainted with justice." Then the morose man thought a moment. "No," he said, "I can't do it."

"Why not?"

"I would be a man of authority. I would be the thing I have hated all my life. The other fishermen would laugh at me for becoming the thing I had always hated most."

"But Tomasino, you've just admitted that I was different from other men of authority. You could be different too. It is possible to make your authority seem to spring from the very people over whom you have authority. And after a while, Tomasino, it actually does spring from them, and you are only the instrument of their will. That is the thing that the Americans want to teach you who have lived under men who imagined that they themselves were authority."

Tomasino thought a long time and then said: "It is too good. There is a trick."

"Yes, as a matter of fact there is a trick, fisherman. The trick is that some men are not good enough for this thing, and that makes it fall down. Right here in this invasion we have a general who is not good enough,

78

General Marvin. He imagines that he is something that ought to be worshipped. Also we have one who may not be good enough, I'm not sure yet, much closer to us than the General. I mean the Captain of the Navy who runs this port. He is a young man and very fond of authority. And Tomasino, we have to get permission from him before you and the others can go out fishing."

"Who is this young man of authority?" Tomasino said with a sullen face. "I will bash his head in with my gaffing hook." And the fisherman's face looked as if he meant it.

"Let's go and talk with him."

And so the Major and Tomasino went to see Lieutenant Livingston in the Port Captain's office. The Lieutenant was feeling very grumpy after the brush-off Major Joppolo had given him because he was in a hurry. Lieutenant Livingston was in no mood to grant requests to an Army man and a meatball.

Major Joppolo, being single-minded, not to say absentminded, was not in the least conscious of Lieutenant Livingston's mood.

"Hi, Captain," he said blithely when he and Tomasino walked in. "Back again."

"So I see," said Lieutenant Livingston without pleasure.

"This is Tomasino, the head of the fishermen here." Tomasino, hearing his name, gave the Lieutenant a Fascist salute.

Lieutenant Livingston said: "Would the old fisherman mind taking a seat out there in the hall? I have a rule that no Italians are to come in this office."

Major Joppolo said: "Tomasino wouldn't mind, but I would. What the hell kind of way is that to run an office in an Italian town?" Tomasino, hearing his name, gave the Lieutenant another Fascist salute.

Quite coolly Lieutenant Livingston said: "I don't

79

know how you run your offices in the Army, Captain, but in the Navy we have something we call security. We can't afford to be careless."

Major Joppolo was indignant. "The hell with security. I'll vouch for Tomasino." Tomasino saluted. He hated authority, but he knew it when he saw it.

Lieutenant Livingston said testily: "Major, after all, this is my office."

The Major said: "Well, goddamit, it's Tomasino's town." Tomasino saluted.

The Lieutenant said: "What do you want, Major?"

Major Joppolo said: "I want the Navy's permission to send out six fishing boats to get fish for Adano."

Lieutenant Livingston said: "Impossible."

Major Joppolo said: "What's impossible about it?"

The Lieutenant said: "We'd have to get permission from ComNavIt and he'd have to refer it to ComNav-Naw, and they're both Admirals. Not a chance."

Major Joppolo said: "What's all that gibberish mean?"

The Lieutenant said: "Commander Navy Italy and Commander Navy North African Waters. Is that gibberish, Major?"

The Major said: "Why do you have to go running to the Admirals? Don't they give you any responsibility at all?"

Lieutenant Livingston spoke very patiently. "You wouldn't understand," he said. "This is a Navy problem."

"Listen, Captain, we're in this damn war together. What's itching you?"

"How do you know this man isn't in the Italian Navy? How do you know he isn't being paid by the German Navy? How do you know he just wants to fish?"

Major Joppolo was too outraged to laugh. "Tomasino?" he said. "Have you ever talked with Tomasino?" Tomasino saluted.

The Lieutenant said: "Can he speak English?"

Major Joppolo had had enough. He said: "Listen, Captain, this town is hungry. It needs fish. If it doesn't get something to supplement its diet, people are going to die here of starvation. Are you going to let these men go out fishing, or aren't you?"

Lieutenant Livingston was surprised by the Major's vehemence. "They might hit loose mines and be blown up," he said defensively.

"I don't care. This is a war. Some people've got to get killed so others can live. Are you going to let these men go out fishing, or aren't you?"

Lieutenant Livingston said uncertainly: "I don't think I ought to."

Major Joppolo said: "Captain, unless you give permission for these men to go out, I'm going to send a separate letter naming each person who dies of hunger in this town to your commanding officer, and in each letter I'm going to say it's your fault."

"Maybe we could work something out," the Lieutenant said.

"You're damn right we could," Major Joppolo said. "By day after tomorrow I want you to have six charts ready showing exactly where these boats can go and not run into our mine fields. They don't have to show where the mines are, all they need show is an area where the boats can go. I'll see that these men stick to that area. Have it ready day after tomorrow."

And before he could catch himself, Lieutenant Livingston of Kent and Yale had said to Major Joppolo of the Bowery and Tammany Hall: "Yes, sir."

Major Joppolo left with Tomasino before the Lieutenant could catch his wits.

Outside, Tomasino said: "I hate him. What did he say?"

"A lot of foolishness, except for one thing," the Major said. "If you go out fishing, Tomasino, you may get hurt. Your boat might hit an American mine."

"What do I care?" said Tomasino. "I am going fishing. Mister Major, if you could know how unhappy the fishermen of Adano have been. All we want in the world is to go fishing. We will go even if we have to pay graft to the men of authority. Now you say we don't have to do that. Thank you, Mister Major."

"No," the Major said, and he decided to try something. "No, Tomasino, I thank *you* for taking charge of the fishermen, and I kiss your hand."

Tomasino looked at this man of authority, and he said: "You are different." And the old fisherman turned and ran out on the mole to the *Tina,* and he shouted as he ran, as if telling his boat: "We are going fishing! We are going fishing! We are going fishing!"

Chapter 9

THE TELEPHONE rang.

"Hello," Major Joppolo said. "Joppolo, Amgot."

"Joppolo, this is Sartorius, up at Vicinamare."

"Oh, hello, Colonel."

"About that bell."

"Yeah, any luck?"

"I'll say. I found the records on it in about fifteen minutes. By the grace of God the Fascists kept their records about things like this by towns, so all I had to do was look in their files under Adano. But boy, those Eyeties sure did a lot of paper work. They had to report to the province every time they took a leak, practically."

Major Joppolo said: "So what about the bell?"

"Well, I found three entries."

"Can we get the bell back? That's what I want to know."

Colonel Richard N. Sartorius was a methodical man. "The first entry," he said, "is dated June fifteenth. It says the bell arrived from Adano by mule cart. It says the bell was very crudely crated, and had to be crated all over again. That took three days."

"Where's the bell now? Did you find it?"

"The second entry is dated June twenty-second. It says the bell was put aboard the motor ship *Alcuri* for Milan via Genoa. It was addressed to the Fecoratta Artillery Foundry, Forty-three Via Edda Mussolini, Milan."

"Oh, hell, they shipped it off."

"Not only that, but the third entry says the Fecoratta Artillery Foundry at Forty-three Via Edda Mussolini in Milan — can you imagine naming a street for that flewsie? — it says that the Foundry acknowledged receipt of the bell. That entry was on July the second. I'm afraid your bell is just a hunk of cannon now, Joppolo."

"Damn."

"Well, at least I found the records for you."

"That's awful disappointing."

"Yeah, I'm sorry. But I'm glad I could set you straight on it." All Colonel Sartorius wanted was one word of thanks.

"These people down here'll be heartbroken," the single-minded Major said.

"Is that a fact?" said Colonel Sartorius. "Well, you're *wel*come," and he hung up hard.

Chapter 10

THE DAY that Mayor Nasta came down from the hills Major Joppolo got his first idea that perhaps the people of Adano really were glad to have the Americans around.

Major Joppolo was having lunch with Captain Purvis at the Albergo dei Pescatori. Joppolo and Purvis had almost nothing in common, but they were beginning to like each other pretty well. It was probably just that they were both officers and Americans, and no matter whether they would have been worlds apart back in the States, here they were blood brothers, and they could talk over their reactions and laugh together and understand each other. Brother Purvis still wanted to get Brother Joppolo drunk, but even that issue, which began bitterly, was now becoming a joke and a promise of some fun.

The Albergo dei Pescatori had the best food in Adano, and the Major and the Captain ate there regularly now. The food was nothing to write home about, but it was better than C Rations. Lunch and dinner were exactly alike and never varied: pasta with tomato sauce, a little fried eggplant and cheese, an omelet, bread, fruit and red wine. The place owned just nine regular customers. Besides the Major and the Captain, there were the owner, his wife, and his son, two prostitutes of the town, and their two men, who were never the same at any two successive meals. At each meal Major Joppolo used to say as he sat down, "I'll have to run them out of town one of these days," but soon the remark became just a habit, like saying a blessing, and there was little chance of its fulfillment.

At each meal there were also some idlers in the place, but they just came in to listen to the noon and six-thirty broadcasts from Rome.

On the day that Mayor Nasta came down from the hills, Major Joppolo and Captain Purvis had just finished their pasta and were talking about the stuffy Navy fellow, Livingston, when they heard an unusual noise out in the street. There were shouts of anger, and whistles.

The Rome broadcast was on at the moment, and some ather outrageous things were being said, so Major Joppolo guessed: "That's the mob down at one of the Dopo Lavoro clubs jeering the radio. I heard they did that a couple days ago. This is the first time I ever actually heard them."

Captain Purvis said: "Why aren't these bums jeering here? What the hell do they think they are, anyhow? Tell them to jeer, pal."

But the noise outside grew, and seemed to be coming up the street. And soon several of the idlers who had been listening to the radio in the restaurant ran out. As the noise grew still louder the two prostitutes picked up handfuls of fruit and ran out, pursued by their paying guests. Then the owner of the place and his wife and son ran out with their mouths full of pasta and eggplant.

Finally Major Joppolo said: "Let's go see what it is." So he and Captain Purvis ran out too, with their napkins in their hands.

This is what they saw:

Up the center of the street a forlorn looking man walked. He was very short, and rather heavy-set. His clothes were dirty and torn. His shoes were covered with dust. His face was very sad, and he walked slowly, hanging his head. There was only one proud touch to his whole figure, and that was a pair of pince-nez spectacles balanced on his big nose.

Behind the man, keeping a safe distance as if there still might be some dynamite in him, a large crowd walked, shouting and whistling its derision. The derision was ten times louder than it would otherwise have been because this was the first time the people of Adano had ever been able to express their feelings toward this man. Even behind their own closed doors they had held their tongues about Mayor Nasta in the past, because he seemed to have ears in every house, and his eyes peeked in every window, and his punishments were sadistic.

But now they shouted what they thought.

"Fascist Pig," they shouted. This was what they shouted most.

But they also shouted: "The murderer always goes back to the scene of his crime!"

They also shouted: "Where is Mayor Nasta's whip now?"

Curiously the two prostitutes shouted, and there was a kind of pride in the way they shouted it: "Son of a whore!"

There was a priest in the crowd, and he shouted: "Blasphemer!"

There were some children in the crowd, and they ran along shouting: "Pig! Pig! Pig!"

The anger of the mob bordered on violence. When the unhappy Mayor got opposite the Albergo dei Pescatori one of the prostitutes raised her arm and threw a plum at him. It missed him and splashed in the street.

A boy of twelve threw a stone. Then several brickbats flew, and the shouts of long repressed hatred became shrieks of revenge.

Captain Purvis looked at Major Joppolo and Major Joppolo said: "We've got to put a stop to this."

Captain Purvis was not a subtle American, but he was a brave one. He ran out in the street between Mayor Nasta and the crowd. He held up his hand and shouted: "Stop! Stop, you ignorant bastards."

The crowd kept coming. A stone flew past Captain Purvis toward Mayor Nasta.

Captain Purvis pulled his pistol out of his pocket. That

was enough. The ones in front held back the others, and the mob halted in the street. Captain Purvis went back to the sidewalk.

Mayor Nasta, seeing that he was saved, ran over to his deliverers, and he stood in the gutter blubbering his thanks. "Americans! Oh God, my friends. Thank you for saving me from these ungrateful people. I have served them for years and see how they behave. I am all alone, Americans. I have been in the hills all alone for days. No one would stay with me. All the others gave themselves up. I have thought everything over. I wish to help you if I can. . . ." And he rattled on, his voice going higher and higher.

Someone in the mob shouted: "Mister Major, if you help that man you are not our friend."

Major Joppolo acted quickly to save the situation. He walked into the street and held up his hand for silence; he was careful to make it his left hand, so that it would not be mistaken for a Fascist salute.

"Go home, people. I will take care of this man as he deserves. He is under arrest."

And the Major said quickly to Captain Purvis in English. "Arrest him, Purvis, show this gang that you're arresting him."

This was the kind of thing Captain Purvis enjoyed, and as he clapped his hand heavily on Mayor Nasta's shoulder he shouted: "Goddam, I wish I understood Eyetalian. This is wonderful."

The crowd broke up slowly, mumbling its protests at being deprived of revenge.

Purvis said: "Who the hell is this little squirt, anyway? Jesus, they sure hate him, don't they?"

Major Joppolo said: "He's the one who used to be Mayor."

"Oh he is, is he? Well according to what Borth says, they've got plenty of reason to hate him." And the Captain kicked Mayor Nasta in the seat of the pants simply because he didn't know the Italian for: "You're a little bastard."

Mayor Nasta whimpered in Italian: "What are you going to do with me? If you are going to kill me, please tell me first. Don't shoot me from behind."

What Major Joppolo did with Mayor Nasta was to take him up to his office. Everyone, even little Zito who had once worked for Mayor Nasta, even D'Arpa, the weasel-like vice mayor who had once worked with him, everyone made faces of disgust when they saw Mayor Nasta, and some made obscene remarks within his hearing.

When word passed around the Palazzo that Mayor Nasta was back, many people stuck their heads in the door at the end of the Major's office, which had once been the Mayor's office, to have a look at him in his disheveled condition, and to laugh at him to his face.

Major Joppolo said to Zito and Giuseppe: "I want to have a talk with Mayor Nasta alone. Go and tell the people in the other offices that I do not want to be disturbed, not even by a cracking open of that door. I do not even want to be disturbed by the brushing of ears on the keyhole."

"Yes, Mister Major," Zito said.

"No, Mister Major," Giuseppe said.

Major Joppolo sat at the desk and said brusquely: "Sit down."

Mayor Nasta sat in one of the chairs in front of the desk.

"Well, what is it that you wish?" Major Joppolo said.

Mayor Nasta brushed his hand along the wood of the desk pathetically, and he said: "It seems strange to be sitting on the wrong side of this desk."

Major Joppolo said: "It may seem stranger to sit on

the wrong side of the bars of your municipal jail. What do you want?"

Mayor Nasta rearranged the pince-nez on his nose, but he did not look Major Joppolo in the eye as he said: "I just want a chance, Mister Major."

"*You* want a chance!" Major Joppolo spoke angrily. "To whom did you ever give a chance?"

"I have thought it over," Mayor Nasta said. "I have been all alone for days. It was awful at night. I have thought it over, Mister Major. I want to help if I can."

"How many years were you in office?"

"Nine, Mister Major."

"After nine years in office, you have thought it all over, have you? After nine years of graft and stealing and keeping these people down, you've thought it over, you want to help, do you?"

"You have other Fascists in office here. I saw the face of D'Arpa a minute ago. I saw Tagliavia who was my Maresciallo of Finance. I saw Gargano of the Carabinieri. If you could use these, why not Nasta, the Mayor?"

"I have a new Mayor, and a better one."

This hurt. "Who is this Mayor?"

"Bellanca the Notary, an honest man, much more honest than the former Mayor."

And the former Mayor said: "Yes, Bellanca is honest. But surely you have something for Nasta to do? I would accept something less than Mayor." Nasta rubbed the wood of the desk wistfully. "There is not much left of the old Nasta," he said. "I would accept something less than Mayor."

Major Joppolo's eyes grew angry. He stood up abruptly. "Oh, you would, would you? Yes, I have something for you to do. You are to report every morning to Sergeant Borth of the American Army. You will find him in the Fascio. That is all you have to do each day. But

89

see that you do it, Nasta, or you will be put in jail."

"You mean that Nasta has become a common probationer?"

"Oh, so Nasta is familiar with the practice of putting people on probation? That is very genteel of you, Nasta. I thought all your punishments were more ingenious than that."

"Please be generous with me," Nasta said. "Please give me some work to do."

"Generous? In the name of God, Nasta, what do you expect? For the crimes you have committed against the people of Adano, you deserve to be shot outright, without a trial. You certainly never would give a fair trial, unless it brought you some kind of profit. I am being more than generous. I am putting you on probation. See that you behave, you Fascist."

Mayor Nasta was obsequious now. "Yes, Mister Major," he said. "What did you say was the name of the American officer to whom I must report?"

"His name is Borth, and he is not an officer. He is a sergeant. You are not worth an officer, Nasta."

"Yes, Mister Major."

This is how it happened that Mayor Nasta reported once every morning to Sergeant Borth at the Fascio. Because four or five people followed the Mayor everywhere he went out of curiosity and hatred, there was a small audience on hand the next morning when he reported to Sergeant Borth for the first time. The audience enjoyed what it saw and heard, for this kind of situation was meat for Sergeant Borth, who thought the whole war was a joke.

The tattered Nasta stepped into one of the M.P. offices, rearranged his pince-nez, and said: "Where will I find the Sergeant Borth?"

"I am Borth."

"I am Nasta."

"Oho," roared Sergeant Borth. He stood up, rubbing his hands. "So you are the Mayor. I understand that you have come to Adano to repent your sins. Is that right, noble Mayor?"

"I was told that I was to report here each morning. I was to report, not be humiliated, Sergeant."

"You will call me Mister Sergeant."

Mayor Nasta snorted, from his long habit of snorting.

Borth said sharply: "Listen, Nasta, I know more about you than you know about yourself. You be careful how you behave here. Now, answer my questions civilly. Is it correct that you came to Adano to repent your sins?"

Mayor Nasta was white with anger, but he said: "I suppose you might say so."

"Thank you," Borth said with exaggerated politeness. "In that case you will repent one sin each morning when you report to Sergeant Borth. Would you like to choose your own sins, or would you like Sergeant Borth to choose them for you?"

Mayor Nasta couldn't keep himself from snorting.

"I see," said Borth, with his over-politeness, "you would like Borth to choose. Very well, let's see. This morning we will discuss the sin of your disgraceful running away from your post in the face of the American invasion. What is this sin called, Mayor Nasta?"

"What do you mean, what is it called?"

"You are at a loss for words? Very well, Borth will answer his own question. It is called the sin of cowardice."

Mayor Nasta snorted.

"No matter what side you were on, no matter if you were on the side of the crooks, it was a sin to run away, was it not, Mayor?"

Mayor Nasta rearranged his pince-nez with a trembling hand.

"Answer my question: did you or did you not give rifles to the Carabinieri and grenades to the Finance

Guards, make them a beautiful speech about fighting to the last man, and then run to the hills?"

Mayor Nasta said with a trembling voice: "You tell me, clever Sergeant."

Sergeant Borth shouted: "Answer me, probationer."

Mayor Nasta said quietly: "I did, Sergeant."

"Mister Sergeant!"

"I did, Mister Sergeant."

"Are you sorry for this disgraceful sin, Nasta?"

Mayor Nasta could hear the people snickering behind him.

He said meekly: "I am, Mister Sergeant."

Borth said: "All right, then, you may go."

The small audience who heard this first repentance told their friends about it, so that the next morning there was a larger crowd in front of Sergeant Borth's office when Mayor Nasta reported.

On the second morning, Sergeant Borth made Mayor Nasta repent for the sin of having had such a big house in this poor town, and for having hoarded money, which was hidden in a mattress in the house, and for being a grafter.

On the third morning, the Sergeant made him repent for being a Fascist, and for having been, as a young man, a member of the Segretaria Federale di Roma.

On the fourth morning, the Sergeant made him repent for the sin of having fought for Franco in Spain, not gallantly, to be sure, but for having fought at all.

On the fifth morning, the Sergeant made him repent for the sin of having taken cuts on the fish market, the bakeries, and the vegetable market, and for stealing twenty-five per cent of the city impost tax.

On the sixth morning, the Sergeant made him repent for the sin of offering to be a spy for the Americans if Sergeant Borth would just stop making him repent.

On the seventh morning, the Sergeant made him repent for having forced his will on two young girls of the town.

And so, day after day, the repentances went. And every day the crowd outside Sergeant Borth's office in the Fascio grew, and the laughter got louder and louder.

Chapter 11

ONE morning Tomasino the fisherman called on Major Joppolo at the Palazzo. As he entered the building, and even as he walked into the Major's office, he looked like an American sight-seer. His neck bent back on itself and his eyes wandered around in dull amazement.

Major Joppolo was pleased to see him and said cheerfully: "Good morning, Tomasino."

But Tomasino's face changed from curious to sullen, and he said: "I did not want to do it."

"Do what, Tomasino?"

"Come to the place of authority, this Palazzo. I have never done it in my life. My wife made me do it."

"Why? What did she want?"

"She said that if you had lowered yourself to come and see me on my fish-boat, I could lower myself to go and see you in the Palazzo. She wanted me to invite you to come to our house tonight to help eat some *torrone* which my daughter Tina made. My wife is a difficult woman. I hate her. She thinks she is the authority in my house."

Major Joppolo said: "Please be so good as to tell your wife that even though her husband was so reluctant in the delivery of her message, the Major would be delighted to accept."

Tomasino said: "I am of half a mind not to tell her. I hate her."

Major Joppolo said: "What time?"

Tomasino said grimly: "You are a man of authority. You decide what time."

Then Major Joppolo suddenly remembered two sentences from the *Notes From Joppolo to Joppolo* in his Amgot notebook. He remembered: "Don't play favorites. . . . Be careful about accepting invitations. . . ." It would be best if he were not seen going to the house of Tomasino. People like the interpreter Giuseppe might misunderstand his motives. It would be a good idea to go after dark. The Major made some quick calculations: let's see, the sun goes down about eight fifteen, it gets dark. . . .

"How would nine o'clock be, Tomasino?"

Tomasino said sadly: "Eight, nine, ten — what difference?"

"I'll be there at nine. What is the address?"

"It is a horrible house. Nine Via Vittorio Emanuele."

Promptly at nine o'clock Major Joppolo knocked on the door at 9 Via Vittorio Emanuele. Tomasino opened the door, but did not show the slightest pleasure at having a visitor.

"Come in," he grumbled.

The Major stepped in and tried to shake his hand but could not find it in the dark.

"We have to climb many stairs," Tomasino complained.

As a matter of fact, there was only one flight. At the top of it they turned into a brightly lighted hallway. Tomasino led the Major through the hallway to a narrow parlor. This parlor belied the unsociability of Tomasino, for its furniture consisted almost exclusively of chairs — a sure sign, in Adano, of frequent and numerous guests. Besides the chairs there were only a large Italian radio in one corner and a round table in the center. The room was so narrow that from the chairs on either side one could reach whatever was on the table.

Two guests had arrived before the Major, and their identity surprised him.

"Hi, Major," said Captain Purvis, who looked as if he had been into a couple of bottles of wine, "Giuseppe told me the old fish-hound here had a couple of pretty daughters. I was getting kinda horny. Giuseppe here told me he'd fix me up. Good old Giuseppe."

"Good night, a boss," said Giuseppe. He was much embarrassed; he had had no idea that the Major would show up.

The Major was just as embarrassed as Giuseppe. He was thinking of those sentences from the Amgot notebook: "Don't play favorites. . . . Be careful about invitations. . . ."

"Why, hello," the Major said.

"Haven't seen the quail yet," Captain Purvis said. "The old lady's out in the kitchen. She's a honey. Taught her how to say 'My God.'"

The Major sat down stiffly.

Captain Purvis said: "Say, I didn't know you were an old hand around here, you dog. Why don't you tell me about these good things? You old bastard, I thought you never did anything but work. Tell me, how are these chickens? Yum, I could go for a little breast of chicken right now."

Major Joppolo said weakly: "I haven't seen the girls, except one of them in church. This is my first time here."

Captain Purvis, who was unquestionably tipsy, said: "Hey, speaking of chickens, I heard one the other day. You remember where Hoover said once that he was going to fix it so there would be a chicken in every pot?

Well, I heard the other day that after the U.S. Army was around these Italian towns for a while there was going to be a pot on every chicken."

The Captain roared with laughter. Giuseppe, although he had no idea what the point was, laughed politely. The Major was horrified. Tomasino sat in depressed silence, understanding nothing.

Tomasino's wife came in from the kitchen with a platter of *torrone* and saved the day. She must have weighed two hundred and fifty pounds. When she put the candy down she raised her two arms, turned to the Major and shouted: "My God! My God!" She pronounced it as if it were spelled G-u-d, and all her fatness shook with laughing. Everyone else except Tomasino had to laugh at her.

Giuseppe jumped to his feet and introduced the Major to Tomasino's wife. Her name was Rosa.

She said in her husky fat lady's voice: "I am delighted to see you here, Mister Major. That wet stone" — she pointed at Tomasino — "almost refused to go and ask you. I am learning to speak English." And she shouted again: "My Gud! My Gud!"

"No, fatso," said Captain Purvis, "it's *Gawd*, not Gud. Gawd, Gawd, Gawd."

"Gud, Gud, Gud," the old lady said, and heaved in ecstasy.

Captain Purvis said: "Goddamit, where are these pretty mackerel the old fish-hound is supposed to have? Say, Major, we got to make a deal here. Giuseppe here says he thinks I'd like the dark one best."

Giuseppe put in a word for his loyalty: "I'm a save a blonde for you, boss."

Major Joppolo really didn't know what to say.

Giuseppe said quickly to the fat Rosa, who was still laughing softly at her triumphs in English: "Where are the girls?"

The mother said: "If you think you can hurry two pretty girls trying to make themselves prettier, you'll find them in the bedroom."

Major Joppolo was alarmed to see Giuseppe get up and go into the bedroom. He wondered what kind of girls these were, anyhow.

But in a few moments Giuseppe came back, leading a girl by each hand. He had apparently explained the situation to the girls, because Tina went directly to Major Joppolo, shook his hand, and sat down beside him, and the dark one, Francesca, went straight to Captain Purvis, shook his hand, and sat down by him.

"Mmm," said Captain Purvis, "not bad." He felt secure in the certainty that the girls did not speak English. "How'd you like to go to bed, Toots?" he said.

"Take it easy," Major Joppolo said.

"You think I'm too previous?" Captain Purvis said. "Hell, why beat around the bush, Major?"

Tina said in Italian: "I heard you breathing in church last Sunday. You ought to take more exercise, Mister Major."

Major Joppolo said: "I was late, I was very late. I got working on something, and I lost track of time. I had to run to church. It was very embarrassing."

Tina said: "You had Father Pensovecchio worried. I could tell by the way he got mixed up in his service."

Major Joppolo said: "Do you go to church every Sunday?"

Tina said: "Of course."

Captain Purvis said: "Goddam you and your wop talk, Major. You'll really make some time. All I can do is make eyes at this piece."

Giuseppe said: "Capatain, Giuseppe's a translate. You talk and Giuseppe's a tell a Francesca what you say." And so for a time Captain Purvis was engaged in conveying nonsense to Francesca by way of Giuseppe's uncertain interpretation. The general idea of Captain Purvis's remarks got across, however, for Francesca blushed more and more frequently.

In the meanwhile Major Joppolo was able to talk with Tina, interrupted only once in a while by bursts of "My Gud!" from the mother and gales of laughter all around the room, except from Tomasino, who stared moodily at the floor.

The Major said: "Do you always go to the Church of San Angelo?"

This time it was Tina who blushed. "No," she said. "Giuseppe told me you were going to be there. I wanted to see what the American Major was like. Most Sundays I go to the Church of the Benedettini."

Major Joppolo said: "What did you think of the American Major?"

Tina said: "He breathes very loudly, like the leaky bellows of the pipe organ at the Benedettini."

The Major laughed.

"Have a piece of *torrone*," Tina said. "I made it."

One could not very well turn down an invitation put just that way, so the Major took a big piece. The candy was passed all around the room, and for a time all conversation stopped. Nothing could be heard except the crunching of nuts between teeth and the smacking sound of boiled sugar coming unstuck from teeth. During this time of chewing, Major Joppolo couldn't help thinking how strange it was to build a whole evening around the eating of *torrone*, but that seemed to be the program.

When he dared, Major Joppolo said "Good."

Captain Purvis could afford to be more honest in English: "Christ," he said, "what did we come to, a glue factory?"

"Another piece," Tina said to the Major cordially.

"In a few minutes," the Major said.

"We must have some wine," the fat and happy Rosa said. "Go out in the kitchen, fool," she said to Tomasino, "and get a bottle of Marsala."

Wine on top of *torrone,* and probably mixed right up with it. Major Joppolo could think of nothing less tempting, but Captain Purvis, hearing the word *vino,* shouted: "*Vino,* hurray for *vino.*" Then he said very seriously, as if pulling himself together: "Jesus, if I have much more of this stuff, I'm going to have to lay one of these girls. If I have to stay in this town much longer, I'll take on the fat one, even if she is the mother."

Major Joppolo stood up and said: "Purvis, either you shut your big trap or I'll throw you out of here."

Captain Purvis said: "Aw come on, Major, don't be a spoil sport. You know you feel the same way, if you were just honest enough to say so."

"Shut up, Purvis!" The Major's eyes blazed. "That's an order. Now you behave yourself."

Captain Purvis stood up and saluted with a wavering dignity.

Tomasino came back with the wine, and Captain Purvis saluted the bottle, bending slightly at the waist and aiming the breakaway of the salute straight at the bottle.

Rosa, sensing that something was wrong, shouted desperately: "My Gud! My Gud!" But nobody laughed.

Tina jumped up and said: "Let's dance," and she ran over to the radio and turned on Radio Moscow. "Moscow always has the best music," she said.

Francesca, with Major Joppolo's help, carried the table from the middle of the room to the end away from the radio. Captain Purvis rushed over to Rosa, held out his arms, and said: "Okay, fatso, let's dance."

Rosa understood from his gestures what he meant, and she stood up laughing. The tipsy Captain and his

huge partner careened around the room. After a couple
of turns Rosa collapsed into a chair, gasping and shouting her English vocabulary.

Then Captain Purvis danced with Francesca, and
Major Joppolo with Tina. They stamped and laughed
and talked above the music until Tomasino said glumly:
"You are making too much noise. You will wake the
girls."

Tina ran over and toned the radio down a little.

"The girls?" the Major said.

Tina blushed. She said: "My sister's daughters."

"Francesca's?"

"Oh, no, of my sister who is in Rome."

Major Joppolo did not think to ask why the daughters
were in Adano and the mother in Rome; or why Tina
blushed; or why she did not seem very anxious to talk
any more about the sleeping girls.

"Let's dance some more," she said.

So they danced until they were both sweating in the
midsummer heat.

It was Tina who said: "Some fresh air, Mister Major?"

He said: "That would be a good idea."

Tina said: "We can go right out here."

She slipped out through wooden shutter doors onto
a narrow balcony over the dark street, and the Major followed her. Behind him he could hear Captain
Purvis saying to Giuseppe: "There goes that bastard out
to make some time with his wop talk. How the hell can
I make love when I have to keep you hanging around,
Giuseppe?"

Tina closed the shutter doors behind the Major.

The two stood against the cool iron of the balcony
railing and looked up at the sharp stars. Tina said: "Do
you like it here?"

Major Joppolo said: "I've never been so happy in my
life."

"That seems strange," Tina said, "when you're so far from home."

"I'm not so far from home, in a way. Florence is almost a home to me. My father and mother were from a little town near Florence."

"Where are you from, in America I mean?"

"The Bronx, Tina."

"Where is that, the Bronx?"

"New York."

"The Bronx is part of New York City?"

"Sometimes I think New York City is part of the Bronx."

"Oh, I should love to go there. Is the Bronx beautiful? Is it beautiful for Florentines in the Bronx? How would it be for someone from Adano?"

"For my Florentine parents, I think it is beautiful, yes, it is beautiful. In Italy they were just poor peasants, and you know it is not very beautiful for most of the peasants here. There my father is a waiter. He has a very good job, in the University Club, it is a very nice atmosphere, all the chairs are leather like in the Palazzo and the walls are all panelled. My mother has a washing machine. Father has a car. It is very beautiful for them, I think. For me, it was not always so beautiful."

"Why not, Mister Major?"

"Well, it's hard to explain. You see, I grew up in America. I could see that the Bronx was not the most beautiful place in America. I always wanted a little more than we had. I don't know, it's hard to explain."

"No," said Tina, "you don't have to explain. I know what it is to be restless. That's why my hair is blonde, I guess."

Major Joppolo had made up his mind that Tina's hair was dyed. But he didn't expect her to talk about it.

Tina sensed his embarrassment. "Oh, my hair is not natural, Mister Major. I dyed it because I was not satis-

101

fied. My dark hair was my Bronx. Every one had dark hair. I wanted something different."

"I thought at first perhaps you were from Northern Italy," the Major said politely.

Tina laughed. "Tell me some more about yourself," she said.

"There's not much to tell," he said.

"Did you go to one of those American colleges? I've seen them in the movies at Vicinamare."

"No, not exactly. I went to school until I was sixteen. Then I lied about my age, I said I was eighteen so that I could get a driver's license and take a job. I worked as a truck driver until I was twenty, then I had an accident, from lifting things which were too heavy."

"What kind of an accident, Mister Major?"

"It was a rupture. After the accident I had no job for two months. It is not very exciting to be unemployed in the United States. Finally I got a job as a clerk in a grocery store at twelve dollars a week."

"How much is that?"

"Twelve hundred lira."

"Twelve hundred lira! You must have been rich."

"No, Tina, twelve hundred lira is all right for Adano —"

"All right! I should say it is all right. Six hundred is high pay. My father used to think six hundred was a very good week — and he hasn't been out for a long time," she added sadly.

"But that's not so much in the States."

"You mean everyone is rich in the Bronx?"

"No, I wouldn't say so, Tina. It's just that our standard of living is higher than yours."

"What does that mean?"

"Well, that's hard to explain, too. It's just that everyone has a little more than they have here. They mostly have automobiles, in peacetime, that is. The food is a.

little better, everyone gets orange juice and milk and things like that. They get paid a little more. They have to pay more for what they get, though."

"In other words, it's just what I said. Everyone is rich in the Bronx."

"Well, have it your own way. Anyhow, I think fate has had a lot to do with my life, because one night a friend of mine told me that they were about to have examinations for jobs in the City Government."

"The City of the Bronx?"

"No, Tina, New York City. He told me I ought to take them. I said I hadn't had enough education, but he said I ought to go ahead and try. So I did and I came out number 177 out of 1,100. That made me feel pretty good, as if I knew something after all. They gave me a job as a clerk in the Department of Taxation and Finance."

"Did this make you rich again?"

"No, being a tax collector did not make you rich in New York. I was earning twenty dollars a week. That's two thousand lira."

"Two thousand, richer than ever."

"I did all right, too, only then they elected a man named LaGuardia, and since he was a different party from the previous man, a lot of people got thrown out, and I was one. I borrowed some money from my mother-in-law — "

"Your mother-in-law? Were you married?"

"Yes, Tina, I'll tell you about that some time. I borrowed this money and bought a grocery store in the Bronx, and it was all mine. Only then about two years later things went badly, we had hard times, and I had to sell out before it was too late. I went back to the City to see if they'd have me back, because they had sent me a couple of notices while I had the grocery store, saying they wanted me. They said: 'Why didn't you answer the notices?' I said: 'I never got them, I must have been in Florida when you sent them to me.'"

"Where is Florida?"

"It's in the south, I wasn't there at all. That was the second time I lied to get a job. Since then I've tried never to lie, the truth is much better and much safer. So they gave me a job in the Sanitation Department. Later I took my examinations for advancement to Third Class Clerk, and afterwards I got to be a Second Class Clerk. I was earning forty-two dollars a week when I went into the Army." Major Joppolo was getting a little boastful about his non-existent riches. "That was four thousand two hundred lira a week."

Tina said: "The wife, is she pretty?"

Major Joppolo said: "Yes, she is very pretty, at least she seems so to me. I miss her very much. She has a mole on the left side of her chin, but otherwise she is very pretty. She is of Italian parentage, so she has dark skin like yours. In some ways you remind me of her."

Tina had been looking up at the stars. But now she suddenly looked down into the dark valley of the street and said: "Let's go in and dance." And she opened up the shutter doors and went inside. Major Joppolo went in after her.

Captain Purvis had gone to work on Tomasino's wine, and he was making a decided nuisance of himself, so Major Joppolo persuaded him to go home. He and Giuseppe led the Captain home.

When he got back to his own villa, and was undressed and in bed, Major Joppolo felt miserable. It wasn't until nearly three o'clock that he realized why. Giuseppe was right. It made a man feel very unhappy to be as far from home as the Bronx, New York, is from Adano, Italy.

Chapter 12

THE NEXT morning Captain Purvis sat with his feet up on his desk. He was in a bad humor.

Sergeant Trapani was out of the office. The Captain spoke to Corporal Chuck Schultz, who was on guard. "That Major Joppolo," he said. "I was beginning to like him, but he's a wet blanket. God, I was just getting a wonderful buzz on last night, and he descended on me, sober as a whitefish, and he made me go home."

Corporal Schultz said: "Was you getting buzzed on that Dago red?"

The Captain said: "Yeah, there's an old fish-hound down here. Giuseppe took me to his house because he's got a couple of nice quail, he gave me some red stuff."

The Corporal said: "That *vino's* murder, Captain, it'll give you the G.I. trots every time."

Captain Purvis said: "Yeah, I got 'em this morning. I feel terrible. But there's no excuse for that Major doing me the way he did."

Corporal Schultz said: "That *vino's* bad stuff, sir, you don't want to get mixed up with that *vino* no more'n you can help. Had some myself last night, and I been having to go every ten minutes this morning."

Captain Purvis said: "Yeah, I've made about six trips myself. I'm still sore at that Major."

Corporal Schultz was not a gold mine of conversation, and pretty soon the two fell silent. Captain Purvis yawned, stretched, stared out of the door into the bright street for a few minutes, yawned again, got up, walked around the room, sat down, yawned and said: "Christ, I'm bored. Wish I had something to do."

He leaned back in his chair, and put his feet up on his

desk again. As he did so, he knocked some papers on the floor.

"Oh, hell," he said, "I suppose I might as well clean up my goddam desk. Got to do it sooner or later."

He reached down on the floor and picked up the stray papers. He began to sort and arrange papers in piles, and he threw some away, and he got up and put some away in his files. He read some of them aloud to Corporal Schultz, who was not in the least interested.

In due course he picked up a purple slip, and he said: "Hell's bells, what's this?" And he read: "On July 19, orders were received from General Marvin, Forty-Ninth Division, to keep all mule carts out of the town of Adano. Guards were posted at bridge over Rosso River and at Cacopardo Sulphur Refinery. Order carried out. On July 20, guards were removed on order of Major Victor Joppolo. . . ."

Captain Purvis banged the flat of a hand down on the table. "Goddamit!" he shouted.

"Hey, Schultz," he said. "Where's Trapani?"

"Said he was just stepping out for a couple of minutes, sir, said he'd be right back. Anything I can do, sir?"

"No, goddamit. Wait till I get that Trapani."

Trapani came in in a few minutes.

"Hey, you, come over here," Captain Purvis said as soon as he arrived.

"Yes, sir," Trapani said.

"What's this?" the Captain said, and he held out the purple slip.

Trapani took it and looked at it. "That's the report on the mule cart situation, sir," Trapani said coolly. "You told me to make out a report, remember?"

"You're damn right I remember, and where did I tell you to send it?"

"It was to go to G-one of the Division, sir."

"Well goddamit, why didn't you send it?"

106

"I put it on your desk for approval, sir."

Captain Purvis huffed and puffed. He knew very well he didn't pay as much attention to his desk as he ought to. "Well, damn it to hell, let's send it out of here. I want to personally see you put that thing in the pouch for Division."

Sergeant Trapani sat right down and addressed an envelope, and put the slip in it, and put the envelope in the pouch which was to leave the next afternoon by courier for Division headquarters. He addressed the envelope to the wrong person at Division, but then, Captain Purvis didn't notice that.

Chapter 13

A PERSPIRING courier brought a note to Major Joppolo's office.

It said in English: "I got to seen you in the immediate." And it was signed M. Cacopardo.

Not five minutes behind the courier, Cacopardo himself showed up, all dressed for traveling. He had leather gauntlets on, and goggles up on his forehead, and he carried a green parasol in his right hand.

The eighty-two-year-old man trotted the length of Major Joppolo's office, leaned forward over his desk, looked over his shoulder at Giuseppe and Zito, then looked at the Major and said in a loud whisper: "I got to talk alone."

Major Joppolo asked his interpreter and usher to step outside.

"I have received a secret messages from the Mafia," the old man said, still whispering loudly. "I have the

A BELL FOR ADANO

military secrets of where are the German troops. You must send your soldiers, Mister Major."

Major Joppolo said: "I have no soldiers, I'm just the administrator of Adano."

Cacopardo said: "I got to go to the General. I am ready."

Major Joppolo said: "Just a minute, Mister Cacopardo, I can't send every Tom, Dick and Harry to see General Marvin. You'll have to give me some evidence that your information is good."

Old Cacopardo reached into his jacket and pulled out a piece of tissue paper. He unfolded it on Major Joppolo's desk. "See," he said, "here is Pinnaro, here is the hills before Pinnaro, here is the Germans. Element here of Forty-Third Panzers, something here out of Hermann Göring. I have all the details."

Major Joppolo decided at once that the chances of the old man's information being right were good enough so that he ought to send him forward to the Division.

"I will send you to the General, Mister Cacopardo," he said, "but I want to warn you. The General is a very impatient man. If your dope isn't straight, he'll be very angry. I don't know what he'll do to you, but it won't be nice. Also, old man, I've got to ask you not to get me in trouble with him. I'm already in Dutch with General Marvin. Promise me that you will be careful, will you?"

"I will be careful," Cacopardo said, "but the informations is important."

Major Joppolo made out a pass for Cacopardo and sent for a jeep from the motor pool.

Cacopardo stepped back, and raised his hand in a Fascist salute. Then, as his aged memory functioned, the hand wavered over to his forehead, and the salute became military. And he said: "Cacopardo is sulphur and sulphur is Cacopardo." He turned on his heel, as militarily as he could, and marched out.

108

Between the Palazzo in Adano and the headquarters of the Forty-Ninth Division, in a villa beyond Vicinamare, old Cacopardo did not say a word to the jeep driver. He sat leaning forward against the wind, his goggles down over his eyes and his parasol straining over his head. The jeep's windshield was down on the hood, with the canvas cover over it, as all jeep windshields should be where there is possibility of enemy strafing attacks, and so the wind was very strong. After a while old Cacopardo decided that sun was preferable to wind, and he moved the parasol down and held it in front of him, to fend off the wind.

The villa in which the Forty-Ninth Division was dug in for the time being had belonged to a friend of Cacopardo's. Cacopardo and this friend had shared an interest in Italian furniture, and the old man knew the value of the things in this villa. The friend was dead now, but Cacopardo had a hard time remembering which of his friends had died and which were still living; he therefore thought of them all as living. It was easier that way.

Because he was entering the villa of his friend, whom he considered to be living, Cacopardo approached the gate in the spirit of a cordial visit, and he expected to be received cordially. He was in for a surprise.

Anyone who has never tried to see a general could not possibly know what Cacopardo's reception was like.

A sentry stopped him at the gate.

"Good morning," said Cacopardo, as if addressing a butler at his friend's door, "is my friend Salatiello here?"

The sentry said: "Ain't nobody here of that name as I know of. What is he, an M.P.?"

"What is these M.P.?" Cacopardo asked his jeep driver.

"Military Police," the driver said.

"Military Police, indeed. He is prefect of Vicinamare

109

and a collector of wooden curiosities. He is my friend. This is his house. Is he here?"

"Say, Buck!" the sentry shouted to a man lounging inside the gate. "Ever hear of a fellow round here named — what was that name again, Bud?"

"Signor Salatiello, he is my friend."

"Saladullo?"

"Hell, no," Buck shouted back. "No one round here with a name like of that."

"No one here that name," the sentry repeated.

Cacopardo said: "Then where is General Marvin?"

M.P.'s are trained to be mysterious with strangers. "Jeez, I can't tell you that, Bud," the sentry said.

"I have a paper to see General Marvin," Cacopardo said, pulling out his pass.

"Oh, hell," said the sentry, "why didn't you say you had a pass? Sure, the General's here." And he shouted: "The Old Man's in, ain't he, Buck?"

"Yeah, I think His Nibs came in about half an hour ago."

"Yeah, he's in," the sentry said. "What you want to see him about?"

Cacopardo pulled out the tissue paper. "I can tell you where are the Germans," he said.

"Right up there," the sentry said, pointing up the driveway to the main door of the villa. "Right in that there door."

The jeep drove up to the main door. There was another sentry there. When Cacopardo tried to go in, the sentry put his bayoneted rifle across the path. Cacopardo jumped back, alarmed. "I am no enemies," he said. "I have the paper to see General Marvin," and he stretched out the pass. Cacopardo learned quickly, for a man his age.

The sentry took the pass. "Brother, I doubt if you can see the General right now," he said. "He don't like to see no one in the mornings. You stand here a minute." The sentry called the corporal of the guard.

The corporal of the guard came right back. "This way, brother," he said.

He led Cacopardo to a man at a desk.

"Name," the man said gloomily.

"Cacopardo."

"Is that a first name, for godsake, or a last name?" the sour man said.

"That is the name of my family," Cacopardo said.

"How you spell that?"

Cacopardo spelled it out. The man wrote laboriously: Cacaporato.

"First name," the unhappy man said.

"Matteo."

"Goddamit, you got to spell those Dago names."

Cacopardo spelled it and the man misspelled it.

"Who you want to see?"

"General Marvin."

"You haven't got a chance of seeing him," the man said. "Hell, there's a war going on, Dago. What you want to see the General about?"

Cacopardo reached in his pocket for the tissue paper. "I can show you where are the Germans," he said.

"You'll have to talk with G-two about that," the man said, and he pointed with his pencil. "First door on the right, where it says Colonel Henderson."

Cacopardo went to the door marked Colonel Henderson, and he knocked.

"Walk in, damn it," a voice shouted.

"General Marvin?" Cacopardo asked.

"Upstairs, upstairs," the impatient voice, which belonged to a full colonel, said. Cacopardo started out. "Say, wait a minute."

Cacopardo turned around. The Colonel said: "Who are you, anyway?"

111

"Cacopardo Matteo, I was sent to see General Marvin."

"General Marvin doesn't like Italians," the Colonel said. "What do you want to see him about? You better not ask him for any favors, he'll kick you out, personally, himself."

Cacopardo reached in his pocket for the tissue paper. "I can show you where are the Germans," he said.

"You've got no business taking that kind of thing to General Marvin. What do you think we have a G-two section for around here? You can just show that to me."

"I was sent to see General Marvin. That is the one I am going to see."

After an argument with Colonel Henderson, Cacopardo was sent upstairs under guard, was stopped and questioned by a sentry at the head of the stairs, was sent downstairs because he did not have a proper Division pass, was given a pass, was taken upstairs again, was questioned as to age, religion, political beliefs and sex by a sergeant, was interviewed by a staff officer who doubted whether the General would be free to see him, was referred to Colonel Middleton, the General's Chief of Staff, was questioned by Colonel Middleton's secretary, who thought the Colonel was busy, was finally admitted to Colonel Middleton, who, after an argument, agreed to see whether the General would see Cacopardo, which he doubted.

At the moment, General Marvin was playing mumble-te-peg with Lieutenant Byrd, his aide. They had found that a certain magohany table took the knife beautifully. The General had just reached the double flip off the forehead.

Colonel Middleton walked in just as the General let the knife go off his forehead. The surprise of Colonel Middleton's entrance was just enough to throw the Gen-

eral off his aim, and the knife clattered on the table and
did not stick in. This annoyed the General.

"Goddamit, haven't I told you to knock, Middleton?"

"Yes, sir. There's an old Italian here wants to see you."

"Middleton, what's the matter with you? Didn't I tell
you I didn't want to see any more Italians?"

"Yes, sir. But this one seems to be above the average.
He was sent to you by one of our people. He says he has
some information you would want."

"Well, dammit, show him in. What are you standing
there for? Show him in."

And so Cacopardo was finally brought into the presence of the General. By this time he was just as angry as
the General, and being some twenty years the General's
senior, he considered it his privilege to vent his anger
first.

He found perfect expression for his anger in what he
saw on the surface of the mahogany table.

"You are a barbarian," he said.

This was not a very good way for old Cacopardo to
begin with General Marvin, especially since he had two
strikes against him to begin with: he had caught the
General in a bad mood, and he was Italian.

"A *what?*" the General bellowed in his famous voice.

"I said, you are a barbarian. How dare you chop and
pick at the surface of my friend Salatiello's table?"

For the sake of argument, it would have made no difference whatsoever if General Marvin had known that
Salatiello had been thirteen years dead. The General
could not possibly have been more outraged. "Jesus
Christ," he bellowed at the walls, "who is this wop, anyhow?"

"That table was made circa 1775, when your country
had not even begun to existed, barbarian. It was carved
by Vincenzio Bianchi of Parma. I cannot calculate the

values of that table. You are a pig to chop and pick at it."

The General shouted: "Take this crazy wop out of here."

Colonel Middleton and Lieutenant Byrd rushed into the room. They grabbed old Cacopardo, and started to push him out.

"Wait!" the General roared. "Who sent that idiot here, Middleton?"

"I don't know, sir, it was some Major."

"You don't know? Goddamit, it's your business to know."

Colonel Middleton asked Cacopardo: "Who was it who sent you here?"

"My friend Major Joppolo, who is not a barbarian."

Colonel Middleton said: "What unit is this Major from?"

"Adano, from Adano," old Cacopardo said. "From my home, Adano."

"Adano," the General shouted. "There's something about that place. What is it about Adano, Middleton? Goddamit, what is it?"

"The cart, General," Colonel Middleton said. Colonel Middleton would never forget Adano as long as he lived.

"The cart? What cart? Goddamit, don't talk in riddles, Middleton. What cart?"

"The cart that we threw off the road, sir. The mule we shot, sir."

General Marvin remembered, and the memory turned his face a shade darker. "So that's the Major who sent you," he roared. "What was that name again? I want to remember that name."

"Joppolo," Middleton said.

General Marvin shouted: "Joppolo. Write that down, Middleton, remember that name. That goddam Major's a wop, too. I remember now, he's a goddam wop himself, isn't he, Middleton?"

In the interests of justice, Colonel Middleton said: "I don't remember, sir."

General Marvin shouted: "Well, I do. Now throw this crazy Italian sonofabitch out of here, and if you let any more Italians in here, Middleton, I'll break you back to a goddam second lieutenant."

"Yes, sir," Colonel Middleton said.

As they started to run him out, Cacopardo said: "But I have informations. I can tell you where are the Germans. It is important. The Germans, the Germans."

But the General was much too far gone in rage. Cacopardo was taken out and sent home. He couldn't get anyone, not even the sentry at the front gate, to listen to a description of the German positions before Pinnaro.

Chapter 14

BEHIND Major Joppolo's back, Captain Purvis was very critical of him. To his face, the Captain was cordial, even friendly.

The two men now had, besides their mere community of tongue, another thing to draw them together: they both knew the same girls. In a foreign land, that is enough to make Damon and Pythias out of two sworn enemies.

One day at lunch they talked about the girls. They talked as American men do talk about girls when they are abroad.

The Captain said: "That younger one, that Francesca, she sure has a nice pair."

Major Joppolo said: "I think the blonde one is more mature."

"Brother," the Captain said, "I'll trade you a nice pair for maturity any day in the week."

"Just a matter of taste," the Major said.

"Yeah," the Captain said, "I'll take a taste of the younger one, thanks. Just thinking about her makes me sharp. What do you say we go up there tonight and see 'em?"

"Let's do that," the Major said. "That would be fun." Then he wondered why he had reacted so quickly and so happily to the Captain's suggestion. The Captain's attitude toward these girls disgusted the Major. The Captain regarded the girls as trash; he seemed to think of them as something to buy and sell, like Italian watermelon and grapes and red wine. The Major refused to believe that he was falling into this way of thinking.

And yet he had jumped at the Captain's invitation. He thought back on the crazy evening at Tomasino's house. He thought of the sticky candy, of Tina's frankness about her unnaturally blonde hair; he thought of his own chattering about his life, and about his wife; and he thought about his loneliness late into the night. He thought the whole thing was very strange.

But it was not strange. It was very simple, really. It was typical of the way most honest Americans feel when they are abroad, and probably most Britons, and yes, probably most Germans and Japanese, too. It was a typical pattern of loneliness. Major Joppolo loved his wife. He missed her terribly. When, after many months, he found himself near a moderately pretty girl who was sympathetic to him, he found himself first excited by her prettiness; then he grew sad, and talked about the one he loved back home; then he was blackly lonely; then he caught himself thinking more and more often about the pretty one who was close by, and he was a little ashamed of thinking about her, and tried not to, but couldn't help it.

Major Joppolo's case was not as unique as he thought. He was just terribly lonely, and he was just behaving the way most men do in the face of such loneliness. (And Captain Purvis, who also had someone he loved back in the States, was behaving exactly like Major Joppolo: the only difference was the difference of his personality.)

And so it happened that the two dissimilar men went that evening to the house at 9 Via Vittorio Emanuele with very similar feelings of excitement and anticipation.

Major Joppolo and Captain Purvis caught the family of Tomasino by surprise that evening. The fat Rosa was sitting on the living room floor plucking a chicken, and there were feathers all over the room. The radio was on, and the two little daughters of the sister who was in Rome were sitting by it, also on the floor. Francesca and Tina were in brightly colored pajamas, lying on the floor side by side, reading together a cheap Italian romance called *Un Cuore in Tre*. Tomasino, who opened the front door, grimly led the two Americans into the room without any advance notice.

Everyone jumped up, the little girls squealing, fat Rosa calling the name of the Lord in English, and the big girls shouting greetings to the Americans.

Captain Purvis had not had a drop to drink, and was determined to be on his best behavior just to show the Major, but he couldn't help saying, when he saw the girls in their pajamas: "All ready for bed, eh, girls? Well, let's go, what are we waiting for?"

The family of Tomasino and their guests spent the next five minutes on their hands and knees picking up the chicken feathers. When that was done Rosa said to Tomasino: "Sad one, put the girls to bed." Tomasino led the little ones out without gentleness. Rosa retired to the kitchen with the feathers and the bird, to finish her job.

As soon as the two officers and the two girls in pajamas were left alone, Tina said: "Mister Major, I want to talk with you," and she stretched out her hand for his and led him into her bedroom. Captain Purvis's sober shouts followed them this time: "Hey, don't desert me. I can't talk to this lovely thing. Where you going?" And he subsided with: "Oh-oh, you lucky bastard," and settled down for an evening of desperate sign language.

Tina sat down on her bed and the Major sat down on a chair by a wooden dressing table.

"I want to ask you something, Mister Major," Tina said.

"Yes?" the Major said. He did not know what to expect, but he expected it would please him, whatever it was.

"How long do you think the war will last? Here on Italian soil, I mean."

The Major found that he was not pleased. "That's a very serious question," he said. "Let's not talk about war. That's all I have all day long, war, war, war."

"But I have a special reason for wanting to know," Tina said. "How long do you think it will last?"

"How should I know?" the Major asked. His voice was a little testy. "If I knew that, I would have to know a lot more about our plans for the campaign, and if I knew the plans, I would know military secrets, and I couldn't tell you secrets if I knew them."

"But you can guess, Mister Major."

"All right, I guess two more months."

"And how long do you think it will be after those two months before our Italian prisoners of war are released?"

Major Joppolo got the point very quickly, and it did not please him in the least. "You have a sweetheart who has been captured?"

"I don't know whether he has been captured or killed or what. That is the bad part. That is why I wanted to talk with you, Mister Major. Giorgio and I were going to be married."

"Well, what do you want me to do?"

"Can you find out for me whether he is a prisoner, Mister Major?"

"What do you expect me to do, go through all our prison camps and ask all the men if they are the sweetheart of Tina in Adano?"

"You must have some lists, don't you?"

"That is none of my business. I am civil affairs officer of Adano."

"Please help me, Mister Major. Not knowing is worse than having him dead."

"A hundred people come in my office every day asking me this. I tell you it is none of my business. The war is still going on, can't you understand that? We have a campaign to fight. We can't just stop in the middle of battle and open up a question-and-answer service for forlorn lovers."

"Oh don't, Mister Major, don't. You had been so nice to me. I thought — "

"Is this why you were cordial to me? Is this why you sent your father to invite me to your house? So that I could track down your lover?" Major Joppolo stood up. "I'm sorry that you have a mistaken idea of how I work. If you have business to do with me, do not invite me to your home and feed me candy. Come to my office. I will give you equal treatment with all the others."

And he turned and went into the living room, where Captain Purvis was shaping a heart with his two thumbs and forefingers and then pointing first at himself, then at Francesca.

"I'm going home, Captain."

"What for? Hell, the evening's just getting warm."

"Oh, I'm fed up with this, I'm going home."

"Well, you'll excuse me if I don't come. Goddam, I

never thought I'd ever get anywhere talking with my fingers, but this isn't bad. See you tomorrow, Major."

The Major left. Captain Purvis tried to pick up where he left off, but pretty soon Tina came in with tears in her eyes and told Francesca in Italian what had happened, and Rosa came in and asked where the Major was, and Tomasino came back from putting the little ones to bed, and Captain Purvis ran out of finger talk, which parents can understand as well as daughters. And so he got up and left too.

Later Major Joppolo was angry with himself for his childish petulance with Tina. He told himself that he had no right to expect anything else. He reminded himself that he had done a little talking the first evening about his wife, and Tina hadn't flown off the way he did. But he couldn't bring himself to apologize to her, and for several days and nights he did not see her.

He had no way of knowing that Tina was just as lonely as he was, and he did not realize that female loneliness sometimes takes exactly the same forms as male loneliness.

Chapter 15

CORPORAL CHUCK SCHULTZ of the M.P.'s used to talk a lot about how much he hated red wine, but it nevertheless had a certain fascination for him. Chuck's two best friends, Bill and Polack, also found the stuff interesting. The three of them drank it together quite often.

They used to buy it from Carmelina the wife of the lazy Fatta for a dollar a bottle. One night they bought three bottles for three dollars, and then they went to their billets to drink it.

It is very rare for an M.P. to drink anything, even *vino*, to excess, but Corporal Chuck Schultz was a rare M.P. His two friends, Bill and Polack, were in the Engineer Battalion which was working around Adano. They were billeted in the same house with Chuck and some other M.P.'s.

Chuck and Bill and Polack did not drink *vino* in order to savor it on their tongues. They did not drink it to compare it with other wines which they had had on other occasions. They did not drink it to complement food. They drank it to get drunk.

Therefore it was not surprising that on the night when they bought three bottles for three dollars, they began quite early in the evening to tell dirty jokes, then sang some songs, then argued a little, then got restless and decided to go for a walk. Nor was it surprising that the walk was rather noisy. It was really not surprising, either, that when they found that their walk was not taking them anywhere except round and round the same block, they should have decided to go back to their billet. This was not surprising, but it was the thing which got them in trouble.

If they had stayed in their billet and not gone for a walk, they would have been all right. So would they if they had not gone home to their billet so soon, but had walked until their drunkenness dulled their vision and blurred their keenness. But doing what they did got them in trouble.

Here is why:

On the way home, Chuck Schultz said: "Hell of a war."

Polack said: "Smatter, Chuck, you gonna get sick again?"

Chuck said: "Oh, hell no, I feel good. It's jus' hell of a war."

Polack said: "Prove it."

Bill said, for the ninetieth time that night: *"Uno due tre quattro cinque."*

Polack said: "Shup, Bill. Prove it's hell of a war, Chuck."

Chuck said: "Major."

Polack said: "Major who?"

Chuck said: "You know the fella. Town Hall fella."

Polack said: "Yeah, I know the one you mean."

Chuck said: "Joppolo, that's fellow. Hell of a war."

Polack said: "What about him? What's he gotta do with it?"

Bill said: *"Cinque cinque cinque cinque cinque."*

Chuck said: "He never gets drunk, never, never gets drunk. But he's good fella."

Polack said: "Oh, he's wonderful fella."

Chuck said: "He's bes' goddam fella whole invasion."

Polack said: "Oh, cripes, he's better'n that. He's perfec'."

Chuck said: "No, he ain' perfect. He don't drink. But he's good. Oh, he's good's hell. These wops, they think he's Jeez Christ. He's bes' goddam thing ever happened to this town."

Polack said: "What's 'at prove? Prove it's hell of a war. Don't change a subjec'."

Bill said: *"Uno due tre uno due tre."*

Chuck said: "Shut up your goddam counting, Bill. I'll prove it's hell of a war. It's all 'cause of the Major."

Polack said: "Goddamit, how's he prove anything if he don't drink?"

Chuck said: "Here's how he proves *everything*. He's bes' goddam thing ever happened to this town, but he's gonna get his ass kicked. Now is that any kind of a war?"

Polack said: "Who's gonna kick it? Show me the sonofabitch who's gonna kick it."

Chuck said: "General Marvin's gonna kick it, that's who."

Polack said: "Oh, hell, he kicks everybody's, I don't see nothin' special about that."

Chuck said: "Yeah, but look, Polack, here you got a guy who's best goddam thing ever happened to this town, I mean he unnerstands these people, and that old fart General Marvin he's gonna bust him down to Corporal, just like me. Now what the hell kind of a war is that?"

Bill said: "*Cinque quattro tre due uno.* Backwards. *Cinque quattro tre due uno.*"

Polack grew suspicious. He said: "How you know? Does the old fart tell you who he's gonna bust and who he's not?"

Chuck said: "I seen the paper."

Polack said: "Bustin' him?"

Chuck said: "No, the paper 'at's goin' to get him busted. Trapani and me, we tried to hide it, but the Cap'n found it. It's surer'n hell goin' to get the Major busted when old fart-face sees it."

Polack said: "Jeez, can you imagine a war like that?"

Chuck said: "Hell of a war."

Polack said: "Goddamit, Chuck, you proved it to me. Hell of a war."

Bill said: "I like *cinque* best. *Cinque cinque cinque.*"

Chuck said: "Rotten dirty stinkin' unfair lousy war."

Polack said: "Hell of a war, you take and ruin the bes' goddam man you got."

Chuck said: "I like that Major, he's a honest sonofabitch. I don't want for him to be busted like that."

Polack said: "I ain't never seen this Major, but if you say he's the best goddam Major you ever seen, I'll take your word for it and I think it's a unfair sonofabitchin' war myself for bustin' him."

Chuck said: "You know, we ought to do somethin'

for that Major. Polack, we ought to do somethin' for him."

Polack said: "You said me a mouthful, Chuck. We surer'n hell ought to."

Chuck said: "What could we do, Polack? Somethin' good. He deserves it, by damn, somethin' good."

Polack said: "What the hell *could* we do, Chuck? You're a goddam Corporal, and Bill and me, we're just goddam P.F.C.'s. What the hell could *we* do?"

Chuck said: "Let's think."

Polack said: "Okay, pal. . . . You thinkin'?"

Chuck said: "Yeah, but I ain't got a damn thing."

Bill said: "*Uno due tre.* We ought to give the guy a goin'-away present if he's all that good."

Chuck said: "First sensible thing you said all night, Bill. We'll give him a goddam present."

Polack said: "What'll we give him, Chuck?"

Chuck said: "Jeez, that's a hell of a tough one. For a goin'-away present, hell, it's got to be good, if it's for him."

Polack said: "It was Bill's idea. What'll we give him, Bill?"

Bill said grandly: "*Uno due tre quattro cinque.*"

Chuck said: "He's no goddam good, him and his numbers. We got to think of something, Polack, we got to."

Polack said: "Let's go back and get those bottles. Maybe they'd help us think of something."

Chuck said: "That's right, let's go back to old Four Eyes' house. Maybe we'll think of something there. Take a drink, think of something."

The billet where Chuck and Bill and Polack lived was in the grand town house of a man named Quattrocchi. This man was a merchant whose family had lived in Adano for generations, and for generations had been wealthy. Their house, except possibly for old Cacopardo's, was the nicest in town. It had been picked as a

billet on the first day of the invasion. In the beginning
a field hospital had moved in, and afterwards the engineers and M.P.'s had taken over. Signor Quattrocchi
had left all of his furniture in the house, merely covered
over with canvas slip covers; he had left some of his
glassware, in glass-fronted cabinets the doors of which
were locked; he had left many of his books on the
shelves; he had left the larger of his paintings still hanging. He had not had much time to arrange his affairs,
but Major Joppolo had tried to assure him that his house
would be well taken care of.

The three drunken boys entered the house and noisily
made their way upstairs to the room where they slept.
Each took a bottle out from his bedroll and they sat for
a time drinking and thinking.

Chuck said: "Take a drink, have a think."

Polack said: "Get a stink, take a drink."

Chuck said: "Jeez, that's hard, to think of somethin'
good enough for that goddam Major."

Polack said: "I can think of a lot of things, but not a
goddam one of 'em is good enough. The trouble with
that goddam Major is he's too damn good. Now you give
me a lousy Major, and I'd have you a present in no
time."

Chuck said: "It's a hell of a war when you can't even
think of a goin'-away present for a good guy."

Polack said: "Say! I just thought of somethin' terrible.
Are you sure this Major's goin' away?"

Chuck said: "Didn't I see that slip of paper?"

Polack said: "Tha's right. Shall we give him a bottle
of ol' lady Fatta's wine?"

Chuck said: "Hell, Polack, you know that's not good
enough. You know damn well this wine gives you the
G.I. trots every time you drink it. You wouldn't want
to send the Major out of this town having to go to the
latrine every ten minutes, would you?"

125

Polack said: "Tha's right. Shall we give him some paregoric an' bismuth? If he's got the trots, that's the bes' goddam thing there is."

Chuck said: "Polack, I think you're drunk. You know he ain't got the trots till we give him this *vino*. What the hell's the matter with you?"

Bill said: "One, two, three, four, five. Why don't you borrow something from old Four Eyes here to give the Major? You'd find a real nice goin'-away present right here in this house if you just got up off your fat behinds and looked for it."

Chuck said: "Bill, why don't you have more ideas? You got the best goddam ideas when you have 'em."

Polack said: "Yeah, good idea, let's borrow something."

Chuck said: "Bill, you don't even know how good your ideas are when you have 'em. Look: this Major, he's Italian himself, speaks it like a goddam native. He sure is gonna appreciate something Italian from old Four Eyes' house. Boy, Bill, I don' know why you aren' a goddam millionaire with the ideas you got."

Bill said: "*Uno* and *tre* is *quattro*. *Due* and *tre* is *cinque*. Jeez, I can even add."

Chuck said: "Let's go an' find something 'fore we pass out."

The three boys got up. They were pretty drunk now. They staggered out of their room and along a long corridor until they came to a drawing room.

Polack said: "Lookit that room, like a goddam Gran' Central Station. There's a lot of Eyetalian junk in there."

Chuck said: "Let's have look."

Polack said: "Why'n we give'm a chair?"

Chuck said: "Good idea. Take the goddam shroud off'n a chair, give 'im a chair."

Chuck and Polack skated across the floor to a chair. They bent over it to take the slip cover off. Their fum-

126

bling hands could not find where to loosen the cover.

"Lif' it up," Chuck suggested. "Look at it from unnerneath."

So they lifted the chair above their heads. Polack reeled. Chuck lost his grip. The chair crashed to the floor, and a leg broke off. Bill picked the leg up.

Chuck said: "Too damn much trouble, lousy chair. Hell with a chair."

Polack spotted a terra cotta bust standing on a marble pillar-like stand in one corner. "Who's 'at?"

Bill said, as if positive: "Garibaldi."

Polack said: "Le's give'm a Garibally." And he went over to the corner, lifted the bust off the pillar, started uncertainly back toward the others, lost his balance, and dropped the bust. It broke into hundreds of pieces.

Polack looked over the mantel at a painting of a fat nude. She was lovely in his wine-washed eyes, and he said: "Give'm a woman. A Major needs a woman."

So the three worked together to get the painting down. They balanced themselves on chairs and grunted and all lifted on the bottom edge of the painting. They managed to lift it off its hook, but they could not keep it balanced. The picture fell, and its canvas hit the back of a chair, and the fat woman was ripped from flank to flank.

Polack said: "Hell with Gran' Central Station. Le's go in 'nother room."

They went into a dining room. In one corner there was a big glass-faced cabinet containing Venetian glassware on shelves. "Give 'im somethin' to drink out of," Chuck said.

He tried the door of the cabinet, but it was locked. "Bill," he said, "open this goddam thing up. Don't just stan' there with that goddam club. Open up."

Polack said: "Case of 'mergency, break glass an' pull lever."

Bill stepped up and poised the chair leg. "*Uno, due, tre,*" he said, and on three he let go. The glass front shivered to the floor. The three boys staggered forward to chose a gift. First they dropped a bowl. Then they dropped a glass swan. Then they dropped a big goblet. Then they knocked the whole cabinet over and broke everything.

The three men went from room to room this way, leaving a trail of ruin behind them. Their disappointment grew as they saw their chances dwindling of getting anything good enough (or durable enough) for the Major.

Finally Chuck said: "Hell of a war, when you can't even find a present in ol' Four Eyes' house."

Polack said: "Hell of a lousy goddam unfair war."

Bill said: "Le's go to bed."

So they went to bed. Polack heard Chuck crying in his bedroll, and he said: "Smatter, Chuck, feel sick?"

Chuck sobbed: "Hell of a war."

Polack said: "Yeah, hell of a war, Chuck, go to sleep."

Chapter 16

WHEN Major Joppolo arrived at his office next morning, two visitors were waiting for him. One was Quattrocchi, owner of the house where Chuck, Bill and Polack were billeted. But Quattrocchi had to wait, because the other was Lord Runcin, one of the Amgot higher-ups. The Allied Military Government was, and still is, a joint British-American affair, and as in the higher echelons of the military command, American and British officers were sandwiched in with each other. Lord Runcin was near the top.

Lord Runcin was a man of about fifty. He had wavy

blonde hair and bright eyes which seldom looked straight at whoever he was talking with. He took snuff. Aside from the fact that he had a purely colonial point of view toward the Italians, he was considered to be a pretty good man for Amgot. Not the least of his attributes was his energy. On this particular morning, it was only five minutes past eight, and yet Lord Runcin had been on the road since six thirty, had taken breakfast on American rations in a wheat field, and had been waiting patiently for his Amgot representative in Adano for fifteen minutes. He was making a round of interviews, to try to pick up the best examples of Amgot work from each of the occupied towns.

Major Joppolo showed him into his office. "Wizard quarters," His Lordship said. Lord Runcin affected the slang of his subordinates, but he always seemed to use American slang when talking to his British men, and *vice versa*, so that many of them understood very little of what he said.

This was the first time Major Joppolo had ever had a *tête à tête* with a real honest to goodness Lordship. He was surprised to find him wearing shorts and an open collar and no hat at all. His Lordship's deferential manner, as he sat on the other side of the Major's desk asking questions, made Major Joppolo, who had once been a clerk in the Sanitation Department of New York City, feel quite important.

By way of making conversation, His Lordship pointed a thumb in Quattrocchi's direction and said: "Your Italian friend is in quite a flap."

The former Sanitation clerk said: "What was that, Lord? I didn't get that."

"Never mind," said His Lordship. "Well, what kind of a job have you been doing here, Joppolo?"

The former Sanitation clerk said: "Well, Lord, I've been doing all right."

129

"Doing all right, eh?" His Lordship smiled and made a note of the expression in his notebook, for future use. "What are the best things you've done?"

Well, there was the subsidy. The Italians used to pay every family with a son in the Army eight lira a day for the head of the family and three lira for each dependent. Because these people really depended on the subsidy, Major Joppolo had started paying it again at the old rate. He now called it Public Assistance, because he thought that sounded more democratic. He paid it out of fines and income from goods that he was selling, and he had a committee consisting of the Mayor, the Chief of the Carabinieri and a local citizen to determine whether each family needed or deserved Public Assistance. On the first day the town had paid out seventy-four thousand lira.

"Bully," said His Lordship. "What else?"

Well, to show how the town was financing itself, there was the muslin. A Liberty Ship had come into Adano harbor, and had discharged a cargo of war materials — bulldozers, bridge girders, tents, and some ammunition. Down in the bottom of one hold the unloaders found six bales of white muslin. The skipper of the ship said he had to unload it. The Quartermaster on the beach would not take it. There were no papers for the muslin, no consignment. The muslin had U.S. Treasury markings on it, so it was obviously Lend-Lease, and it was obviously lost. Major Joppolo heard about it, and seeing the rags on the people of his town, he said he could use it. He called his Civil Supply director and told him about the muslin, and the director gave permission to sell it at a fair price. Major Joppolo put two rolls up for sale, and held the other four in reserve. There was such a shortage of cloth in the town that the two rolls were gone in that many hours.

"Good work, Joppolo," His Lordship said. "What else?"

There was the refugee problem. On the day of the invasion, there were only six or seven thousand people in the town; the others had all run to the hills. Within a few days there were thirty-two or -three thousand. The town got badly crowded, and one reason was that there were a lot of refugees from the town of Vicinamare. These people had come down to Adano because the Allies had been bombing Vicinamare pretty hard before the invasion. Now that the battle had gone beyond Vicinamare, they wanted to go home, but there was no transportation. One day the Major saw a German bus driving down the street. An American soldier was driving it. Major Joppolo said to himself: "I could use that bus." He asked around and found out it belonged to the Engineers. So he called the Motor Officer and said: "I'd like to use that bus of yours one day a week." The Motor Officer said it would be okay with him if the Major had proper permission. So Major Joppolo called the Adano base commander, who said it would be all right. And a few days later one busload of cheering, laughing people had started home. Now Colonel Sartorius, head of Amgot for the Province of Vicinamare, heard about the bus a few days later, and he got sore, and told Major Joppolo not to do that any more. "Sometimes," Major Joppolo said, "I think Colonel Sartorius is an awful dope."

Lord Runcin said: "Do you mean you think he takes harmful drugs?" And his Lordship dipped into his snuffbox.

Major Joppolo said: "Oh no, Lord, I just mean he's stupid."

"Dope, eh?" His Lordship said, and put the expression down in his book. "Very good, what else?"

Well, Lord, the people of Adano were so contented under the Americans that they offered of their own accord, without anybody suggesting it, to maintain the little American cemetery on the outskirts of town. So they built a fence around it and painted it white, and Russo the old stonecutter was making headstones, and every Sunday the people took flowers up and put them on the graves of the boys who had died taking the town.

"I say," His Lordship said, "damned touching. What else?"

Food was pretty good. In the first days, the Major had found five cars of wheat on a siding at the railroad station, had had it ground into flour, and had been able to spare some for the neighboring hill towns, which were starving. He had given one baker a very heavy fine, three thousand lira, for baking soggy bread, for refusing to sell it on credit, for refusing to take American invasion lira, and for having dirty hands; and since then the bread had been pretty good from all the bakers. He had taken steps to send the fishermen out. He had arranged for the people to have pasta, which they had not had for eight months. Food was all right.

"Good," said Lord Runcin. Every time His Lordship took snuff, Major Joppolo's eyes nearly popped out of his head and he almost forgot what he was talking about. "Anything else?"

Well, cleaning this town up was something like Hercules and that stable of his. But fortunately the Major had some experience with sanitation. When the Americans came into the town, one old man was charged with keeping it clean. All he had the strength to do was sweep off the sidewalk in front of the Palazzo and carry away Mayor Nasta's garbage. Now Major Joppolo had a crew of forty-five men working. They had eight refuse carts and an Italian truck which had been converted into a water truck. It sprayed the streets every morning.

"Water," said His Lordship. "Positively pansy."

The Major didn't understand that expression, but he took it as a compliment.

"Oh sure, Lord," he said, "this town is much better off than it was before we came in. You can't imagine how these people were ground down. Why, they're so used to being afraid of officials, and so used to making out forms and being hauled up to court and having carabinieri ask them their names, that they all put their last names first and their first names last, the way it goes on official papers, all the time. Just like the Chinese.

"Lots of them have told me that they're better off now than they were before. For one thing, they can congregate in the streets any time they want and talk about whatever they want to. They can listen to their radios. They know they can get a fair trial out of me. They can come to the City Hall and talk to me any time they want. Mayor Nasta had office hours from twelve to one each day and you had to apply for an audience weeks in advance. I told you about the streets being clean. Oh, there are lots of ways, Lord, and if I have anything to do with it there'll be lots more."

His Lordship was getting a wee bit bored. He dipped more and more frequently into his snuffbox and looked out the window. "Fine show, fine show," he said. "Anything bad in this town?"

"Yes, there is, Lord," the Major said. "One thing."

"I wish all of our towns had just one thing wrong, Joppolo."

"Well, this isn't exactly bad, Lord, and maybe it'll sound a little silly to you."

"My job," said Lord Runcin, taking snuff grandly, "is to make sense out of silly things. What is it, Joppolo?"

"Well sir, this town needs a bell."

"A bell? Why, Major, I heard such a jangling of bells

133

at eight o'clock this morning, you might have thought
it was Christmas day."

"Yes, but this is a special bell, Lord."

"I didn't know they had any special bells except in
Hell."

"This one was seven hundred years old. It was just
about the most important thing in the town, to hear
these people talk. Mussolini took it away . . ." And Major Joppolo told how the bell had been crated up and
shipped away to make gun barrels, and how the people
had come to him about it, and how he had tried to track
it, and had found that it was almost certainly melted
down, and at any rate was in unoccupied territory.

Lord Runcin's colonial attitude cropped up. "Surely,"
he said, "these people can get along with the bells they
have. We can't afford to be too sentimental, you know,
Joppolo. Can't afford to let these people be *too* happy,
you know. Can't afford to let discipline get too loose."

"Lord, I can't see that happiness and discipline don't
go together."

"Young man," said His Lordship, taking a sniff for
emphasis, "I think I've had a little more experience in
these things than you have."

"Every time I've done something for these people,"
Major Joppolo said, "I've found they did two things for
me just out of thanks."

"Well, what do you want *me* to do about this bell?"

"I just wondered, Lord, if you could suggest a way to
get them another bell. Not just any bell, you know, but
one that could take the place of the one they lost."

"Every time I need something out of the ordinary,"
His Lordship said, "I make application to the United
States Army. They have the most extraordinary things,
you know. They gave me a jeep. They gave me my choice
of pipes, damned good briar, too, went from Scotland to
the U.S.A. and all the way back here to Algiers, by way

of the U.S. Army. Some one told me about these electrical razors, and they even got me one of those, but I can't use it because of this damned Italian current, wrong current, you know, not like our current. I suggest you try the U.S. Army, Joppolo."

"I haven't had quite the same kind of luck with the Army, Lord. You got some friend, or something? Who do you ask for all these fancy things they get you?"

"Just write General Wilson, W. B. Wilson, Quartermaster Depot, Algiers. General Wilson told me he'd try to get me anything I wanted. Just use my name, Joppolo, he'll find you a bell. I'm sure of it."

Major Joppolo wrote down General Wilson's name and address. "Thank you, Lord," the Major said. "That sounds like it might work. I sure want to get a bell for this town."

Lord Runcin clapped his snuffbox shut and stood up. "Well, Joppolo, sounds to me as if you were doing a wizard job here. Keep it up. If you have any troubles, just give me a buzz." And His Lordship left, on the verge of a delicious sneeze which he had been saving in his nostrils for ten minutes.

Major Joppolo stared out of the window, and he was wonderfully happy, with the double happiness of accomplishment and praise for it. He was drawn back from his pleasant daze by a torrent of Italian.

It came from Quattrocchi.

"You Americans think you are so civilized, you think you are doing us a favor by disembarking on our shores. You are no better than the Germans. The Germans never did anything in this town such as your men have done. I gave you my house. I did not mind giving you my house. I thought the Americans were civilized. You are the one who told me they are civilized. You said they would take care of my house as if they owned it. You are a liar."

Having been praised so recently, Major Joppolo was stung by this dispraise.

"What do you want?" he said sharply. "Stop this babbling and tell me what you want."

"I don't want anything. What I have lost I can never get back, so how can I want anything?"

"If you don't want anything, why are you taking up my time?"

Quattrocchi spoke sarcastically: "I'm sorry if your time is so valuable, Your Worship." And then he spoke angrily: "I have lost some things which were valuable to me, too. I went to my house this morning, to get some things I had left behind. And what did I find? I found that your barbarians had smashed my terra cotta head, it was done by the Florentine Camilliani in the sixteenth century. What value can you place on that? They tore my Venus; it was by Giorgione. What is the price of that? They smashed the glasses in which my mother drank her bridal toasts in Venice. How many lira do you think they were worth to me?"

Quattrocchi began to cry, and became incoherent.

Major Joppolo was furious. He called up Captain Purvis and said: "Purvis, what the hell's the matter with your men? Did you know they'd been behaving like a bunch of wild men in their billet? This fellow was good enough to let them use his house and some of the stuff in it, why the hell did they have to abuse it? I want you to find out who busted up the stuff down at your billet and have them in your office in fifteen minutes." And he hung up without waiting for the astonished Captain to take a deep breath.

Major Joppolo walked around to the other side of his desk and patted the sobbing Quattrocchi on the shoulder. He said: "Come, Quattrocchi, let's go down to your house and see exactly what they did."

So the two men walked down the street to the beautiful house. Quattrocchi led the Major through the rooms on the second floor and showed him the broken things.

Major Joppolo was terribly depressed by what he saw. "There is no excuse for it," he said softly to Quattrocchi, who was beyond fury.

Major Joppolo took Quattrocchi up to the M.P. headquarters. Captain Purvis had Chuck, Bill and Polack there. As soon as the Major came in, the three boys stood at attention.

"At ease," Major Joppolo said, "but listen."

The three boys stood at ease.

"You fellows ought to be sent home to the States," he said. "What kind of an example do you think you men are for the people here? How do you think we'll ever persuade them that we're decent people if you behave like we all live in the woods and have shaggy fur?"

Polack said: "We didn't mean no hurt, Major."

The Major said: "Your intentions don't make the slightest bit of difference. It's the result that matters."

Polack said: "We was doin' it for you, Major."

"What do you mean, doing it for me? How could you think I would want you to do anything like that?"

Polack said: "We was lookin' for a present for you, sir." Polack thought that if the Major stacked up to all the boasting Chuck Schultz had done about him the night before, he ought to be able to talk their way out of this fix.

The Major said: "Why in God's name would you want to get me a present? I've never seen you before."

Polack said: "We're just enlisted men. We seen you before."

Major Joppolo said: "I still want to know how you thought you were getting me a present, and why you were."

Polack said: "It was goin' to be a goin'-away present."

The Major said: "Who's going away?"

137

Polack said: "Well, Corporal Schultz here said —"

Chuck Schultz said: "You let me handle this, Polack."

Major Joppolo turned on Corporal Schultz: "Say, what is this all about anyway?"

Chuck Schultz saw that there was no way out. He said: "There wasn't no excuse for what we done, Major. We was very drunk. I think Polack here's still a little drunk."

Polack raised a threatening fist and said: "Why you . . ."

Major Joppolo said: "What's all this about a present?"

Chuck said: "Sir, we just got some kind of a drunk idea that you was about the best officer we ever seen, and we figured we wanted to give you a present. We thought maybe we could find a present for you in the house. We knew you was Italian, more or less, and we thought you'd like something Italian from the house. That's all there was to it."

Major Joppolo said, and his voice was much softer: "I'm not Italian, boys. I'm American, and sometimes I'm not as proud of it as I'd like to be."

Then the Major turned to Quattrocchi, and he said in Italian: "I hardly know what to tell you. I know that no apologies and no payment can ever return what you have lost. I wish to tell you that these men who committed the crime are sorry for what they did, now that they realize how cruel they were to you. I wish to tell you, Quattrocchi, that I feel less proud of being an American than I did yesterday. These men will be punished justly and severely for what they have done. I want you to file a claim for payment for what was destroyed, and I wouldn't blame you for doubling the prices. That's all I can say, Quattrocchi."

Quattrocchi said: "I don't know about most Americans, but I know I can always get justice from you, Mister Major."

The Major said: "Good day, Quattrocchi. From now on your house will be kept nicely, I can promise you that."

Quattrocchi left. The Major turned to the three boys. He said: "I don't know whether you realize yet what you've done to this Italian. It's as if you had cut his arm off. He loved those things you busted up. Now I just told him that you three would be punished severely — as severely as you have hurt him."

The three boys stiffened up a little.

The Major said: "I'm going to make this your punishment: to have this man's unhappiness on your conscience, and from now on to keep his house as clean as if everything in it belonged to your own mother. That's all. You're dismissed."

Chuck said: "Yes sir, thank you, sir."

Polack said: "Thank you, sir."

Bill said: "Thank you, sir. We'll take care of the house."

Polack said: "Yes sir, we sure will."

As soon as they were outside, Chuck said: "What'd I tell you about that guy?"

Polack said: "That's the best goddam guy I ever seen in *this* Army."

Bill said: "The thing that got me down was what he said about my mother. Mom was always so proud of her glass. Cut glass it was. I feel like I busted it last night."

Chapter 17

HAVING weathered eighty-two winters, Cacopardo was not the least cooled in his desire to help the Americans by General Marvin's behavior.

Every two or three days he would send a note to Major Joppolo. Many were silly suggestions. Many were about things Major Joppolo had already done. But one day he sent a note which caught Major Joppolo's interest.

"To the Officer of CIVIL AFFAIRES:

"I beg to notify, for the necessary steps: Since several months, the small people at Adano does not receive the ration of olive oil, or other fats, but the officials both of commune, civil & military staf, have been largily provided for the families & personal friends.

"I am informed, that the small population is therefore compelled to pay at the black market any price, up to Lire 80 per liter (equal to 800 grams). The price fixed by the Fascist government for the supply is Lire 15 & an half per kilo (1,000 grams).

"You cannot allow any longer this tiranny against the poors!"

"Respectfully,
"Matteo Cacopardo."

The thing which interested Major Joppolo in this note was the fact that old Cacopardo blamed the black market on Fascist graft. Now Major Joppolo was acutely aware of the black market. He had intended for some time to investigate it. Now he did, and what he found was disturbing.

The black market was not the fault of corrupt Fascists. It was not even the fault of the merchants who jacked their prices out of all bounds. It was the fault of the invaders. Demonstrably, it was the fault of the Americans.

There were two reasons why the Americans gave Adano its black market, and the inflation which inevitably went with it. One reason was American generosity.

Apparently the Italians thought the Americans were coming to their soil armed mainly with cigarets and candies, for every grown person asked for cigarets and every child shouted in the streets for candies. And the Americans gave what was begged. They also gave C Rations, both cans which they had opened and had been unable to finish, and unopened cans. When they bought anything, they figured the price by their heart. And the second thing was that when they bought anything, and could not find an Italian-speaking pal to dicker for them, they just paid what they figured they would have paid in the United States.

Here are four examples that Major Joppolo dug up, which show exactly how the black market and inflation grew up:

He traced the black market in wine to the house of Carmelina, wife of the lazy Fatta. The very first person who bought wine from Carmelina, on the very first night of the invasion, was Corporal Chuck Schultz. Carmelina's story to the Major was that the Corporal had just handed her a dollar and walked away. Schultz's story was that the Italian lady had haggled and shouted and threatened to call the police. In any case, Schultz paid a dollar. The regular price for that grade of wine before the invasion had been twenty lire, or twenty cents.

Four soldiers sauntered into a barber shop one morning, and made motions with their fingers around their skulls that indicated they wanted haircuts. None of them could speak Italian, so they based their payment on what they had last paid for haircuts in the States. Each plunked down a fifty cent piece and said: "Keep the change, Joe." The regular price for haircuts had been three lire, or three cents. Shaves had cost two lire. Here in one morning's work, the barber had made two hundred lire. He retired to a life of leisure, and refused to cut any hair for three weeks, till his money gave out.

The black market in prostitution was serious. Demand was naturally high, with a newly arrived Army. Supply was rather low, what with the timid girls who had run into the hills. Now their standard price before the invasion had been, believe it or not, five lire, or five American cents. In making their propositions in the early days, American soldiers who could not speak Italian had used what they thought to be international sign language: they had raised two fingers, representing an offer of two bucks. There was some confusion at first, when the girls thought they meant two lire, or two cents, and for a time they refused to do business. But later they caught on: two hundred lire a piece. Business flourished then and so did the black market.

The welfare of the town was really threatened by the black market in food. Peasants, instead of bringing their grapes and melons and fresh vegetables into the town market, would go to the various bivouac areas and hang around the edges until they could catch a straggler. Then, in the heat of the day, they would tempt the Americans with cool-looking fruits, and would sell them for anywhere from ten to twenty times the proper prices. It got so bad that city people would buy what little fruit did reach the town market, and would take it out into the country to sell it to the foolhardy Americans.

To stop, or at least to curb, the black market, Major Joppolo did three things: he put the town out of bounds to American soldiers, who from then on could enter only on business; he had the Carabinieri stop all foodstuffs from leaving the town; and he fined anyone caught selling over-price or under-measure three thousand lire — a lifetime's savings for a poor Italian peasant.

Chapter 18

SERGEANT TRAPANI's having addressed the purple slip reporting the countermand order on the carts to the wrong person did not help much. As soon as the wrong person opened up the envelope and read the slip, he forwarded it to the right person.

The right person was Lt. Col. W. W. Norris, G-One Officer of the 49th Division. The wrong person put the purple slip on his desk. Col. Norris, who was burdened down with much too much paper work, did not even read it all the way through. He just read the first part, about General Marvin's issuing the order that carts should be stopped on the outskirts of Adano.

Then he wrote in pencil on the upper left hand corner of the slip: "Usual copies for Division files. One extra copy to be sent to Colonel Middleton marked 'For General Marvin's Information.'" And then he tossed the slip in his outgoing basket.

A couple of hours later a Technical Sergeant emptied Col. Norris's outgoing basket, and in time got around to making three copies of the purple slip for the files of the 49th Division, where they would be buried, never to be seen again. One copy went under M.P.'s, one copy into the Personnel file, and the third into the Intelligence files under Occupied Territory, Disciplinary Measures. The Technical Sergeant recopied the purple slip, so that he could make a clean top copy for Colonel Middleton and the General. He wanted to get ahead. He didn't want to do anything sloppy. He was so careful in his typing that he didn't even notice what the purple slip said.

The Technical Sergeant put the four copies and the original purple slip into Col. Norris's incoming basket.

It happens that Col. Norris had an assistant, one Lieutenant Butters, who was very inquisitive. He annoyed the Colonel often by reading over his shoulder. He always wanted to know what the Battle Order was the moment it was drawn up, before it even went to regimental commanders.

The only advantage of Lieutenant Butters' curiosity was that he usually read Colonel Norris's mail more carefully than either Colonel Norris or his Technical Sergeant.

The morning after the Technical Sergeant put the purple slip and the four copies into the Colonel's incoming basket, Lieutenant Butters got up bright and early, dressed, shaved out of his helmet, and before breakfast went to Colonel Norris's desk and went through his incoming basket.

When he came to the purple slip and the four copies, he took the papers out of the pile, read until he had finished, put the pile back into the incoming basket, and then tucked the purple slip and the four copies into a portfolio on his own desk.

Later in the day, when the Colonel was out to a conference, Lieutenant Butters took out the purple slip and the four copies. He called the Technical Sergeant over to his desk.

"Did you see these?" the Lieutenant asked.

The Technical Sergeant, who was afraid he had made a mistake in typing, said merely: "Yes, sir."

"Well, that Major was right," the Lieutenant said.

The Technical Sergeant, who hadn't the faintest idea what the purple slip was about, said: "He was?"

The Lieutenant said: "Sure he was. It's easy to see he was. And if General Marvin ever lays eyes on this Information copy, it'll be just too bad for the Major."

"Yes, sir," said the Technical Sergeant, to be on the safe side.

Lieutenant Butters said: "Here, you file these, I'll take care of the Information copy."

"Yes, sir," the Technical Sergeant said, taking the copies.

The Lieutenant said: "That Marvin trimmed me down once for something I didn't do. I never have liked him. I don't know this Major, but I think it would be a shame if he caught a trimming just for this."

"Yes, sir," the Technical Sergeant said. Then he frowned and added: "You aren't going to get me in trouble, are you, sir, like when that letter to Colonel Norris from the P.R.O. got 'lost'?"

"No, don't worry," the Lieutenant said.

But the Technical Sergeant did worry for several days, until he got up the courage to ask the Lieutenant: "Sir, what did you ever do about that Information copy I made for General Marvin? You didn't throw it away, did you? Colonel Norris is liable to ask me about it."

"I wish I had thrown it away," Lieutenant Butters said. "I didn't have the guts. I put it in the courier pouch for Algiers. You know how much stuff we've been losing on that run. I thought maybe — "

The Technical Sergeant, relieved of his worry, smiled and said: "It might get lost accidentally on purpose?"

Chapter 19

MAYOR NASTA had just come out from his daily repentance before Sergeant Borth. He walked across the way to the broad sidewalk in front of the Palazzo. Every day knots of people gathered on that sidewalk, some just to pass the time of day, some to air their perennial com-

145

plaints, some to get in touch with the town's mean little lawyers, whose office was that sidewalk.

Mayor Nasta walked up to one such knot. There were about ten people, and he found that they were discussing the war.

He waited for his chance, and said: "I got some news from the interior yesterday afternoon."

Mercurio Salvatore the crier was so far gone in boldness that he said: "We have no desire for news from the one who is no longer Mayor."

Mayor Nasta remembered the time when he would have put the crier in jail for a whole year for saying something like that, but now he said: "This news came from the son of your friend Afronti, the noisy cartman. The boy deserted on the first day of the invasion and he is now here. Perhaps you know him. He is an honest boy."

The Mayor's poison was beginning to take hold. "If that is the case," said the lazy Fatta, who was to be found on this stretch of sidewalk every morning, "if that is the case, what did he say that was so interesting?"

"He said that our friends the Germans are mounting a counterattack."

"There is nothing new in that," said Father Pensovecchio. "They have counterattacked before. They counterattacked near Vicinamare and it did them no good. They were thrown back. They will be thrown back again."

"Not this time," said Mayor Nasta. "This time they will employ five fresh divisions. They have the crack 29th Panzers and the Pilsener Division. These are good troops. This time they will not be thrown back. They intend to push the Americans into the sea."

The lazy Fatta, who had no sense about the news, said: "When will this attack come? I think I will go to the hills."

Mayor Nasta looked very important, as he used to in

the old days. "I should not tell you this," he said, "but the attack will begin on the morning of the twenty-third, at four o'clock in the morning. You can expect the Americans to be pushed into the sea between the twenty-fifth and the twenty-eighth."

The impressionable ones were beginning to believe him. Laura Sofia, the unmarried one, who stood about on this sidewalk in the belief that she might catch a husband that way, said: "The twenty-third, that is next Wednesday."

But Mercurio Salvatore, who had been treated well by the Americans, refused to believe that they were leaving. "I do not believe it," he said. "The Americans will stop the attack." Even the crier was now willing to believe that there was going to be an attack. All he would not believe was that the Germans would succeed.

Mayor Nasta said: "The Americans will not stop it. The Americans may be friendly, but they are not good fighters."

Margherita, the formidable wife of Craxi, said with a threatening look: "Liar!"

But Mayor Nasta said: "This is not my opinion. This is the opinion of the son of Afronti, the noisy cartman. You know the boy. You know that he is honest. He says that the Americans are timid in battle. He says that our own troops could even beat the Americans."

Mercurio Salvatore, the crier, was reduced to saying: "I do not believe it."

Mayor Nasta said: "It is true. This boy fought in Tunisia. He says that at the place called El Guettar the Americans did not press their attack, he says that they behaved like frightened men and were defeated. The British can fight, perhaps, but not the Americans."

The formidable Margherita said: "It is a dirty lie," but there was no anger in her voice, it was nearly drained of conviction.

This man Nasta was a very persuasive man. He had persuaded himself into office, and he had persuaded the people into fear of him, and now it was easy for him to persuade them to mistrust the Americans.

Mayor Nasta said: "The son of Afronti told me that in the interior the Americans behaved themselves very badly. They were generous to us along the coast because they had to have a beachhead, but in the interior they have been different. Negro troops have raped seven Italian girls. There has been much looting."

The lazy Fatta said: "I hear that the Americans looted the beautiful house of Quattrocchi right here in Adano. They did much damage."

Mayor Nasta said: "Yes, that is true, I talked with Quattrocchi yesterday."

The formidable Margherita said: "What happened?" This was something close to home, and she considered anything that happened in Adano more or less her personal property, to use as gossip.

Mayor Nasta said: "The American vandals destroyed four hundred and seventy thousand lira worth of stuff in Quattrocchi's house. Heirlooms, paintings, sculpture, glassware. They said that Italian art is degenerate; they did all this because they wish to impose American ideas of art on Italy. That is what Quattrocchi told me the American Major had told him."

Mercurio Salvatore, the crier, said: "That I will not believe. The Mister Major is our friend." The crier was annoyed enough to say this in very nearly his crying voice. He spoke loudly enough to be heard inside the Palazzo.

"Quiet," Mayor Nasta said. "He will hear you and punish you."

"Why should he punish me?" Mercurio cried. "I am defending him."

"He is unpredictable," Mayor Nasta whispered. "Also,

148

he is lecherous. He is trying to seduce the daughters of
Tomasino the fisherman. I have this on good authority.
You will see, in a few months the daughters of Tomasino
will have big bellies."

The formidable Margherita was beginning to enjoy
this. "If I know the daughters of Tomasino," she said,
"they may have big bellies without the help of the Mister Major," and she laughed harshly.

"You will see," Mayor Nasta said. "I must be going
now," he said, bowing to the circle, as if the fact that it
was beginning to grow embarrassed him. "Good day,"
he said, "do not forget the twenty-third."

Each day when he came out from his repentence before Sergeant Borth, Mayor Nasta would go across to the
sidewalk in front of the Palazzo, and he would approach
a different group, and he would tell them pretty much
the same thing.

Sergeant Borth allowed this to go on for several days,
because Sergeant Borth was a careful worker. He waited
until he was sure of all his facts. He had his informers
trap Mayor Nasta into new exaggerations and accusations. He made sure that the son of Afronti the noisy
cartman had not deserted. He checked with Intelligence
at IX Corps to make sure that the Germans were not
expected to counterattack on the twenty-third. He even
went so far as to check with Captain Purvis as to the intentions of Major Joppolo toward the daughters of Tomasino. "Hell," the Captain said, "I don't think the Major
knows what a pushover they'd be, talking wop the way
he does."

When he was ready, Sergeant Borth went to Major
Joppolo. "Major," he said, "we've got to put Nasta away."

The Major said: "What's he done?"

"He's been planting rumors against us. I hate to admit
it, but he's done it very systematically and very skill-
fully."

"What kinds of rumors?"

"Oh, all kinds. He has quite a few people thinking that the Germans are going to put on a major counterattack next week. He even has some of them believing that you haven't been doing right by certain young ladies in this town."

Major Joppolo blushed. "That isn't true," he said.

"I know," Borth said. "I checked into it. But they tell me the Mister Major could make time if he wanted to."

"Cut it out," the Major said.

"That's what they tell me," Borth said. "They say these particular girls don't smell of fish, but their old man knows a good fish when he sees it."

"Cut the kidding," the Major said, and that echo was in his voice. He changed the subject quickly. "When are you going to arrest Nasta?"

"In the morning, when he comes in for his daily worship."

"Okay," the Major said. "Let's keep him in the prisoners of war cage for a few days, and not send him to Africa till we've questioned him a bit. I'm sort of glad to have him put away."

The next morning Mayor Nasta was somewhat surprised to see, besides Sergeant Borth in his office, two other men wearing brassards marked M.P. He said, as suavely as ever: "Good morning, Mister Sergeant."

"And what crime would Mayor Nasta like to repent this morning?" Borth asked.

"Is it not the Mister Sergeant's turn to pick a crime?" the Mayor asked.

"Perhaps it is, perhaps it is. Well, let's see. This morning I think Mayor Nasta will repent the crime of not having made good use of his freedom. He will repent the crime of having talked against the Americans."

Mayor Nasta turned pale. Borth stood up.

"He will repent the crime of having invented false ru-

mors, of having told the gullible people here in Adano
that the Germans were planning a counterattack for next
week."

Mayor Nasta turned his head and looked at the door.
Borth motioned to the M.P.'s to step into it, and they did.

"He will also repent having said slanderous and false
things about Major Joppolo. Also he will be very sorry
that he lied about the son of the cartman Afronti."

Mayor Nasta was white as a sheet. "Lies! They are
lies!" he said.

Borth said: "Mayor Nasta is excitable this morning.
And he had grown so calm about his repentances. Why
is he excitable this morning?"

Mayor Nasta was excitable because he knew he was
caught. "Lies," he shouted. "My enemies have been lying against me."

Borth said: "Is this a lie? Is it a lie that you said yesterday morning, before fifteen people on the sidewalk in
front of the Palazzo: 'The Americans are such cowards
that they had to be pushed from their transports into
landing barges when they came here'? Is it a lie that you
said. . . ." And Sergeant Borth repeated word for word
ten sentences that Nasta had said, as informers reported
them. Sergeant Borth had a very good memory, and he
enjoyed deflating this man, and he made a very terrifying show of it for Mayor Nasta.

After ten sentences, Mayor Nasta did not shout anything more about lies. He resorted to ridiculous, hollow
threats which echoed his days of power: "I will have
you killed," he shouted. "I will have you put in prison."

"No," Borth said, "you have that just backwards,
Mayor Nasta. *I* will have *you* put in prison."

Mayor Nasta shouted: "You can't do that. I will report
you to the authorities. You will be sorry. When you are
beaten, you will be sorry."

Borth said: "I think you really believe that the crooks

of the world can win this war. You'd better think that one over a little. We are going to give you a chance to think it over, Mayor Nasta. You are under arrest."

Then Borth said to the two M.P.'s in English: "Take him away, boys. He's getting noisy."

The M.P.'s took Nasta by both arms. Borth said: "I'm going to miss your daily visits, Mayor Nasta. I hope you will come to see me when you get out, I mean *if* you get out."

Mayor Nasta said stubbornly: "You will be sorry."

The M.P.'s took Nasta away to the prisoner of war cage.

The p.w. cage was simply the walled park opposite the Church of the Benedettini, with all but one of its gates boarded up and a little barbed wire strung along the top of the wall. When Mayor Nasta was admitted, there were some two hundred Italians and about twenty Germans in the enclosure. Several of the Italians were from coastal defense divisions, and a number were from Adano itself, and as soon as they saw Mayor Nasta, they told their friends from other towns: "There is the Fascist pig we were telling you about."

And from that moment on, Mayor Nasta was addressed by all the Italians in the p.w. cage as Fascist Pig.

Mayor Nasta did not make a very good start in the cage. The Americans had a forty-year-old, Italian-speaking Top Sergeant in charge of the guard. The first time Mayor Nasta saw the Top Sergeant walking in the enclosure, he rushed up to him and said: "This is a mistake. I should not have been imprisoned. It was all a mistake."

"Is that so?" the Top Sergeant said in a slow, Brooklynese Italian. "You are another mistake? We have several mistakes here. All mistakes here must clean the latrine. You are our newest mistake, so you will have the privilege of cleaning the latrine this week."

Life in the p.w. cage was not very pleasant for Mayor

Nasta. None of the men had blankets, and the nights were pretty cold, so they slept in close rows, keeping each other warm with their bodies. But no one would sleep next to the Fascist Pig. They said he had a peculiar smell. As a matter of fact, he did have a peculiar smell for several hours each morning; it came from being a mistake.

At last Mayor Nasta found a man who would talk with him. This was a German who spoke Italian.

Mayor Nasta told him that he was still Mayor of Adano, that he had been treacherously arrested by the Americans, that he was trying to do all he could to help the Germans win and that, in short, he was a pretty important person who ought to be helped. The Italian-speaking German told his friends all about Mayor Nasta, and they decided they ought to help him escape.

For a couple of days Mayor Nasta moved over and lived with the Germans. They made plans for the escape. There was nothing elaborate about the plans. They just decided to lift the Mayor up over the wall. They asked him if he had the courage to sit on barbed wire for a few minutes. He said yes, anything to escape. They asked him if he had the courage to jump down twelve feet on the other side. He said yes.

So in the middle of a dark, clouded night, the Germans made a pyramid of their bodies and let Mayor Nasta climb up it to the top of the wall. He sat on the barbed wire on top of the wall, quiet as a cat, until he was sure that the sentry outside had marched to the other end of his beat. Then he turned facing the wall, let himself down as far as he could, and let go. He hurt one knee a little; it hit the wall as he landed on the ground. But he was able to get up and run off silently.

The Top Sergeant at the p.w. cage called up Sergeant Borth at eight-thirty the next morning and told him that Nasta had escaped.

Sergeant Borth borrowed Corporal Chuck Schultz and a jeep from the M.P.'s and went hunting. By this time Sergeant Borth had so many voluntary informers and informers-on-informers that the job of tracing Mayor Nasta was not too hard.

He soon found out that Mayor Nasta had been sheltered for a few hours in a house on Via Favemi. He had then left town by the Via Roma. He had stopped in at a farmer's house near the Casa Zambano to change into peasant dress. This was one of the easiest things to check, because the peasant turned up wearing Mayor Nasta's loud powder blue suit, which was dusty from several nights on the ground.

Mayor Nasta had then been seen at several points along the Vicinamare road. One farmer had given him a lift in his cart. Mayor Nasta had evidently had enough of the hills, and was trying now to get to Vicinamare, where friends would be able to hide him.

Sergeant Borth picked him up three miles short of Vicinamare, at about ten-thirty.

Jeeps had been passing Mayor Nasta all morning, so that he was not particularly alarmed when Sergeant Borth's jeep drove up alongside him, and even when it stopped, he waved crudely and shouted: "Good day, good day," in what he thought was a thick peasant accent.

Sergeant Borth mimicked the accent: "Good day, good day, farmer."

Mayor Nasta, who still did not recognize Borth, shouted again: "Good day."

Borth shouted: "Good day. You are the first farmer I have ever seen with pince-nez glasses on."

Then Mayor Nasta knew Borth. Mayor Nasta's spirit, which had been strained by the arrest and by the days in the cage and by the escape, suddenly broke. He turned and ran out across the fields, squealing crazily, just like a soldier who had broken under shellfire.

Sergeant Borth got out of the jeep and went out onto the fields. He did not hurry, because Mayor Nasta was running in circles, wishing to run away from himself more than anything else. By the time Sergeant Borth caught him, he was exhausted and limp, and his eyes were milky with fear.

As Borth half walked, half carried him to the jeep, Mayor Nasta jabbered and mouthed his fear. "If you are going to shoot me, tell me first. Don't shoot me in the back. Tell me if you are going to kill me. I want to know, I want to know. . . ."

Sergeant Borth slapped him sharply in the face, and for a few seconds he was silent.

But when he was seated in the jeep, and the jeep began to move, Mayor Nasta began again. "Don't shoot me in the back. I will do anything to be shot from the front, where I can see the gun. I will tell you everything I know. I can give you names. Don't do it from behind."

Borth said: "How can I shoot you from behind when I am in the front seat and you are in the back seat?"

But Mayor Nasta was not pleading rationally. "I will tell you secrets," he babbled. "D'Arpa the vice mayor is a traitorous man, he is not to be trusted, watch out for him, but please do not shoot me in the back. Tell me first if you are going to kill me, tell me, tell me, I must know. Bellanca the Notary is not on our side, and he is strong with the people, watch out for him. You see, I can give you names. Do not shoot me in the back."

Borth knew that Mayor Nasta was dragging up accusations and suspicions out of the past, that he meant that these men were not to be trusted by the Fascists. His talk was crazy, for he was overcome with fear.

Therefore Borth gagged Mayor Nasta, and tied his

hands behind his back, and let his milky eyes speak his terrors. At least his eyes were silent.

As the jeep passed the Cacopardo Sulphur Works on the way into town, Borth looked at his watch. It was just before twelve o'clock. Major Joppolo would be either at lunch or on his way there. So Borth told the driver to go to the Albergo dei Pescatori.

Since it was the noon hour, scores of people had drifted to the Doppo Lavoro clubs along the street near the Albergo dei Pescatori to listen to the radio and wait for lunch. When they saw Borth's jeep, with a man tied up in the back seat, they clustered around, and called for their friends. And when they saw that Borth's cargo was Mayor Nasta, and that after all these years the Mayor had a gag in his mouth, they cheered and laughed at the man.

These noises increased Mayor Nasta's terrors, and he kept twisting and trying to look behind him.

Borth went into the restaurant and found Major Joppolo and brought him out.

Major Joppolo held up his hand to silence the crowd. "I want to speak to Nasta," he said to Borth. "Can he hear me with that thing on his face?"

"Yeah," Borth said; "you've got the rare pleasure of being able to speak to Nasta and he can't talk back."

Major Joppolo said: "Nasta, you are a disgrace to your people. There is goodness in your people, but not in you, not a bit. The world has had enough of your kind of selfishness."

It was one of Major Joppolo's greatest attributes in his job that he could speak pompous sentences with a sincerity and passion so real that his Italian listeners were always moved by what he said. Now all the listeners except Nasta were moved by his words to shout: "Kill him! Kill him! Kill him!"

Here was one time when Major Joppolo's sincerity

and passion bounced back on him, because the people's shouts frightened Mayor Nasta so badly that he fainted, and Major Joppolo was the first to see the ridiculousness of trying to spell-bind an unconscious man.

There was nothing left to say except one sentence to Borth: "We'll have to send him to Africa."

And to the music of Adano's delighted cheers, Borth and his limp companion drove down the street.

Chapter 20

THERE was no better index to the state of mind of Adano than the activities of the painter Lojacono. If one had made a graph of the spirits of the town and then put beside it a graph of the number of commissions Lojacono received, the two would have exactly corresponded. Whenever the town was optimistic, Lojacono worked. When the town was blue, Lojacono was idle.

Lojacono could paint anything. He could paint a house or he could paint a saint. He was the one who painted panels in the churches. He was the one who painted the fat and holy people on the fat Basile's two-wheeled cart.

The white-haired Lojacono suffered when he painted. First he suffered the pangs of creation, then he suffered when the people of Adano criticized his work. His work was beautiful and everyone in the town loved it, but for some reason they always criticized it first.

Major Joppolo had not been in Adano very long before Lojacono was busy. His first efforts were a little crude, because the town had been depressed, and his right hand idle, for so very long. But soon he warmed to the town's happiness, and he did things he had never been able to do in his life, which had not been short.

The same morning that the crowd stood around Borth's jeep in front of the Albergo dei Pescatori, another, smaller crowd stood on the Molo Ponente in the harbor and watched Lojacono work. He was painting new names and little figures on the bow surfaces of the fishing boats, and the crowd consisted of fishermen and their families.

Except for Lojacono's work, the boats were all ready to go. Their seams were calked, and they were tight as wine-bottles. The barnacles and the whiskers were off, and the bottoms had been given a little lead paint. The rigging was smart, for Major Joppolo had persuaded the Navy to give the fishermen some bright cable and some unsoaked hemp rope.

The fishermen were impatient to have Lojacono finish.

"Lojacono is talented but slow," said the fisherman named Agnello, on whose boat the painter was working just then.

The white haired painter said: "Would you rather have me quick and messy?"

One of Agnello's three helpers, Merendino, said: "It will have to be proved that you are not messy before we answer that."

Lojacono stopped working and looked at the fishermen standing there. He pointed at his work and said angrily: "Have you ever seen a porpoise less messy than that one?"

Agnello said: "The porpoise is not bad, but he will die of loneliness unless you hurry and give him some company. Porpoises like company, you know that, Lojacono. Have you ever seen a porpoise play alone?"

"He will have company," Lojacono said impatiently. "The Mister Major is going to be riding on his back. If you would be silent, I could get on with my work."

Merendino said: "Work then, old man, do not be so slow."

The old man went back to his work. Tomasino, sitting with his head in his hands on the afterdeck of his boat, which was moored next to Agnello's, said gloomily: "I cannot see the point of all this painting. It is frivolous. My boat has been named *Tina* since the girl was born. It will remain *Tina*. The leaves and the fruit which dangle from the name are good enough for me, even if they are not new. You would think that Christ had come again, with all this fresh paint."

Agnello shouted to Tomasino: "What is the matter with you, sour one, do you have gas in your bowels this morning? Cheer up, we are going fishing again."

"In the next century," said Tomasino glumly, "after all this painting is finished."

Lojacono stuck his head up over the side of Agnello's boat and shouted: "Be quiet, Tomasino, you know that the only reason you are so impatient is that you like what I did twenty years ago and you have no desire for anything new."

Tomasino said: "If I have to wait another day for the slow painter I will blot out the name *Tina* and the leaves and fruit with some lead paint I have, and I will go fishing alone in a nameless boat."

Lojacono started painting the Mister Major, and the little crowd came in closer to see the details. He resolved a difficult point by making the Major's hat rather big and by tilting it so that it covered most of his face. At least the hat was definitely American.

"His leg is too short. The leg of the Mister Major is longer," Agnello said.

"I was about to say that the leg is too long," Merendino said.

"In other words," Lojacono said, "the leg is precisely right."

"He does not have a hunch-back like that," said Sconzo, another of Agnello's helpers.

"He is bending forward because of the speed of the porpoise," Lojacono said.

"The color of his skin is too white," said the wife of Agnello. "His skin is more Italian-colored."

"You are dull," Lojacono said, "you do not see the symbolism of the white skin."

This is what the criticism was always like. And this shows the purpose of the criticism: it was not so much that the people did not like what Lojacono was doing, as that they wanted to know exactly what was in his mind. In future, showing off his boat, Agnello would be able to say: "You can see how fast the porpoise is going by the way the Mister Major is leaning forward. And do you see how white his skin is? That is because of the symbolism in the Mister Major's skin."

In due course Lojacono finished his work, and everyone pronounced it quite good, although, one said, it would be hard for a porpoise to jump that high out of the water with a man on his back, and, another said, should not the name of the boat, which was now *Americano,* be a little lower? Lojacono attributed the former highness to good spirits and the latter highness to the way the name American had been raised in everyone's esteem by the Mister Major; and everyone went away satisfied.

The next morning the boats went out. Major Joppolo went down to the harbor to see them off, and the people in town were all excited at the prospect of eating fish.

The catch that day was excellent. When the boats were all in and the fish all weighed, it was estimated by Agnello that a total of three thousand two hundred pounds had been taken in. Better than that, the fish were mostly of good grades. It was the custom to sort the fish into four grades, the biggest to be sold for five lira, the next for four, the next for three, and the smallest for one. More than half of that first day's catch were of the five lira grade.

The second day's catch was even better — nearly thirty-five hundred pounds.

On the third day it was still over three thousand.

There were near riots at the fish market, and in the Albergo dei Pescatori, which in the old days had specialized in fish for fishermen (and that is the most delicate and finicky of all fish cookery), the crowds were bigger than they had ever been, and lots of people went away disappointed, not because of a shortage of fish, but simply because there wasn't time to feed them all.

The fishermen were wildly happy. The mere fact of going out again would have made them happy, but to have the catch so good, and their boats in such good condition, and their income so high for a change — they were delighted.

On the evening of their third day, some of them went to Tomasino, and Agnello said: "Tomasino, don't you think you ought to go to the Mister Major and thank him for making it possible for us to go fishing?"

Tomasino was as happy as he could ever be, but that did not mean that he smiled, or that he would answer happily. "I have been to the Palazzo once to see him, because my wife Rosa forced me to. Never again. I hate that place."

The young man named Sconzo said: "Then don't you think we should send Agnello? We think that we owe our thanks to the Mister Major. We were talking about it while we were out today."

Tomasino was not pleased with the suggestion that Agnello should go in his place. "Is Agnello the head of the fishermen?" he said.

"No," Sconzo said, "but if you do not wish to go . . ."

"The best fishing boat in this harbor is named *Tina*,"

A BELL FOR ADANO

Tomasino said, and though he spoke gloomily, there was a kind of gaiety in his idea. "Therefore the one for whom that boat is named ought to be the one to go and thank the Mister Major."

The other fishermen thought that that was a fine idea, but Agnello said: "We would all like to be present when you give instructions to your daughter as to what she is to say to the Mister Major." He was afraid that grim old Tomasino would tell her to say something begrudging.

So all the fishermen went up to Tomasino's house and found Tina, and Tomasino said: "Tina, we have an errand for you. The fishermen of Adano want you to go to see the Mister Major for them . . ."

Tina surprised everyone by blushing and refusing to go.

"But why not?" Agnello asked. "We thought it would be nice if a beautiful girl took our message to the Mister Major instead of a man who stinks of fish."

Tomasino did not like that remark and he said angrily: "Tomasino does not stink of fish any worse than certain other fishermen he knows."

Agnello said: "I did not have any particular fisherman in mind, old gassy bowels. Do not forget that it was suggested that I should go. I stink too."

"That is true," Tomasino said with a puckered face.

Tina said: "I just do not wish to go."

Tomasino turned on her: "Girl, by the same reasoning which made your mother force me to go to the Mister Major against my will, I now order you to go to him also."

Tina lowered her head and said: "Well, if you order me . . ." Agnello said afterwards that he thought by the way she said this, she really wanted to go all along.

Tomasino said: "I want you to tell him that we are glad to be able to go fishing . . ."

162

"And that we are thankful to him for making it possible," Agnello said.

"And that we are very grateful for the new rigging," Merendino said.

"Also if he has had anything to do with sending so many fish into our nets, we thank him," Sconzo said.

Tomasino said: "Tell him those things but don't make a fool of yourself, daughter."

She said with more vehemence than was necessary: "Don't worry, I won't."

Tina went to see the Mister Major at eight o'clock the next morning. When Zito led her to Major Joppolo's desk, she said defiantly: "You said that if I had business with you, I should come to your office. I have come."

Major Joppolo had the discretion to wave Zito out of the room before he said: "I am sorry I said that. I have been miserable about it ever since."

Tina said: "Have you?" That much she said softly, then she added harshly: "You ought to have been. You were very rude."

The Major said: "I know I was. I'm really very sorry. I have been trying to find out the thing you wanted to know."

Tina was all softness now: "Do you mean about my Giorgio? Have you found out? Is he a prisoner?"

"I don't know yet. But I may have some word for you on all the prisoners in a few days."

"You may? Good word, Mister Major?"

"Good word, Tina."

"Oh, Mister Major, I thank you, I thank you and I kiss your hand."

Major Joppolo hardly had time to think vaguely that he wouldn't mind kissing Tina's hand before she had run out.

She ran all the way home and when Tomasino asked

her if she had said what the fishermen had told her, she said that she had, oh yes, she had, and she threw her arms around her father's neck and kissed him on both cheeks, and he put his arms around her and pressed her a little and said glumly: "My little Tina, I think you are crazy."

Chapter 21

THE TROUBLE with Errante Gaetano was that he couldn't keep his mind on anything. Or to put it the other way around: whatever had his mind at the moment seized it so wholly that he couldn't think about anything else. It made no difference what his mind *ought* to be on; whatever it was on, it was really on.

After General Marvin ordered his good mule shot, Errante got another. This one was not as amiable as the first, and was more stubborn in its mind. But it was a mule, and it gave Errante both pleasure and work.

One afternoon Errante was driving this new mule through the town. It was late in the afternoon, the hour when most of the children of the town got out on the Via Umberto the First and shouted for caramels. American military traffic seemed to be particularly heavy at that hour each evening.

As he thought back on it later (and he had plenty of time to think it over in jail), it seemed to Errante that a great number of things happened very quickly. Actually it was just that quite a few things flashed across his mind in fairly rapid succession, giving him an illusion of great activity.

First he looked ahead down the Via Umberto the First and he saw the bridge over the Rosso River, and he shied, like a sensitive horse seeing a place where it has hurt itself once before. Errante shuddered every time he saw that bridge, because it made him think of the rude awakening he had had there and of the shooting of his mule.

Next he saw a row of amphibious trucks come toward him across the bridge. These amphibious trucks fascinated Errante. He had recently spent one entire day sitting on a knoll near the beach about five miles west of Adano watching these fat creatures waddle out across the sand, let themselves gingerly down into the water and then churn off to the cargo ships lying offshore; and then churn back again, and climb up out of the sea, like any amphibious animal looking heavier and clumsier on land than in the water. Errante loved them and called them Swimming War. "Here comes Swimming War," he thought to himself when he saw the amphibious trucks crossing the bridge.

After the trucks, his mind focused for a few moments on the figure of Gargano, Chief of the Carabinieri, who was directing traffic about half way down the Via Umberto the First. Errante said to himself: "Even if Gargano can talk three times as fast as anyone else — once with his mouth, once with his left hand, and once with his right — I do not like him."

Errante's mind did not dwell on the distasteful subject of Gargano for long, because Errante's ear transmitted to Errante's mind the sound of many children shouting: *"Caramelle! Caramelle!"* Errante liked children even more than he liked Swimming War.

Errante's slow mind swung his eyes around to the direction of the sound. He saw the children on the sidewalk, and his mind concentrated on the pleasing sight.

His mind noted that there were approximately fifty children running up and down the sidewalk, that about six or seven leaders, somewhat older and taller than the average, were always out in front, that the others tagged willingly behind, and that all of them, from the rich little great-grandson of old Cacopardo all bright in blue, to the numerous beggar children in brown tatters — all of them laughed with a tinkling laughter and shouted for caramels as if they really expected to be rolling them on their tongues in no time at all.

What the mind of Errante did not note was that his new mule, either following an accidental whim or fascinated, like its master, by the children, had turned at right angles to the street and had stopped walking.

Swimming War was coming up the street. Gargano the Two-Hands had a vigilant eye out for traffic on the street. The new mule of Errante stood stock-still right across the road. And Errante stared at the children, thinking only of them and not noticing that anything was wrong.

"How nice it would be to be a child!" Errante's one-track mind thought. "Look at the fat little son of the fat Craxi! Look at the thin son of stupid Erba! See how Erba's ragged child holds the hand of the rich little sulphur boy in blue! Noisy old Afronti was shouting to me the other day about democracy. He said my mind was slow. He said I would never understand. I wish he were here now. Here are the true democrats of the world. Childhood is the real democracy!"

It gave Errante a great sense of importance to be thinking thoughts like these.

All of a sudden a terrible confusion burst in on his thoughts.

Errante's slow eyes saw only a flash of uniform. The uniform hurled itself at the head of his mule, wrenching the head to one side. The mule reared and screamed.

That scream did something to Errante's mind. He saw a vision of his other, beloved mule dead beside the road. That awful thing would not happen again while Errante survived to prevent it.

He leaped from his cart. He saw the blur of a uniform running at his mule's head again. He charged at the uniform. Where a head should be at the top of the blur he struck with the heel of his hand. He hit something and heard an angry roar.

The roar, he realized in a few moments, came from Gargano the Two-Hands. It said: "Imbecile! Pile of turd! Get out of the road, can't you see the trucks coming? Don't you know that blocking traffic is sabotage? Don't you know that you can be shot for blocking traffic?"

Errante's one-track mind played him a funny trick now. It stopped in the middle of its fury to think: "Look at Two-Hands! Trying to talk and catch my mule at the same time. He has to use his hands to catch my mule, and he has to use his hands to talk. He cannot do either."

But when Gargano gave off trying to talk and concentrated on the mule, Errante's mind went back to its business. He threw himself at Gargano again. He struck another blow with the heel of his hand that was to decorate Two-Hands with a purple spot under the left eye for several days.

Two-Hands roared again with pain and anger. But he did not try to argue now. He grabbed the mule's reins near the bit and tried to pull him to one side. The mule, however, had decided not to move until this hullabaloo was over. Two-Hands could not budge it, so he kicked the flank of the mule.

Errante decided to retaliate in kind. He kicked the flank of Two-Hands.

Gargano roared again, and beat the mule in the head.

Errante beat Gargano the Two-Hands in the head.

Gargano was roaring continuously now. He grabbed the mule by the ears and tried to pull him that way.

Errante grabbed Two-Hands by the ears, even though Two-Hands' ears were not as handy to grab as the mule's, and he pulled.

167

Gargano the Two-Hands would have lost this battle, for he was fighting against two beasts, but at this moment some American soldiers from the amphibious trucks came running up.

One of the soldiers pulled Gargano the Two-Hands aside. Three of the soldiers went to work on the mule, and succeeded in making it get off to one side of the street. It took four soldiers to put Errante off the street.

When these things were accomplished, the American soldiers went back to their amphibious trucks. All they wanted was to pass.

Since a large crowd had gathered, it remained for Gargano the Two-Hands to assert his authority. He whispered to someone in the crowd to run up to the Palazzo and get a force of about six carabinieri. Then he engaged Errante in argument until the reinforcements should arrive.

"Saboteur!" he shouted, pounding one fist on the other.

"Murderer!" shouted Errante. "All authorities are murderers."

"You are the murderer," Gargano said, drawing a finger across his throat. "How do you know how many innocent American boys you may have killed by holding up this military traffic?"

"Murderer," shouted Errante Gaetano of the one-track mind. "Killer of mules."

"Whose mule was killed?" Gargano asked, spreading his hands, palm upwards, in the attitude of a question. "Do you see a dead mule around here?"

Errante could see that his mule was alive. He went over to it, and inspected it from the tip of its nose to the tip of its tail. He was determined that if he found a single wound, he would inflict an exactly similar wound on Two-Hands.

Gargano followed Errante in his inspection, just to make sure that he did not try to run away. "Does a dead mule breathe? Does a dead mule stand up in its shafts? Show me a dead mule that snuffles its nostrils that way."

In time the six carabinieri came. Gargano said: "Stupid cartman, you are under arrest," and he clapped his right hand around his own left wrist.

The six carabinieri surrounded Errante. To Gargano's surprise he did not resist at all. He just asked to be allowed to speak to his mule. He went over and patted the side of the mule's jaw, and said to it: "Be patient, Mister Major. The man for whom you are named is just, they tell me. You will see your master again before long."

Chapter 22

IN the middle of the avalanche of mail which old Cacopardo poured at Major Joppolo, another letter came which interested the Major. It said:

At one or two kilometers from the beach of the sea in sector of Adano, in shallow water, with the tops of masts out of sealevel, is liing the motor ship Anzio.

Real proprietor Galeazzo Ciano, son in law of Mussolini, who made the alliance with Hitler, a ridicoulos minister for Foreignes Affaires.

The ship had taken the cargo of nafta and lubricating oils for Trieste, at Adano, & then completed TEN THOUSAND tons of crude sulphur at Vicinamare. Retourning in the waters of Adano, in the way to Trieste, neared to this harbour, & whilest awaiting communications from the semaphore, was hit at the stern by a torpedo of a submarine, which evidently has watched his loadings at Adano and Vicinamare.

A cloud of white smoke (sulphuric anidride) developped at once & the master, very capable seaman, tried at full speed, steering at zigzag, to reach the shallow waters beside Molo di Levante (breakwater) when a second torpedo, perhaps at the tunnel of the propollershaft, sung she.

The cargoes are the great value for the civil life of Adano & other towns in the neighbour hood.

I am informed of the presance in this harbour of a floating dock, which, yesterday, is said, has taken from the bottom of the sea, a small smack, sunk in a recent bombardment of british plains.

Abstraction of other political considerations, I beg, that you submit to the consideration of H.E. the Admiral of naval forces in these waters, the convenience of oisting in the floting dry dock the Anzio, discharging on shore the cargoes, so urgent here for the civil normal life. If so, I would like to sell the sulphur, at profit to Adano and cause of all free menkind.

Respectfully,
M. Cacopardo.

The phrase "at profit to Adano" caught Major Joppolo's eye. He was having a little trouble meeting his Public Assistance payments out of income from fines and out of moneys left over from other projects. Perhaps if the Navy would be willing to raise the *Anzio*, he could sell the cargo and use the proceeds for Public Assistance. It was worth a try.

Major Joppolo had not had occasion to talk with Lieutenant Livingston of the Navy since the day he politely blackmailed him into letting the fishermen go out. As he called up this time, he remembered that other conversation, and he decided that a new tactic might be advisable.

The Kent-Yale voice said: "Livingston, Port of Adano."

Major Joppolo said: "Hello, Captain, this is Joppolo. Say, I just called to tell you that a lot of people have told me that this whole town's grateful to you."

The Kent-Yale voice was suspicious. "What for?" it asked.

The Major said: "For being able to eat fish. You'd be amazed at what a difference it makes around here. A lot of people have come in and asked me to thank the man down at the Navy, and I guess that's you. Just this morning old Bellanca, the guy I have as mayor now, asked me if he ought to write you a personal letter of thanks."

Lieutenant Livingston expressed a warming interest: "Is that a fact?"

Major Joppolo said: "Yeah, I told him I'd thank you for him. I want to thank you for myself, too. Boy, it makes a difference to get some fresh fish after weeks on end of nothing but C Rations."

Lieutenant Livingston grew cordial. "Yeah," he said, "those C Rations sure are terrible."

Major Joppolo said: "I have fish every day for lunch now, and every mouthful I take, I say a little word of thanks to the Navy for sending the fishermen out."

Lieutenant Livingston was in the bag. "As a matter of fact," he said, "we had some fish down here at the Navy Club last night. It was all right, too. Did you know I'd organized a little Club down here? Took over a little house, just a place for the officers who come into this hell-hole to drop in at." The Kent-Yale voice was lowered to a confidential murmur. "I got ahold of some Scotch, a few cases. Come on down and have a drink some time."

Major Joppolo said: "I sure will. I feel like I could use one every once in a while."

The Lieutenant said: "God, so do I. This place is such a dump."

Major Joppolo did not like to hear his town referred

171

to in that way, but he was doing a job just now, so he said: "It sure gets boring, doesn't it?"

The Lieutenant said: "Boring? Say, if they ever give this old world an enema, this is where they'll put the tube in."

Major Joppolo did not get the point, and so he did not laugh as the Lieutenant would have liked him to, but he said: "But you Navy fellows certainly do get yourselves fixed up nice."

"Well," the Lieutenant said modestly, "we figure it doesn't hurt any to live comfortably."

"Well," the Major said, "just called up to thank you for that fish deal. You certainly have made yourself a popular fellow with these Italians."

"Nothing to it," the Lieutenant said, "glad to help 'em out."

"Well, anyhow, thanks a million. . . . Oh say, before I hang up, I just happened to think. I heard the other day of another way you could use your initiative and earn yourself some more friends, and do a hell of a lot of good in the bargain."

"How's that?" said Lieutenant Livingston, rising like a famished trout to a well-cast dry fly.

"Have you seen those masts sticking up out of the water near the breakwater on the east side of the harbor? Well, I heard that they belong to a little motor ship that has a cargo of sulphur and some other stuff this town really needs. I just thought that maybe one of these weeks when your floating dry dock isn't too busy, you could raise her and the town would have the cargo and you'd probably have to drop your job and be mayor, you'd be so damn popular."

"Say," the Lieutenant said, "that's a hell of a fine idea. I'll have to get permission, but that shouldn't be hard. Thanks a lot for the idea."

"I called up to thank *you*," the Major said. "I'm going

to take you up on that Scotch invite one of these days."

"Sure thing, any time," the Lieutenant said.

When he had hung up, the Lieutenant thought to himself, what a good guy, you never can tell about a meatball until you get to know him.

Chapter 23

BRIGADIER GENERAL WILLIAM B. WILSON of the Quartermaster Depot in Algiers leaned back at his desk and shouted across the room to his deputy in a rich Southern accent: "Ham, listen to this, goddamit, sometimes I think those English think they *own* us."

The Colonel addressed as Ham looked up from the *Stars & Stripes.* "What have the limeys done now?" he asked.

"Just got this letter, damnedest thing I ever saw," the General said. "It's from an American major, too, just goes to show how those glib bastards can put it over on us if we don't watch 'em."

The Colonel called Ham said: "Yeah, they sure are good talkers."

"Listen here, now, he says: '*Am writing you at the suggestion of Major General His Excellency Lord Runcin'* — that fancy bastard. I met him one time down at the Aletti, and I just happened to say, like anyone does who's a gentleman when he says good-bye, I said to him: 'If there's anything I can ever do for you, just let me know.' He came right back at me and said: 'I may,' he said, 'you Americans have everything, you know.' So damn if I didn't get a letter from him about two weeks later reminding me of what I said and asking me if I'd get him a jeep. Well, this Amgot thing sounded pretty important to me, so I just about busted my neck to wangle him a jeep. Soon as he got that he wrote me a thank-you note and asked me if the Americans had any pipes, that he was lost without a pipe, and could I get him one? So I got him a pipe. Then I had to get him an electric razor, for godsake. Then he wrote me that chewing gum was such a curiosity among his staff, would I get him a large box of chewing gum? He even had the nerve to ask me to get him a case of whisky, he said he got a ration of rum and gin, but all the Scotch was imported to the States, so would I mind terribly nailing him a case of Scotch? I made up my mind I was never going to get him another thing after that, even if I got sent home."

"What's he want now?"

"He doesn't want it, this Major of ours wants it, that's what makes me mad. Old Runcin seems to think I'm a one-man shopping service, and he goes around recommending to people to write me all their screwy things they want."

"Well, what does this guy want?"

"Jesus, Ham, he wants a bell."

"What the hell for?"

"He says here: 'I consider it most important for the morale and continued good behavior of this town to get it a bell to replace the one which was taken away as per above.' I don't know, something about a seven-hundred-year-old bell. But that's not the point, Ham. The thing that makes me mad is this English bastard thinking he owns us."

The Colonel named Ham, who was expert at saying Yes to his superiors and No to his inferiors, said: "Yeah, I see what you mean."

"They do it all the time, Ham. You watch, an Englishman will always eat at an American mess if he gets a chance. Look at Lend-Lease, why hell, we're just *giving*

174

it to 'em. And don't you think they'll ever pay us for it. They won't even thank us for it, Ham."

The Colonel named Ham said: "I doubt if they will."

"I know they won't. And look at the way they're trying to run the war. They got their officers in all the key spots. Ham, we're just winning this damn war for the British Empire."

The Colonel named Ham said: "That's right, I guess."

"No sir, I'm damned if I'll root around and find a bell for this goddam sponger of an Englishman. Where the hell does he think I'm going to find a seven-hundred-year-old bell? No sir, Ham, I won't do it. Write a letter to this Major, will you, Ham?"

"Yes sir, what'll I say?"

"Lay it on, dammit, tell him the U.S. Army doesn't have a stock of seven-hundred-year-old bells, tell him he should realize there is a war on, tell him to watch out for these goddam Englishmen or they'll take the war right away from us."

"Yes sir."

Chapter 24

MAJOR JOPPOLO enjoyed his afternoons as judge, partly because he liked to see the happy effect of real justice on the people of Adano, and partly because Gargano, the Chief of Carabinieri, acted out every crime as if it were a crime against himself.

Major Joppolo's trials were impressive, because he managed, by trickery, by moral pressure and by persuasion, to make the truth seem something really beautiful and necessary.

"The truth, I want the truth now, not next week," he would say, and the accused would find himself telling the truth and discarding the elaborate lie he had devised.

Trials began at about three in the afternoon, each Monday.

Gargano brought in the first culprit, one Monday afternoon, and as he led him in, he said: "We will take the light cases first."

"You have some serious cases, then?" Major Joppolo asked.

Gargano held up his forefinger, and said angrily: "One."

"Then maybe our fines will be high this week," the Major said. He thought he was joking, but he had become almost miserly on behalf of Adano, and each Monday afternoon he used to try to see how much he could net in fines.

"I hope so," said Gargano, vehemently. Then he said: "First case."

The Major took the name, age, birthplace and sex of the accused and had Giuseppe make him swear that he would tell the Italian counterpart of the truth, the whole truth and nothing but the truth. Gargano read the accusation. The man had made a public nuisance of himself while drunk.

The Major questioned the man. He was poor, where did he get money to drink with? From his wife. Where did she get it? From the Public Assistance. Did the man not know that it was very degrading to get drunk on charity? He did, but the pleasure offset the degradation. Did the man plead guilty or not guilty? Guilty. "Very well," the Major said; "I see you're too poor to pay a fine. I will give you your choice of losing the Public Assistance money for two months or going to jail for one."

Without hesitation the man chose losing the Public Assistance.

"If that choice is so easy," the Major said, "you don't need the Public Assistance at all." And he directed Gargano to have him taken off the list.

"Second case," Gargano said.

This was the case of a woman who was accused of selling goat's milk both overprice and underweight. The woman denied everything. The Major told her he wanted the truth, and that she would make out better if she were honest than if she were not. All right, she said, she had sold a little bit underweight. The Major said he would call in the woman to whom she had sold the milk and question her, and if the accused were lying, he would triple the fine. All right, she said, she also sold the milk overprice, for eight lire instead of six. This woman looked just as poor as the man in the first case, but her error was far more serious. The Major fined her three thousand lire, to be paid within a week.

The third case was a theft. A peasant was accused of having stolen some cigarets from an Army bivouac near his farm. Major Joppolo asked him to tell his side of the story. He said that some soldiers had given him one carton of cigarets, which he put under this jacket, and that he then started home. Major Joppolo called up the bivouac and got the Army story, which was that the man had stolen two cartons and some C Rations. The Major then made his speech about the truth, and by a series of adroit questions got the man to admit everything. Major Joppolo gave the man a fine of a hundred lire and a lecture.

When the theft had been disposed of, Gargano stood up and said: "And now the important case."

The case which Gargano considered serious was the case of Errante and his mule cart.

Errante was sworn in. The Major asked for the accusation. Gargano pushed Errante to one side and stood before the Major.

"Honorable Mister Major," he began, "this is a case of interference with the American military. I consider it one of the most serious we have yet had to handle."

The Major said: "That is for me to judge, Gargano. What is the accusation?"

Then Gargano told, or rather acted out, the story of how Errante Gaetano's cart had blocked traffic on Via Umberto the First. Gargano the Two-Hands leaped and swore and shook his two fists at Errante, and he made Zito act as the mule, and he attacked Zito fiercely, and then he reeled back from sham blow after sham blow. He did not ask anyone to act out the part of Errante, but let his own dodging and staggering give the idea.

He painted a terrible picture of the unknown but possible consequences of Errante's holding up the procession of amphibious trucks. He himself seemed to die several times as he imagined the deaths of American boys which resulted from the bone-headedness of this cartman.

Gargano went on to show how Errante had defied authority and had tried to make it ridiculous in the eyes of the people. He stepped to one side and acted out the part of the people, giggling at authority because of the rudeness of this cartman.

He wished to impress on the Major that this cartman's crime was doubly serious because it all took place in the full view of fifty-odd children. What kind of idea of law and authority would these children grow up with? As he put this point across Gargano himself ran up and down shouting for caramels.

He wound up by attacking Zito again, staggering some more, giggling on behalf of the people, and pointing to the ceiling as he swore by the Heavenly God that he had never been so humiliated in his life.

It was clear to Major Joppolo from this exposition that the seriousness of this crime was closely bound up in Gargano's mind with the embarrassment of Gargano. He asked for the cartman's story, and he let Errante tell just as long a story as Gargano had, even though his own mind was already made up on the case. Errante's slow, painful story was a beautiful thing to hear, and yet it was tragic. It was the story of any Italian peasant who had lived so many years in the realm of fear.

"I am poor, Mister Major," he began. "I have a cart. A cart is all I have."

He looked around the room and thought.

"My wife died of the malaria," he said. "My wife was a serious woman. She did not laugh for eighteen years. However, she cooked rabbit well. She died of the malaria."

Errante paused again. His mind had to reach out for each memory.

"I do not like the place where I live. I have to brush the goat droppings aside each night before I lie down. It is crowded living with four goats in my room. It is not as crowded as it was before the invasion. Five other goats were killed by the bombardment. I was sorry that they were killed, but I look at it this way: there are less droppings to brush away at night."

The cartman paused for a long time. Gargano muttered: "Come to the point, stupid one."

Major Joppolo said: "Tell it as you wish, cartman."

Errante said: "I still do not understand why they shot my mule. I was asleep on the cart. Perhaps it was because I had had too much to drink. But that is a fault common among cartmen, and I have not heard of any other mules being shot. To say nothing of the necessity of repairing the right wheel of my cart. I do not understand it, Mister Major."

Major Joppolo realized for the first time that this man

was the victim of General Marvin's rage. There was nothing he could say to the cartman to explain, but then, Errante did not seem to expect the Major to explain.

He went on: "There are many things I do not understand, Mister Major. When I was young, I was handsome. At least that is what my wife, who was able to laugh then, told me. Why am I ugly now, Mister Major? That is something I cannot understand. What has happened to my face?"

He stopped and thought. "My son looked well in his uniform," he said. "That is, he looked well before he was killed. After he was killed, he looked badly. He had no legs and he only had half a head. That is what his Captain told me. Was it necessary for his Captain to tell me all that?"

Gargano burst out: "We are trying the case of a cartman who blocked military traffic. Must we listen to this kind of talk, Mister Major?"

Major Joppolo said: "Yes, Gargano, I think we must. It is my opinion that what the cartman is saying is relevant to his case."

"You are the judge," Gargano said, with both hands in the air, in resignation.

The Major said: "Go on, cartman."

Errante said: "I do not like this man. It seems to me that he waves his hands too much. God gave us tongues to talk with. For several years I have not liked this man. I have never liked him since the day he spat in the face of my wife. That was long after she had stopped laughing."

The cartman turned then away from the fuming Gargano to the Major. After a pause he said: "I ate a watermelon the other day. It was the first fresh fruit I had eaten since the disembarkation. I stole it. All the good things are being sold to the Americans at high prices. There is not much left for a cartman except goat's milk.

With every good there is an evil. With goat's milk one has to accept goat droppings."

He paused and said: "With Americans I suppose one has to accept hunger."

He paused for a long time. Then he said: "At that, hunger is better than some other things. I would like to have heard my wife laugh again."

After another pause he said: "It seems to me that I have heard more laughter since the disembarkation. This is especially true among the children. You see, I have been trying to think out what made me stop and listen to the children the other afternoon, when I did not notice the Swimming War."

"The what, cartman?"

"I call them Swimming War. They are American vehicles which swim."

"Amphibious trucks, yes, go ahead."

"Among the children there is more laughter. There is something else among the children which I never noticed before, too. In that crowd of them the other afternoon the thin child of Erba was holding the hand of the little Cacopardo. I do not know if you realize what that means, Mister Major. Erba is a cartman like me, only more stupid, Mister Major. Everyone knows the name of Cacopardo."

"Yes, I know they are rich," the Major said.

"I am almost as stupid as Erba, Mister Major, but I have noticed something. The things that children do are right on top of the children, and easy to see. The same things in older people lie deep down inside. Therefore at any time what you see happening among the children is also happening among the older ones, only you cannot see it, since it is deep. I mean the laughing, and the holding of hands. And yet —"

Errante Gaetano paused. This time it did not look as if he would come out of the pause. He frowned.

"And yet what, cartman?"

"And yet I still do not understand why they shot my mule. This need for sitting in jail I can understand: I simply did not notice the Swimming War, and I am sorry I got in its way. But about the mule that was shot, there is no explanation."

At this moment Major Joppolo hated General Marvin with a bitter flash of hatred. He said: "Yes, cartman, there is an explanation. It isn't a very good one, I know. You are a student of human nature, I can see that. You must have noticed that human beings often make mistakes. The shooting of your mule was a terrible mistake by one human being. I am very sorry that he happened to be an American."

Errante scratched his back and said: "If it was a mistake, well, if it was a mistake . . ." And tears came into his eyes.

Major Joppolo covered up this embarrassment by saying to Gargano: "We are going to have to dismiss this case, Gargano. I regret that it caused you embarrassment. But after what this man has said, could you see any justice in punishing him?"

Gargano protested: "American soldiers might have been killed by the delay."

The Major said: "I doubt it, Gargano. All he was guilty of was being too interested in the children's laughter."

Errante had recovered from his moment of emotion. He said: "There is more laughter. I think my wife would have laughed at my description of this man" — he looked at Gargano — "talking about my cart. It is too bad she died of the malaria. Now that you Americans are here, I think she would have laughed. In spite of the mistake about the mule. Yes, I think so, Mister Major."

Chapter 25

"WELL, here's what happened," Major Joppolo was saying. The other people in Tomasino's living room were laughing and talking loudly, but Tina and the Major paid them no attention.

"When the batch of prisoners came in last week, they had a new kind of paper. All it said was: 'For release at p.w. cage nearest bearer's home,' and it was signed by somebody at Ninth Corps. Well, we wanted to check and make sure because we hadn't heard anything about letting all the Italian prisoners loose.

"So I wrote a note to this guy at Ninth Corps, and I got his answer this morning. He said there was a new policy, they'd decided that it would be best for the morale of the people if we let the Italian prisoners free. He said the risk we might run of letting out a few fanatical officers who would continue to work for the Germans would be offset by the good that would be done for most towns."

Tina said excitedly: "When will you let them free?"

The Major said: "We have to sort them out, and send them to the prisoners' cage nearest to where they live. We have quite a bunch from Vicinamare that we have to send up there. It will take about a week, I guess."

Tina said: "Have you been to the enclosure recently?"

The Major said: "Yes, I was there today."

"Are there several men from Adano there?"

"Yes, quite a few, I understand."

"Oh, Mister Major, did you talk with any?"

"Yes, I did."

"You didn't happen — ?"

"He's not here, Tina. I looked for his name on the list. Also I asked some of the men from Adano. They said

183

they had not heard anything. I went down to the cage specially to find out.

Tina said: "You are very kind, Mister Major."

He said: "I was very rude before." He wanted to tell her why he had been rude — that there are certain things a lonely man doesn't like to listen to, that he had begun to like Tina, and that he didn't like the feeling of being used by her just to get something she wanted. But he didn't. He didn't because she pulled him up short.

She said: "Do you think my Giorgio is in one of the other prisoners' camps?"

The Major said: "There's no way of telling," and his voice was suddenly cool.

"When will I know?"

"Next week some time. I've told you all I can. I shouldn't have told you this much."

"Be careful," Tina said, and her smile teased the Major, "you are getting rude again."

The Major smiled too. "I could tell you why, but I won't," he said.

Chapter 26

MAJOR JOPPOLO's desire for popularity in Adano stuck out all over him. It was not just that he wanted to do a good job, and felt that popularity was one sign that he had. It was not much tied up with wanting the Americans to be well received, though he did want that. It was mainly that he himself wanted very much to be liked.

He did not let this desire show itself blatantly, in

184

back-slapping and flattery and other usual means of achieving popularity. He was not especially a politician.

But in everything he did, in every decision he made, he was swayed just a little by the way that act would affect his popularity in the town.

By the same token, in everything that the town did, or the officials of the town, Major Joppolo hunted out little signs that he was liked, and watched vigilantly for warning signals that this thing or that thing was making him disliked.

For this reason it made him uneasy, one morning, to have the usher Zito come to him and say that all the officials of the town wished to have a conference with him some time that morning. He wondered if they wanted to express their displeasure at something he had done.

He said: "Right now, Zito, if they can all come in now."

So in a few minutes they began coming in. As usual Bellanca the Mayor came in first, and it seemed to the Major that the old man's eyes, which were sad from his years of conflict with bad men, were even sadder than usual. D'Arpa the vice mayor came next, walking fast and somehow low, like a weasel, and his little animal eyes looked sad to the Major too. The Major scanned each face as it approached him: the face of Tagliavia the Maresciallo of Finance, looking prosperous but worried, the Major thought; of Panteleone, the Municipal Secretary, looking unctuous but perhaps a little less unctuous than usual, the Major thought; of the pear-shaped volunteer health officer, Signora Carmelina Spinnato, too efficient and fat to have any expression with meaning in it; of Rotondo, the lieutenant of Carabinieri, blank as a wall; and of Saitta, the man concerned with cleaning up the town, himself the cleanest man in town, a face scrubbed with pumice until it shined but even in its cleanliness a little sadder than usual, the Major imagined. The face of Gargano the Two-Hands especially concerned Major Joppolo, for he knew that he might have offended the Chief of Carabinieri in the trial of Errante. And indeed, Gargano did seem to look a little severe.

Honest old Bellanca was spokesman for the group. He said: "We have something to ask of you, Mister Major."

"I'll try to oblige you," Major Joppolo said.

"You may not like it," the old man said.

Major Joppolo said: "Is there something I have done you wish me to correct?"

Gargano the Two-Hands pointed both forefingers at the Major and said: "It is something you have not done."

The others laughed at that remark, and Major Joppolo became more uneasy than ever.

"Something I have forgotten to do?" he asked.

"No," said Tagliavia, the prosperous-looking Maresciallo of Finance, hooking his thumbs in his waistcoat, "you did not forget to do it because you did not know you were supposed to do it. It is something you did not think of doing, and we are very angry with you for not having thought of it."

The others all laughed again, and Major Joppolo began to suspect that they were in a rather gay mood, and that they had put on the glum faces to fool him. But he did not show his suspicion.

He said: "Tell me what it is. I am sorry to have made you angry."

Signora Carmelina Spinnato bounced over to his desk and looked gravely at his profile, and then bounced around front and set up a frame with her thumbs and forefingers and looked through it at his full face. "Which do you think it should be?" she asked the others. "From the side or from the front?" Major Joppolo had never imagined that Signora Carmelina Spinnato could be playful, but she looked as if she were trying to be now, bouncing around with that look of mock gravity on her face.

"From the back!" shrilled D'Arpa the vice mayor.

All laughed again.

Major Joppolo said: "Stop laughing at me. You can laugh at me behind my back, but this is my office, not here."

Old Bellanca said: "We are not laughing at you. This is something which is important for Adano."

"Then tell me what it is."

"You will forgive me," old Bellanca said, "for giving you orders, Mister Major, but you are to go to the house at Number Twenty-three, Via Favemi, and there you are to climb to the second floor and ask for a man named Spataforo. He will tell you what to do."

"He certainly will," Gargano said, and all of them laughed.

"You will find this man Spataforo somewhat opinionated," old Bellanca said.

"Some people call him rude," Signora Carmelina Spinnato said, and all laughed.

"You must not mind him," old Bellanca said. "Just do as he tells you."

The Major said: "I do not like all this mystery, but I'll go. What was the address again?"

"Number Twenty-three, Via Favemi," old Bellanca said. "Go to the second floor, look for Spataforo, and forgive him his manners."

Major Joppolo took down the address and the name.

"When must I go?" he asked.

"At your convenience, Mister Major," old Bellanca said.

And the officials of the town of Adano trooped out of the Major's office, looking like so many bad children.

The Major did not wish to seem too curious, so he waited until after lunch to go to Number Twenty-three, Via Favemi.

He found that the house at Number Twenty-three, Via Favemi, was just another three-storey grey stone house like all the others. By the front door there was a box-like frame with a glass cover. Inside the frame there were about five portrait photographs of that quaint style with the background touched away so that the heads seemed to float in small private clouds. The frame evidently leaked, for streaks of rain and grey dust had run down the pictures. One of the pictures seemed to be of Tina when she had dark hair.

The Major tried the door and found it unlocked. He went up some stairs to the second floor where he found a door in a serious state of disrepair. It sagged from its hinges and one of the panels gaped and was warped. He knocked.

There was no answer, so he knocked again. There was no answer the second time, so he went in.

Through a dark little entrance hall he went into a large room. It was an old photographic studio, in utter ruin, it seemed.

In the middle of the room there was a huge, wood-framed portrait camera, covered with dust, and beside it a high four-legged stool. Between the stool and the box-like camera there was a spider's web, laden with dust and the carcasses of flies and moths. At the end of the room which the camera faced there was an iron and wood bench, like an old park bench, and behind the bench there hung a faded backdrop, an out-of-scale painting of St. Peter's Square in Rome. A pile of dusty wooden film packs lay on the floor, and in one corner there was a heap of cuttings of developed film.

The last thing he saw in the room looked as if it were made of cobwebs and old clothes. It was a man.

He was lying on the floor under a window. Major Joppolo hurried over, because he thought he was dead.

But when the Major got near, the corpse spoke: "Go away," it said. "If you want to look at your own face, look in a mirror."

Major Joppolo said: "I was told to come here and to look for a man named Spataforo. Are you Spataforo?"

The man said: "Spataforo is my name."

The Major said: "They said you would tell me what to do."

Spataforo said: "Oh Lord in Heaven, deliver me from vain people . . . Go and sit on the bench."

Major Joppolo went over to the bench, leaned over and blew away the dust from a spot big enough to sit on. He sat down.

Spataforo still did not get up from the floor. He said: "You are like all the others. You can look at the faces of thousands of your countrymen, but you think your face is more beautiful than all the others. You want to take your face and put it in a frame and put it on a shelf and stare at it. You are disgusting."

Major Joppolo said: "I don't know what you're talking about. If there is something you wish to do, do it. I do not have all day."

The old man began slowly to get up. His knees cracked as he moved them. "Vain and in a hurry," he said. "What is your hurry, vain man? Can't you wait for your image to be made?"

Spataforo moved slowly over to the stool beside the camera. He sat on it, being careful not to disturb the spider's web.

"I have been in this business a long time," Spataforo said. "Eighty years, ninety years, a hundred years, I don't know how long. Manufacturing faces, so that people can stare at themselves. What do you think of that as a life's work? Bah!"

The old man got down from the stool and went and stood in front of the Major. "What a face!" he said. "What an ugly thing a man is!"

Major Joppolo was not disproportionately fond of his face, but he did trim his mustache once every three days, he did pull the hairs out of his nose once every fortnight, he kept his hair cut regularly, he washed; he kept care of his face and, without being immodest, thought that it was not too bad. So when the old man called him ugly, the Major said: "Old man, if the idea is that you are to take my picture, do so and stop insulting me. I am a Major in the American Army. I was sent here by some people of this town. I suppose they sent me to have my picture taken. Please take it if you are going to."

The old man said: "So you are an American. I did not know the Americans were so ugly. I thought they were taller and whiter."

Slowly the old man went around behind his camera. He took a cloth which had once been black but now was grey with dust from the top of the camera, and he bent over and put the cloth over his head and the camera, and he peered into the camera.

His muffled voice came out from under the cloth. "Even upside down you are ugly. Usually I like faces much better upside down, but not yours. You are ugly right side up and upside down. Too puffy in the cheeks. The lips are too full. Nothing that can be repaired by turning you upside down."

Finally the old man came out from under the cloth. He went around the spider web and sat on the stool again. He reached for the shutter bulb and sat there with it in his hand.

"See how the ugly young man tries to make himself beautiful for the photograph!" he said. "Look at him lick his lips, so they will be moist and shine! Look at him try to make his eyes look bright by opening them a little wider than usual, so that they look like marbles to play with! Look at him fix his face in half a smile, which is frozen and false!" The old man laughed a creaking, dusty laugh.

Major Joppolo did not dare speak his annoyance, for fear the old man would squeeze the shutter bulb, so he sat there getting redder and more and more frozen looking.

Spataforo said: "It is a funny thing: men are more vain than women. Women are said to look at themselves in mirrors all the time, and comb their hair, and paint themselves. But it is the men who are really vain. Look at you! Rooster! Peacock! You think you are so handsome."

At last the old man squeezed the bulb.

The Major was so relieved that he did not say any of the things he had thought a few seconds before. He just sat waiting for the old man to change the film and take another.

But the old man said: "What are you waiting for, ugly young man? Do you want to put half a dozen pictures of yourself on your mantelpiece?"

The Major said: "Photographers usually take two or three pictures, to be sure of getting one good one."

Spataforo said: "Not this photographer. After you have been in this hateful business for so many years you cannot count them, you do not have to practice on each sitter. No, that is all, thank the Lord in Heaven."

Major Joppolo did not waste any time in leaving. Back at the Palazzo, he met Bellanca the Mayor and D'Arpa the Vice Mayor in the upstairs hallway.

"I have been to see your friend at Number Twenty-three, Via Favemi," the Major said, and he was just able to smile.

Bellanca said: "Did he tell you that you are ugly?"

191

"He certainly did."

D'Arpa made motions of cranking at the side of his head, and Bellanca said: "He tells everyone the same thing. He even tells the most beautiful girls in town, like Tomasino's daughter Francesca, that they are ugly and vain. He is crazy."

The Major transferred his annoyance from Spataforo to old Bellanca — for citing Francesca instead of Tina as an example of beauty. He said: "What in the world did you send me to the old crack-brain for? What do you want the picture for?"

"You will see," old Bellanca said. "It will be the nicest picture you have ever seen."

Bellanca looked at D'Arpa. D'Arpa looked at old Bellanca. The two of them laughed delightedly.

Chapter 27

TACTFULLY Major Joppolo left the project of the raising of the motor ship *Anzio* entirely in Lieutenant Livingston's hands.

The Lieutenant made fine headway. By the twenty-first, he had acquired the use of the floating drydock. By the twenty-fourth, the *Anzio* was up. By the twenty-seventh, gangs were ready to go to work unloading her.

At ten forty-five on the morning of the twenty-seventh the foreman had just finished making his speech of instructions to the workmen. There were about forty men. Some of them were good men and some were not so good. Things were going so busily in Adano that the labor supply was getting pretty low. Some of the men in these gangs were from out of town, and even the lazy Fatta was here, at work for the first time in years.

When the foreman finished his speech, he told the men that there would be a wait of about fifteen minutes before the donkey engines had enough steam to start hoisting the cargo.

Among the laborers there was one stranger to Adano who seemed above the average. He was a handsome man, and he did not have the pouches under his eyes which are usual among heavy lifters. He spoke good city Italian, too. He had a likable smile, and persuasive ways.

When the foreman was finished speaking, the stranger engaged four men in conversation. One of the four was the lazy Fatta.

"Did you hear the news?" the stranger said.

"News about what?" one of the four said.

"About the German counterattack. I am uneasy this morning, because of what I heard."

"What did you hear?" one of the four said.

"This sounds like the real thing. It started on the twenty-third, and it's apparently reaching its peak this morning. The Germans are trying to throw the Americans into the sea."

Fatta was not too lazy to wish to seem impressive. "Oh, I heard about that," he said.

One of the others from Adano, who knew that Fatta never knew anything, turned on him and said: "Where did you hear that, lazy Fatta?"

Fatta said: "Let me think. Oh yes, it was Mayor Nasta, before he was sent away. He said that the Germans would begin their attack on the twenty-third and that they planned to throw the Americans in the sea between the twenty-fifth and the twenty-eighth."

One of the Adano men said: "Mayor Nasta was a liar. The Americans sent him to Africa."

The stranger said: "Maybe the Americans sent him away because they knew that what he said was true, and they didn't want him spreading fear in the town."

Fatta, who was too lazy to think it through, said: "Yes, that may be so."

But one of the others said: "How would the Americans know of the German plans?"

The stranger said: "They have spies. They have agents."

Fatta said impressively: "It is possible. I heard about the attack several days ago."

The stranger said: "You said between the twenty-fifth and the twenty-eighth? Today is the twenty-seventh. That checks with my information. Today is the big day, I guess."

One of the men of Adano said: "What do you think will happen?"

The stranger said: "Well, that's what makes me uneasy. I'd rather not talk about it."

One of the men said: "Why not?"

Another said: "Tell us."

The stranger said: "No, it would not be fair to you, or to the Americans either. I would rather be uneasy by myself." This stranger was a clever man, as you can see.

One of the men said: "We are uneasy now. Fatta has made us that way, and so have you. We would rather be uneasy about something specific. Tell us what you have heard."

"No," the stranger said, "it is too terrible."

The men insisted: "Tell us, tell us."

The stranger, who was clever, and who had spotted the lazy Fatta as a fool and a potential rumor-monger, said: "Well, I will tell this man" — indicating Fatta — "since he had heard the news previously."

He took Fatta aside. The others saw the man whisper to Fatta, and they saw Fatta's face go pale. Then they saw the stranger leave Fatta and move off into the crowd of workmen.

Fatta came over to them directly. He blurted out at once: "The Germans are going to put on an attack on the harbor of Adano at eleven o'clock — poison gas. It will come from a single plane."

In a very few moments the crowd of men had begun to stir uneasily, and the rumor moved among them like a vapor: "Poison gas at eleven o'clock, . . . Gas at eleven. . . . Gas, eleven, a plane. . . . Gas, eleven. . . . Gas. . . . Gas. . . . Gas. . . ."

By two minutes before eleven, the simple Italian workmen were full of fear. At that time the foreman shouted out that all should be ready to go to work at short notice: the donkey engines were warmed up: the men should split into gangs as instructed.

The men divided themselves, and whenever two who had not been talking together met, one would say: "Have you heard . . . ?" and the other would nod.

Eleven o'clock passed. At three minutes after eleven, just as the men were moving toward the *Anzio*, to take their various stations, the drone of a plane could be heard.

This plane was the regular courier, which was due to pass over Adano each morning at eleven o'clock — as any enemy agent could easily ascertain, and as any Italian laborer could easily forget. It was a few minutes late this morning.

As the plane flew over Adano harbor, keeping about a thousand feet above the barrage balloons, all the workmen beside the *Anzio* looked up at it. The stranger strolled over to Fatta and murmured: "That is it."

Fatta passed the word along. The crowd literally seemed to shudder.

Some asked each other: "What shall we do?"

Others said: "The harbor is the target. We are right in the middle of the target."

Others said: "Does gas drop in bombs? Or does it just spray on us?"

The stranger, who had apparently had some experience in this kind of thing, waited for the exact moment when fear reached a kind of climax among the men. Then he threw up his arms and screamed: "I can smell it. Oh Christ Jesus, I can smell it."

And he turned and ran toward the town.

The panic of the workmen was immediate. They all ran. The lazy Fatta ran for the first time since 1932, when his wife Carmelina implored him for the love of God to run for the midwife.

Someone screamed: "Into the water! Save yourselves!" And about eight men jumped into the sea. Two of them could not swim and had to be rescued.

The lazy Fatta found himself running beside a strong young man named Zingone.

"What shall we do?" Zingone said fearfully.

The lazy Fatta said: "Let us not run quite so fast. We must save our strength, we might have to run a long way."

So they slowed down a little.

"What do you think we ought to do?" Zingone asked again.

Fatta saw someone up ahead who had covered his face with his handkerchief, so he said: "Put your handkerchief over your face. That will keep the gas out."

So both of them clapped handkerchiefs over their faces.

"Did you smell it?" Zingone asked through his handkerchief.

"Oh, yes," Fatta said importantly, "I smelled it plainly."

"What did it smell like?" Zingone asked as they ran.

"It smelled a little like the smoke from the Cacopardo Sulphur refinery."

Zingone was silent for about thirty feet, then he said: "Are you sure it wasn't smoke from the Cacopardo Sulphur refinery?"

"It was poison gas," Fatta gasped.

Fatta was gasping from running, but Zingone, who was in good condition and not yet gasping, thought he was choking from the gas.

"Are you all right?" he asked Fatta.

Fatta said: "I think we should not run quite so fast. I understand that gas affect's one's endurance. Let us save our strength."

So they slowed down to a trot.

Their route took them past Fatta's house. Carmelina his wife had been attracted out of doors by the sound of the first fleet-footed workmen running past. She had shouted to later ones to ask what the trouble was. They had shouted back through their handkerchiefs about the gas. But Carmelina was a skeptic, and she did not believe what they said — until something changed her mind.

"Mary Mother of Jesus!" she exclaimed. "Can my eyes deceive me or is that my husband running?"

It was indeed Fatta, trotting heavily toward her beside Zingone.

"Something terrible has made him run," she said to herself. "Perhaps it is true about the gas."

When Fatta came alongside she moved out into the street and with an easy lope, trotted alongside him.

"What terrible thing is making you run?"

"Gas," he said between heavy breaths. "Poison. Germans."

Zingone, who was not winded at all, explained to her: "We were attacked as we worked in the harbor. Some of the men could smell it. It smelled like sulphur smoke. I think it may have been sulphur smoke."

Carmelina said: "Who said it was gas?"

Zingone said: "A stranger. He repeated the story of the German counterattack."

Carmelina said: "You'd better not run so fast, Fatta, you will explode."

Fatta was in truth turning purple, and he gladly slowed down a little more.

Carmelina said: "I do not believe there was any gas."

But at this time several things happened to make her begin to believe it. For one thing, they came on a knot of people around a man who was lying in the street and vomiting. This man was a certain Buttafuoco, who was sick from having drunk a bottle of wine before going to work. But when he was able to say a word between retches, he groaned: "Gas, the gas."

The knot of people evaporated, and they all started running. The sight of the first gas casualty had everyone terrified.

One of the workers was a young fellow named Lo Faso who until a few weeks before had been an acolyte in the Church of the Orphanage, and the first thing he could think of was ringing the bell of the Church. When he did that, and people through the town heard a bell ringing alone and at the wrong time, alarm spread. Those who knew about the gas became more frightened, and those who did not, ran through the streets asking what the matter was. Soon hundreds of people were running up and down the streets asking each other what the trouble was. Seeing these people helped to persuade Carmelina.

Then Mercurio Salvatore, the crier, heard about the gas, and he felt it his duty to spread the word. He ran into the Palazzo and up the stairs to the third floor and through the little trap door up the ladder leading to the clock tower and finally out onto the platform where the ancient bell had hung. He stood there and at the top of his crying voice he roared: "Gas! Poison Gas! Hold your noses, people of Adano! Gas! Poison Gas!"

The crier's voice was audible through two thirds of the town, and when Carmelina heard him, she was convinced. She began to scream, as many other women were already doing: "Gas! Poison Gas!"

Fatta gasped: "Slower, slower."

Carmelina thought he was beginning to fail from the gas. Actually the only gas he was failing from was on his stomach, but Carmelina began to scream: "Help! My husband is dying from the gas! Medical aid! Help!"

Carmelina, Fatta and Zingone trotted into the Piazza, where a huge crowd was already milling in fear. Fatta staggered and fell, Zingone fanned him with a handkerchief and Carmelina wept over her poor gassed husband. There were other scenes like this all through the square.

At this moment Major Joppolo came out on the balcony of the Palazzo, held up his hand and tried to shout for silence. But there was such audible nervousness in the square that he could not make himself heard.

He sent Zito to get the crier, who was still roaring from the clock tower. It had been the crier's voice which brought the Major out to see what was going on. Zito hurried up into the tower and got Mercurio Salvatore.

When the crier reached the balcony, the Major shouted: "Tell them to be quiet."

The crier roared: "Silence. Be still. The Mister Major has an announcement to make about the gas."

Gradually the hubbub subsided.

"There is no such thing as this poison gas," the Major shouted. "It is a ridiculous rumor."

Old Bellanca the Mayor came up beside the Major and said: "Are you certain, Mister Major? It would be a disaster to put them at rest, and then find that there really had been a gas attack." This showed the infectious power of fear, for old Bellanca was one of the steadiest men in town.

The crowd meanwhile shouted such things as: "How do you know? . . . Fatta here is dying. . . . I smelled it. . . ."

Major Joppolo said to Mercurio Salvatore: "Tell them to be quiet for a minute. I want to telephone."

The crier silenced the crowd again, and Major Joppolo went to his phone and called Lieutenant Livingston.

"Hello, Captain," the Major said. "How are you?"

"Fine, fine," the Lieutenant said cordially. "When you going to come down and have that drink with me?"

"Any day now," the Major said. "Say: is anything unusual going on down there?"

The Kent-Yale voice was a little strained as it said: "Yeah, funniest thing, you know that motor ship I was having raised?"

"Yes indeed," the Major said, "that sure was a swell idea you had."

The Kent-Yale voice was unsure of itself: "Yeah, but this morning I was just getting the workmen going on unloading it, when they all up and ran away. Do you think I wasn't paying them enough, or what? I don't know much about these wops. What do you think the trouble was?"

The crowd outside the Palazzo was beginning to get anxious again, and it hummed. The crier shouted it down again.

The Major said: "You haven't had any casualties or anything like that down there, have you?"

"Just two crazy bastards who fell in the water and couldn't swim. We're giving them artificial respiration."

"You haven't had anything that would make you think there was a gas attack on, have you?"

"Say, are *you* crazy? What the hell are you trying to do, pull my leg?"

"No, Captain, not at all. The reason your workmen ran

200

out on you was because some agitator told them there was a gas attack on and they all got scared."

"Is that a fact? Well, gee, I'm glad it's nothing I did."

"I'll try to have your workmen back to you in an hour."

"Golly, thanks a lot, fellow. That sure takes a load off my mind."

"Well," the Major said, "I want to thank *you* for going to work on that thing so fast. The Navy sure can get things done when it tries."

"Aw, that's nothing," the Lieutenant said. "Say, how about coming down this afternoon and having that drink with me?"

"Don't mind if I do. Matter of fact, I've got a little problem I want to talk to you about. You seem to be the only guy that can get anything done around here."

"Be glad to help you if I can," the Lieutenant said. "Five thirty?"

"Make it six," the Major said. "Doubt if I can get away before six."

"Six it is. Thanks a lot for fixing me up."

"Thank *you*, Captain, you're the fixer."

Lieutenant Livingston shook his head as he hung up, and he thought, you sure can't tell about a guy from the first impression. . . .

The Major went out on the balcony again and said: "I have definite information that there is no poison gas attack going on or expected. You are perfectly safe."

There were shouts of disbelief.

The Major said: "Look: I can breathe deeply and it has no effect on me at all." And he heaved two or three exaggeratedly big breaths.

A voice shouted: "It is all very well to breathe on a balcony. The danger is in the street."

"Very well," the Major said: "I will come down in the street with you and show you." And he went down into the street and breathed deeply there.

By this time Fatta was convinced by the solicitude of his wife and friends that he had been gassed. "I am paralyzed from the waist down," he shouted.

Major Joppolo shouted back: "That is nothing new, lazy Fatta." The crowd laughed. The people were beginning to be with the Major.

One of the workers said: "I smelled it plainly at the corner of the Via Barrino and the Via Dogana."

"All right," the Major said, "come with me."

And he led the huge crowd down the Via Dogana to the corner of Via Barrino. There he stood on the curb and breathed deeply. "All you smelled here," he shouted, "was the fish market three doors down."

Another of the workers shouted: "I smelled it at the corner of Via Vittorio Emanuele and Via Favemi, near the Cathedral."

So they all went to that corner, and the Major breathed deeply again, and he shouted: "All you smelled here was the fumes from the sulphur refinery. If you look you can see the yellow smoke coming toward us."

Another shouted: "I smelled it in the alleyway called Piccolo."

But the Major shouted back: "I am not going to spend all morning sniffing at this town. I am already too familiar with the smells. That was probably horse dung that you smelled."

Another workman shouted: "But the center of the attack was the harbor. That is where the gas really was."

So the Major went and breathed deeply in various points of the harbor. His final breathing point was alongside the motor ship *Anzio*. "And now," he said, "who is for going back to work?"

All but two of the workmen reported back to work. One was the stranger, who had disappeared. The other was the lazy Fatta. He had had enough for one day.

Chapter 28

"Oh dear," said Private First Class Everett B. Banto, clerk in A.P.O. 917, in a second floor room in one of the annexes of the Saint George Hotel in Algiers.

He was reading somebody else's V-mail letter, the envelope of which was open. Private Banto was a mail clerk. He had also been a mail clerk in Greenton, Vermont, before the war. Even in Greenton, he had been very concerned about the way America was behaving herself in the world.

"Oh dear," he said, "I don't see how we're ever going to win the war."

"What's itching your pants now?" said Sergeant Walter Frank, another clerk, who was reading somebody else's copy of *Collier's*.

"Listen to this," said Private Banto. "It says here: 'Why the hell do we have to give the Frogs and the Limeys and the Chinks all the stuff we make? Seems to me we've played Santa Claus long enough.' Oh dear."

"Christ almighty," said Sergeant Frank, "what's a matter with that? God, it makes me vomit to see these Frenchmen driving all over the place when my folks at home can hardly even drive to the A. & P. to get their food."

"Walter, that's not a very good attitude, is it? We won't make many friends in the world that way."

"Well, the hell with 'em."

"Goodness, Walter, that's a selfish way to talk."

"I say the hell with 'em."

Private Banto put the V-letter back in its envelope, and put the envelope in its proper cubbyhole. He picked up one of the mail pouches from the front, cut the wire binding and began to sort the contents, most of which consisted of tempting memoranda, not enclosed in envelopes.

"Gosh, Walter," he said, "we Americans certainly go in for a lot of paper work. Look at this stuff from the front — from the *front,* where they're supposed to be fighting. I don't see how we're *ever* going to win the war."

Sergeant Frank, who was trying to read a story, said testily: "So what the hell's the matter with a little paper work?"

"And look at this. Gosh, but we're inefficient. Look here, this is supposed to be addressed to someone in the 49th Division which is over there, and it's from someone else in the 49th Division, right there too, and they sent it all the way back to Algiers. Isn't that terrible?"

"Oh yes, it's just terrible!" said Sergeant Frank, imitating Private Banto's voice.

"Well, what should I do about it, Walter?"

"You can jam it up your ass for all I care," Sergeant Frank said harshly.

"Why, *Wa*lter," Private Banto said. When he had recovered from the shock, he said: "Seriously, Walter, what should I do with it?"

"Well, if it don't look important, you can throw it in the dead letter basket, that's what we usually do."

"You couldn't do *that,* Walter."

"Hell you couldn't. You just said yourself there's too goddam much paper work. What the hell's one paper more or less?"

"It might be important."

"Well, look at it. What the hell is it about?"

"It says: 'For information. Re carts, Adano.' And then it has something about an order that General Marvin issued, and then apparently a certain Major Joppolo countermanded the order, or something."

"It's about General Marvin? Throw it away! That son-ofabitch."

"Oh no, I wouldn't dare." And Walter put the memorandum in the pouch to go back to the front.

"Now don't bother me," Sergeant Frank said. "I'm reading."

Private Banto kept on sorting. "Oh dear," he said in a few minutes, "listen to this, here's a thing about a captain that's being sent back because of behavior unbecoming to an officer. I don't see how we're *ever* going to win, dear me."

Chapter 29

MAJOR JOPPOLO showed up at the Navy Club for his drink at exactly six 'clock.

There were about twelve officers sitting around in the upstairs room of the villa that Lieutenant Livingston had fitted up as a club. There was the port operations officer, his exec, the port communications officer, the mine, boom and net officer, two or three men from an SC boat, and the rest were from a destroyer that had helped escort some merchant ships across from the mainland. Lieutenant Livingston introduced Major Joppolo around, and he had apparently been telling the others what a good guy the Major was, because their responses were cordial.

"What'll you have?"

Major Joppolo, who was not much of a drinker, said: "What've you got?"

"Well, Scotch mostly. Little bourbon, couple bottles of gin, and Lieutenant Commander Robertson here

brought us a bottle of rum. You can even have some wop
wine if you insist, though why anyone would drink that
stuff beats me."

"Let's see," the Major said, "what's everybody drinking?"

"Different things, whatever you want," the Lieutenant said. "How about some Scotch?"

"If that's what you have the most of."

So the Lieutenant poured out some Scotch for Major
Joppolo. He made it strong and the Major coughed on
the first gulp.

"Say," the Lieutenant said, "you sure have these wops
charmed. How'd you ever get 'em back down here so
fast this morning?"

"Guess I'm a kind of pied piper," the Major said. "I
had to pipe through my nose this morning." And he told
how he had sniffed all over town to disprove the gas
attack.

The Navy enjoyed this story and decided that Major
Joppolo was all right.

They talked for a while about how the invasion was
going, and about a destroyer that had been hit by a
Jerry divebomber, and about the Italian Navy, and then,
as Major Joppolo started in on his second drink, about
the big part the U.S. Navy was playing in the whole
operation.

One of the officers said: "That first landing was really
something. Thousands of ships from God knows how
many ports, all going at different speeds and on different courses. Jesus, I don't see how they did it."

Another said: "And I hear that every ship was on
station within ten minutes of H hour."

"Yes *sir*," said Major Joppolo, whose tongue was becoming pleasantly loose in his head, "I take my hat off
to the Navy." And he raised his glass.

"God's teeth," said Lieutenant Commander Robertson, "that's the first Army man I ever saw that was willing to give the Navy credit."

"Navy's the only bunch that can get anything done around here," the Major said. "Don't know what I'd do without this fellow Livingston."

Livingston glowed but said: "I haven't done anything, Major."

"Don't hand me that stuff," the Major said to Livingston. Then he turned to the others. "Listen, every time I try to get anything out of the Army, they tell me to put it in writing. Now Livingston here . . ."

"That reminds me," Livingston said. "You said you had something on your mind this morning."

"Matter of fact, I have. Since you've been getting all the results, I thought maybe — "

"Want to go in the other room?" Livingston asked politely but importantly.

"Nothing hush-hush," the Major said. "Might as well tell you right here."

And he told about Adano's seven-hundred-year-old bell. He told how it had been taken away, and about what he had done to try to get another. Two drinks had made his mind relax, and he told his story beautifully.

He made the town's need for a new bell seem something really important, and he made the bell seem a symbol of freedom in Adano. He made it seem as if the people of Adano would not feel truly free until they heard a bell ringing from the clock tower of the Palazzo.

And not just any bell. He described what he thought was needed in the bell: a full, rich tone; no crack of any kind; and a touch of history that would mean something to the Italians.

His story was nicely told and his audience was just right. The Navy has a quick sense of tradition. All the folderol — saluting the quarter deck, the little silver buck to mark who should be served first in the wardroom, still calling the captain's court of justice going before the mast, the marvelous poetic orders like: "Sweepers, man your brooms: clean sweepdown fore and aft" — these things made Navy men able to grasp the idea of the bell, and be moved by it.

Major Joppolo finished: "And that's all it was, Livingston. I think I want to get this town the right bell more than I've ever wanted anything in my life."

Commander Robertson was the first one to speak: "Seems to me we ought to be able to find a bell," he said.

"Lots of bells in the Navy," said Robertson's communications officer.

"It's got to be just the right bell, though," Livingston said.

"Yes," Major Joppolo said, "that's the important thing. It's got to be the right bell. I wouldn't want to give these people anything but just the right bell."

Commander Robertson stood up and said: "Let me think, seems to me," and he walked around the room.

Then he said: "I think maybe I can get just the kind of bell you want, Major."

Major Joppolo said: "Do you really think you can?"

The Commander said: "I think maybe."

Major Joppolo said: "If you can, I'm going to switch over to the Navy."

The Commander said: "How would this be, Major? There's a ship, a destroyer, she's named for an Italian-American, the U.S.S. *Corelli*, you know her, boys. Well, all destroyers have ship's bells, they have to be loud and clear so that the men can hear them all over the ship, to tell the hours of the watches. I don't know about you boys, but I think the sound I love better than anything in the world is the sound of the bell aboard the *Stevenson*. Of course we can't ring it all the time while a war's going on, but I don't know, the sound of that bell means the whole ship to me. I think a ship's bell could get to be that way for a town."

Major Joppolo was looking out of the window. He was thinking. "Maybe it could," he said.

Commander Robertson went on: "There's a reason why the *Corelli's* in on this invasion. You see, the Navy thinks about that kind of thing. There was something about Captain Corelli, the guy it was named for, he did something in the last war over here in the Mediterranean. Italy was our ally then, you know."

Commander Robertson's communications officer said: "We were talking about that the other day. Bradshaw seemed to know all about it, what'd he say, Red?"

The officer addressed as Red said: "I didn't listen very carefully, it was something about going to the assistance of an Italian ship that was being attacked by a U-boat."

"And was probably running away from it!" the communications officer added. "I guess the Navy had Corelli over here because he was a wop."

Commander Robertson said: "There's a good tie-in there, Major."

Major Joppolo said: "Maybe it's all right."

Lieutenant Livingston, who didn't want to miss out on the credit which Major Joppolo had been handing out, said: "Do you think we could get the *Corelli* to give up her bell? You said you liked your bell so much: would *you* give it up?"

Commander Robertson said: "For a thing like this, if it was put to me in the right way, I think I would. The good thing is that Toot Dowling, he has the *Corelli,* he was in my class at the Academy, he used to substitute for me in football. Hell, I'm sure I could persuade him, if I could just find him."

The communications officer said: "Wait a minute, I

think I remember seeing something about the *Corelli* in that intercept that I decoded last night. Do you remember that, skipper?"

Commander Robertson said: "Yeah, that's right, she was mentioned. That was all present whereabouts and future movements, wasn't it? Can you remember what it said?"

The communications officer said: "No sir, I couldn't possibly remember, there were too many ships in that thing. But I remember the *Corelli* was mentioned."

Commander Robertson said to the communications officer: "Farley, would you mind going out to the ship and finding that order. I think we ought to tell the Major here whether there's any chance of our helping him out. If the liberty boat isn't at the dock, you can take my gig."

"Yes sir," the communications officer said.

While Farley was on his way out to the ship and back, the others talked about new things, but the Major did not enter much into the conversation. He was thinking. He was trying to imagine the sound of the new bell, and he could see the people crowding in the square to hear it for the first time, and he saw himself on the balcony, making a little speech, not too much, just telling them the meaning of the bell and saying that he hoped that they knew now the meaning of freedom. . . .

Farley came back with the order in his hand. "It's secret, sir, equal to British 'most secret.'"

"Okay," Commander Robertson said, and he began to read the message to himself. "Let's see, *Corelli*, *Corelli*. Here it is." He smiled.

He looked up. "Major, I think we'll get you your bell."

Major Joppolo stood up. "Gee," he said, "I didn't expect action like this. If you think you could. . . ."

Commander Robertson said: "Leave it to me, Major. I'll get all the details from Livingston here."

Major Joppolo turned to Livingston: "I don't know how to thank you," he said.

Lieutenant Livingston said: "Well, it's all the Commander's doing. But I'm glad it's working out the way you wanted."

Major Joppolo left quite abruptly.

Commander Robertson said: "If that bugger thinks the Navy is efficient, he's really going to get a surprise this time. We'll get him that bell within a week. The *Corelli*'s putting in day after tomorrow at that port just up the line, I never can pronounce it, begins with a V."

"Vicinamare," said Lieutenant Livingston, mispronouncing it.

"That's the place," the Commander said. "We'll have time to run up there while these teapots are unloading here, and maybe we can bring the bell right back with us."

"Do you really think you can get it?" Lieutenant Livingston said.

"From Toot Dowling?" The Commander laughed. "Hell, he's a pushover."

Chapter 30

THE IDEA of a party for Major Joppolo grew up in a peculiar way. It came up partly because of real affection for the Major. But it was also partly because Captain Purvis wanted to see if he couldn't make some time with one of the daughters of Tomasino.

Giuseppe the interpreter stopped in to see Captain Purvis at the M.P. command post one afternoon. Giuseppe was just keeping his butter evenly spread. "How's a thing, a Cap?" he asked. He called Purvis Cap because his tongue always tripped on Captain.

"Okay," the Captain said.

"You like Adano?"

"Okay," the Captain said.

"You like a little more fun?"

"Who wouldn't?"

"Why you don't a go see Francesca no more?"

"There's nothing there, Giuseppe, the family's always hanging around."

"I'm a no so sure. You don't a try very hard."

"Besides, I think the Major's falling for the blonde. He's a good guy, I wouldn't want to mess him up any."

"How you mess him up? You fool around a Francesca."

"No, Giuseppe, I think the Major's serious. I don't know, he didn't say anything, I just got a hunch. If I fooled around with those girls, it would be strictly for fish. No, I don't think it's a good idea."

"You mean a Mister Major, he's a fall in a love?"

"I don't know. Maybe. I think so."

"What a for? Can he have a no fun without a fall over like a that?"

"Doesn't look to me like you can have much fun with a whole bunch around, including you, Giuseppe, and having to eat that godawful candy, and the old lady sitting there. No, Giuseppe, if I play house with a little dolly, I like a little privacy."

"Giuseppe's a fix."

"I doubt if you could."

"Never mind. Giuseppe's a fix. I tell a you something. These a girl, these a Tomasino's girl, she's a not, uh how you say uh — not a scrupulous. All a three, nobody's a scrupulous. You know those a two little a babies in a house?"

212

"You mean those little girls?"

Giuseppe nodded. "Belong a sister. She's a you know." Giuseppe winked.

"You mean she takes in washing and that's not all?"

"She's a bad a girl. Rome." Giuseppe nodded and winked at the same time.

"Francesca's not a scrupulous. Tina's not a scrupulous. You can have a some fun."

"How? What can you fix, Giuseppe?"

"Fix a party."

"There you go with a crowd again. Hell no, let's have a little privacy."

"How about a Major?"

"Yeah, I suppose we got to think of him. You know, Giuseppe, he's a funny guy. Sometimes I think he's an awful wet blanket, and sometimes I can't help liking him. He was telling me the other day at lunch that the main thing he really wants around here is to have these Italian people like him. You know what I think we ought to do? I think we ought to throw a party for him. Or rather I think we ought to rig it so these Italians throw a party for him." Captain Purvis never thought of Giuseppe as an Italian, because he spoke English.

"Giuseppe's a fix."

"I mean a real good party, Giuseppe. With people like the Mayor and that old sulphur crackpot, and some nice girls of course."

"Giuseppe's a fix."

"And some wine. Couldn't we get some champagne for a change?"

"Giuseppe's a fix."

"If we really had a big party, then a certain Captain and a certain young lady could do a disappearing act, couldn't they?"

Giuseppe winked again.

"That's what I hate about a small party, anyone goes

out, everyone else notices it. We ought to have a big party for a change."

Giuseppe said: "How many you want, a Cap?"

"Oh, I don't know, you can get some of these Italians together and decide. I'll put up whatever dough you need. We could have it down at the villa where my men stay, that Quattrocchi guy's house. Lot of spare rooms down there with beds in 'em, heh, Giuseppe?" And this time it was Captain Purvis who winked.

"When you want a party?" Giuseppe asked.

"Well, pretty soon, how about next Friday?"

"Giuseppe's a fix."

And so it happened that in his mail, two or three days later, Major Joppolo got a card, on which was written in Italian: "A Committee of the people of Adano request the pleasure of your company at a party in honor of His Excellency the Mister Major Victor Joppolo on Friday evening, July 29th, at Villa Rossa, 71 Via Umberto the First, at 8:30 p.m."

Major Joppolo propped the card on the inkstand on his desk where he could read it, and often did: ". . . in honor of His Excellency. . . ."

Chapter 31

THE MORNING the prisoners were released the sun was bright and Adano looked its best.

Major Joppolo's street-cleaning truck had just swished up the Via Umberto the First and turned along the Corso Vittorio Emanuele, with the Chief Street Cleaner, Saitta, spick and span in his white suit, at the wheel. And now the paving blocks glistened from their rinsing, and the smell of wet horse dung was clean on the morning air.

It was a fine day for coming home.

The released prisoners came up the Via Umberto the First in a body. They were still in uniform, but their uniforms were dirty from sleeping on the ground, and many of them were unshaven and had long hair.

They stopped by at Zapulla's bakery on their way up the street, and as they approached the square almost every one of them had half a loaf of good white bread in his hand. They sang and shouted: "Going home! Going home!" as they walked up the street.

They did not march. They had had enough of lining up for inspection and lining up for chow and lining up to shoot and be shot at. They were just a mob of boys going home as they walked up the Via Umberto the First. There was laughter in some of their throats and some of them were crying.

The war aim of most men is to go home. And so for these Italian boys the hateful war was fulfilled, and they were incredibly happy as they walked up the street.

Their eyes were open wide, like the eyes of small children who notice everything. They noticed that Mussolini's pompous inscriptions were painted off the walls. They saw that the street was clean. The bread tasted better in their mouths than it had ever tasted before. They had hardly turned into the Via Umberto the First from the Via Favemi before their ears heard a woman sing. The horse dung was not even sour any more, according to their noses, but was new and sweet on the morning air.

Any day would have been good for coming home, but this home and this day were best. They sang and shouted: "Coming home! Coming home!"

There had not been any advance notice of the prisoners' release, except what Major Joppolo had given

Tina, and she told no one. But somehow the word spread
far ahead of their actual approach, like gusts of wind
ahead of an oncoming cloud.

Women far up the town heard the murmur of their
approach and instinctively knew what it was. They
shouted to other women. Those standing on the sidewalk in front of the Palazzo saw them turn into Via Umberto the First from Via Favemi, and instead of rushing
down the street toward them, they clutched their emo-
tional throats and ran off to find their friends to tell them
of this wonderful thing: the boys of Adano were coming home!

And then the women who had heard the murmur and
the women who had stood there and actually seen the
approach, and also the women that these others had
summoned, all ran back to the sidewalk in front of the
Palazzo and watched.

War is awful for men but it is not too good for women.
In their bedsheets these women had ached for their men.
The nipples of their breasts had hurt from wanting them
so badly. There had been days when certain of these
women did not get letters from their men, and then, in
talking with their friends, had found that those others
did get letters, and those had been bad days. Some had
had their small ones, just old enough to talk, slip up
to them shyly with frightened eyes and say: *"Papà:
where is my little father?"* and there had not been any
answer except in the pit of the stomach.

The women who stood on the sidewalk in front of
the Palazzo had lived in daily dread that their men
might be hurt, or worse. Women who had argued with
their men, and been impatient with them when they had
them securely, forgot the arguments and thought only
of the nice things, the being waked up in the middle of
the night by a man crawling clumsily into bed, the loud
laugh with the head thrown back, the smell of a certain

216

smoke, the sound of a certain kind of wine clucking out of the bottle.

And so the women stood there on the sidewalk in front of the Palazzo with their hands at their throats, or reaching vaguely for loose wisps of hair.

The men walking up the street saw the women standing there. They did not break into a run. Their happiness was terrifying; they walked slowly toward their women.

When the men had reached a place about five hundred yards from the women, the crowd of women started moving forward, slowly at first, the feet just shuffling on the sidewalk, then stepping forward as necks craned and eyes darted, then walking to be closer, and finally running and shouting wordless sounds.

The men did not break into a run. The women ran toward the men. There was equal happiness on both sides, it just happened that most of the men knew their women would be there, whereas some of the women were not sure that their men would be there. That was the difference. That is why the women ran.

There were among those women some who knew that their men were dead. They were just running forward in order to share the incredible happiness, or even the doubt, of the other women. Doubt was better than what they had.

One of the women in the crowd was Tina. She had been expecting this thing ever since the Major had spoken to her about it, and she kept herself very available. She was one of the women who had been brought out by the mere murmur.

She was dressed in her nicest dress, a blue thing that the gay sister had sent from Rome. Her hair had been combed until it shone and its blondeness looked almost real.

She ran forward with the others. Her eyes explored

the crowd of men half lovingly, half fearfully. She pushed at the women in front of her and struggled for a better view.

You can be sure that Major Joppolo was down in the street. He wanted to be there to savor the happiness in Adano. But he also shared the specific curiosity which drove Tina forward. He too wondered whether Giorgio was there.

At the first murmur of the crowd, which he had easily heard through the French doors of his office, he had run down into the street, and he had walked rapidly down it toward the group of men even before the women started moving. Therefore he had just about reached the prisoners when the women started running.

When the prisoners saw the Major, some of them ran forward, shouting: "American! American!" They hugged him and some kissed him, and there were bread crumbs on his face when they got through with him.

Here was the final crazy touch of war. Men who for months had been chosen and trained and ordered to commit the worst of all crimes, murder, were now showering their affection on the very kind of man they had been out to kill.

The women came close. Some had recognized their men, and were screaming the names with trembling voices.

Now at last the men broke into a run. They had only about ten paces to go.

The two crowds mingled.

It was a crazy sight at first. The couples who had found each other embraced each other. Some laughed and some cried, some whispered and some screamed, some pounded and some caressed.

Some of the women with dead husbands embraced the first men they reached, just to taste a little of this sensation that they had wanted so much. But the men rejected them and went looking for their own.

You could begin to see the ones who were not going to find their men at all. They darted faster and faster from couple to couple, repeating the name, asking, looking two and three times at faces already seen just to make sure. The faces of these women went paler and paler and finally they began to cry. Curiously most of these women did not scream, but cried silently; the tears just coursed down their empty faces.

Tina did not have to dart from couple to couple. Major Joppolo happened to be standing close beside her when she found out.

A young man left his woman. He went over to Tina and stood before her and shook his head. That was all he had to do, Tina knew.

Major Joppolo forgot all the injunctions about behavior in public which he had put down in *Notes from Joppolo to Joppolo*. He stepped forward and took Tina's hand. Her hand was cold and loose in his, and she did not seem to realize that he was there.

"What happened?" Tina asked the young man.

He said: "I will tell you later, Tina. Please not just at this moment."

Major Joppolo said to the young man: "We will have lunch together, at the Albergo dei Pescatori."

The young man did not question Major Joppolo with his eyes at all. He said: "Bring Tina at twelve o'clock. I will tell her everything then." He kissed Tina on the cheek.

The kiss made Tina start crying. She buried her face in her hands and shook silently.

The crowd did not break up for a long time. The men stood right there in the street and told many of their experiences. Couples melted into quartets and quartets into laughing circles, and the women who did not find their men went off alone. Fathers held sons in their arms for the first time. A few men hurried off with their women in a desire to become fathers as quickly as possible. Idlers and curious men who had stayed behind began to mix with the crowd. Laura Sofia the maiden lady circulated in the crowd, hoping that the hunger induced in men by war might be in her favor, but she had no luck.

Major Joppolo did not hurry Tina. He let her cry until the tears were all gone and her sobs grew dry and awful. He touched her all the time, with a hand on her shoulder or the back of a hand against her bare arm, just to let her know that someone was there.

Finally the Major took Tina home. A little before twelve he went back to get her. By that time she was all right. Her eyes were red, but she was in control of herself.

They went to the Albergo dei Pescatori. Giorgio's friend, whose name was Nicolo, was already there with his girl. Nicolo had changed into civilian clothes. A few minutes after Tina and the Major joined Nicolo and his girl, Captain Purvis came in. Since he and the Major usually had lunch together, it was quite natural that he should join the group, though the Major regretted it later.

For a time they ate silently. Tina asked Nicolo how things had been and Nicolo said they had not been bad, and Captain Purvis asked the Major where he had been hiding this new quail and he tried to flirt with her a little, and the Major made some polite advances to Nicolo to try to cover up his embarrassment over Captain Purvis. But on the whole the conversation was either nonexistent or meaningless.

It was not until the fruit came on that Tina said: "Nicolo, tell me what happened."

Nicolo had been waiting for her to urge him. "It isn't very nice, Tina," he said. "War isn't ever very nice."

"I know," Tina said. "Tell it to me just as it happened."

Nicolo said: "I will have to tell it that way, Tina. That is the way I remember it and I couldn't lie to you about it. It didn't happen nicely."

Major Joppolo said: "I guess it never seems very nice."

Nicolo said: "It never does."

Captain Purvis, who did not speak Italian, said: "What the hell is all this wop talk about? Let me in on the good news."

Major Joppolo decided it was best to ignore the Captain. The Captain started trying to make eyes at Nicolo's girl.

Tina said: "Did he ask for me, Nicolo?"

Nicolo said: "I'd better begin at the beginning."

Tina said: "All right."

Nicolo looked Major Joppolo straight in the face: "You will see that what happened to Giorgio was a very complicated thing. It was all tied up with what we Italians felt in this war, and I guess with what any man thinks about a war, or even about a game that he thinks he must win. You will see, it was complicated."

Major Joppolo said: "I will understand. My mother and father came from Florence."

Surprisingly Tina took the trouble to say: "He will understand."

Nicolo said: "I don't know whether I understand myself. It began in the battle for Beja, in Tunisia. It was a kind of infection, like something a soldier gets in his bowels, only it was in the heart. Our hearts went all watery, and we were through with the war, although we were still supposed to be fighting. It was the artillery."

Tina said: "Did he ask for me, Nicolo?"

Nicolo deliberately kept himself from being too sympathetic. He said: "You'd better let me tell it from the beginning, Tina. It'll be better that way, I promise."

She said: "All right."

Nicolo said: "The artillery was bad. They say you stop living for a moment when you sneeze. When a shell goes off near you, you have the same kind of paroxysm, and when you come out of it, you know you have been dead for a moment. You can't go on dying like that many times a day, day after day, and be the same. Think what it would be like if you sneezed twenty times an hour, twenty-four hours a day, for days and days on end. Even that would be terrible, and there is hardly any fear in a sneeze."

Captain Purvis said: "Cutie, how would you like to dance the dance of the sheets?" But Nicolo's girl was listening to the story. The Captain said: "Goddamit, I'm going to have to start taking lessons in dago, I can see that. Pass me the *vino*, will you, Major?"

Nicolo said: "We all changed, except Giorgio."

Tina gasped a little when she heard the name.

Nicolo said: "Giorgio used to argue with us. He said we had to go on fighting until we were consumed, and he talked about our honor, and he used to say that even if war made you think that men were just animals, you had to remember that animals often fight each other to the death. I remember he often used to say: 'Have you ever tried to figure out what makes two dogs fight each other?'" Nicolo turned to the Major and said: "Have you ever thought about that, sir?"

The Major said: "No, I hadn't."

Nicolo said: "It is worth thinking about."

Tina said: "Did he ever talk about me?"

Nicolo ignored her. He said: "It makes war a little more sensible if you think about the dogs. Anyhow, Giorgio was tenacious, and I used to admire him for it, though I always argued with him. I thought we ought to give ourselves up. He was so tenacious that he made me help him kill two Germans and we put on their uniforms and came back to Sicily on a Siebel ferry. We had to be careful to pick two Germans just the right size for uniforms. Giorgio made me do it with him because he said otherwise we would be taken."

Nicolo's girl spoke for the first time: "Tell Tina about the night before you left Tunisia."

Nicolo said: "Oh yes, just before we killed the Germans I wanted to back out. I was afraid. I tried to tell him that killing the Germans was dishonorable, and he said that in a war a man's honor was not measured by medals, because they were given out unjustly, but by the amount he could do for his nation. He said that killing two Germans helped rather than hurt Italy (perhaps, as things have turned out, we should have killed more) and that the best thing we could do would be to preserve ourselves for our country's next battle. So we slipped into a bivouac and picked out two Germans and killed them in a quiet way which Giorgio showed me, and we got back to Sicily."

The Major said: "Didn't you have any trouble on the Siebel barge? Do you speak German?"

Nicolo said: "Giorgio spoke a little German, but anyhow we got in with an engineer unit they were apparently trying to save, and they just herded them on the ferry and us with them, and no questions asked."

Major Joppolo said: "Were you attacked on the way across?"

"We came by night. It was only a ten-hour trip. The Germans got quite a bit across by night without being attacked."

Captain Purvis said: "Major, you going to sit here jabbering dago with these people all afternoon? How about cutting me in on this pretty little squiff here?"

The Major said: "He's telling a story, Captain."

The Captain said: "My pants aren't hot for him, the hell with him, what I want to know is, where you been hiding this little piece?"

Major Joppolo ignored the Captain and the Captain took some more wine.

Nicolo said: "The ironic thing was that the Siebel barge landed us just down the beach from Adano here."

Tina said: "Why didn't you come home? Why couldn't he have come home to me then?"

Nicolo said: "But the whole point of our coming across was so we could fight again. We turned ourselves in to a division in the hills just this side of Vicinamare, it was General Abbadessa's division. Tunisia fell just then and so we were congratulated for getting away and they made us both sergeants. Giorgio was wonderful in those days before Sicily was attacked. Most of the soldiers were for faking resistance and surrendering, but Giorgio used to talk about the anguish Italy had had for so long, and he told about Garibaldi and Mazzini and Cavour, and when men said that Italy was beaten, he brought up Britain after Dunkirk. I remember one night a glib one was arguing with him and said that Fascism was evil and so why fight for it, and Giorgio said: 'If Fascism is evil, why haven't you been fighting against it for twenty-one years?' "

The Major said: "Was Giorgio a Fascist?"

Tina turned angrily and said: "He certainly was not."

Nicolo said: "No, that's the funny part of it. He was in jail a lot here in Adano for nothing in particular except being against the Fascists. And yet in 1940 when Mussolini put us in the war, he was one of the first to go."

Tina said: "But what happened?"

Nicolo said: "I was getting to that. The troops fought badly at the coast, as you know, and fell back on Marenisseta. It was the night of the fourteenth of July. Word came that the Americans were going to hit us the next morning. We were bivouacked in the grounds of a villa just east of the town, and as soon as the news came about the attack, most of the troops went crazy. A bunch of them went into the villa and broke into the cellar and brought out some wine."

When Captain Purvis heard the word *vino*, he said: "Hurrah for *vino*! That's one word of Italian I sure can understand. Say Major, what's the word that we begin with *f*? I'd like to know if this little dolly understands it."

Major Joppolo ignored the Captain. Niccolo said: "The men began drinking the wine, they said they were going to be captured in the morning, the war was over for them, why shouldn't they have a good time? About twenty of them got very drunk, and they began throwing bottles against the wall of the house. Giorgio got furious and said he was going to stop them. I tried to tell him not to try, because the men were much too drunk to listen to reason."

Major Joppolo began to suspect what happened to Giorgio and he said: "Do you think you ought to tell Tina the rest of this story?"

Nicolo said: "I think I owe it to Giorgio. I told Tina it wasn't nice."

Tina said: "Yes, Nicolo, go ahead." But she did not sense, as the Major did, what was coming.

Nicolo said: "I tried to stop him, but I never had much influence over him, he was much stronger than I was. He ran over to the place where they were throwing bottles. They had lit a fire, which was against all rules, and Giorgio stood beside it where they could see him and shouted at them. These men had only been in one battle, but they were crazy with fear, and also with the wine. One of them would get up and shout: 'To hell with the son of a frog, Mussolini!' and he would throw a bottle as if he were throwing it at Mussolini. Then the next one would get up and he'd shout: 'To hell with the she-dog in heat, Edda Ciano!' and they would all laugh and he would throw his bottle. Giorgio shouted but they either didn't hear him or wouldn't listen. He got in a kind of a frenzy. Remember: he had been through a lot."

Tina began to realize what was coming. She put her hand up over her mouth and her eyes grew wide.

Nicolo said: "Giorgio ran over to the wall, to the very place where they were throwing their bottles, and he screamed: 'Stop, stop! You are traitors! For the love of Mary Mother of Jesus, stop!' At first just the fact of his being there made the drunkards stop, but then one of them shouted as if it were a big joke: 'Isn't that Benito Mussolini over there?' and they all laughed and another one shouted: 'Yes, the war has shrunk him!' and they laughed some more. Then one of the crazy ones shouted: 'I hate him! I hate him!' and threw his bottle at Giorgio."

Tina put her head down and said softly: "Oh, not that way, not that way."

Nicolo said: "The first bottle missed, but it broke against the wall and several pieces cut Giorgio. I could see the blood running down his face. He had so much courage, Tina, you would have been proud of him, he did not move away."

Tina said softly: "Yes, I am proud, yes, yes."

Nicolo said: "I shouted to him to come away but he wouldn't. He screamed at the men: 'We must fight! The only chance for our nation is to go down fighting. The only chance for us as men is to die in battle.' The men stepped up in turn now and threw their bottles. They were not laughing any more now. Giorgio had touched some spring of guilt in them and they wanted to kill him. The men were so drunk that I don't see how any of them hit him, but the third one did. The bottle hit him in the right shoulder. Of course the bottle didn't break and didn't knock him down, but it must have hurt terribly. But he went right on trying to scream to their brains, but they had none now."

The Major said: "It must have been awful."

Nicolo said: "After he was hit for the first time, he

screamed louder and louder, but the pain must have done something to him, because he screamed religious things. He screamed: 'Oh Christ Jesus lamb of God heart of Jesus,' and things like that. The drunkards kept on throwing their bottles. Several of the ones that broke on the wall cut him and soon his face and hands were covered with blood and his uniform began to be torn and blood seeped through. The second one that hit him struck his groin and that apparently hurt him so much that he couldn't shout any more. When he stopped shouting the drunken men closed in toward him and began throwing their bottles from close and closer." He stopped and asked Tina: "Do you want me to stop, Tina?"

She said: "No, Nicolo, I've got to hear it now."

Nicolo said: "He finally fainted and the drunken men took bottles and beat him." Nicolo turned to the Major again. "They were crazy, sir. Their one battle and the air raids and what they had had to drink. They were not Italians any more, sir. They were not even men."

Major Joppolo said: "A thing like that could happen in any army, if the men were frightened enough."

Nicolo said: "Thank you, sir."

Then he went on: "I had a pistol. Giorgio and I each had a pistol that we had taken off the Germans we killed. I couldn't stand it any longer, so I took out my pistol and fired a shot in the air. That only seemed to frighten the men more and didn't stop them, so I went right up to one and knocked him over the head with the butt and he fell down. Another one who was much bigger than I am turned on me with a bottle, so I fired a shot into the air right in front of his face. He was bringing the bottle down and the shot hit the bottle and cut him up and he started to squeal and that made the others think I was going to kill them all so they ran off."

Tina looked up with a question in her eyes.

"He was alive," Nicolo said. "He spoke a little. I tried

to do what I could for him, but he had lost too much blood."

Tina said pathetically, knowing what the answer would be: "Did he speak my name?"

Nicolo said: "Tina, I have been beside many men who died in this war and no one of them ever mentioned a woman when he died. Men do not talk that way when they die. They talk about their stomachs and they swear, but they do not mention the names of women. I remember he said a snatch from the Litany of the Blessed Virgin, and he asked me to move his head to one side, it would be easier that way, but when I did he asked me to move it back. And then he died, Tina."

Tina put her head down again and said: "Not even in battle."

Nicolo reached out his hand and took Tina's hand and said: "Oh, yes, it was in battle. It was Giorgio's battle, Tina. When I fired the shots officers came and they thought Giorgio was one of the drunks, so he will never get a medal. But Tina, no Italian has died more bravely in this war. Look at me! The drunks and I, we were all captured in the morning. I am ashamed of myself, and the shame I feel and the awful shame the drunks feel and all Italian soldiers feel — we were weak, Tina — the shame will hurt our country for many years. Our only chance is to remember men like Giorgio. If we couldn't go down fighting the way he wanted us to, we can remember the ones like him who did."

Major Joppolo wanted to help. "That's right, Tina," he said.

Nicolo said to the Major: "You see, we are very mixed up. We had no cause to fight for that appealed to us. Do your men?"

Major Joppolo said: "I don't know, Nicolo. I think the cause is there, all right. We've got to get rid of the bad men, and the Germans have some, and I'm afraid you did — and of course we have some, too. I just don't know whether our soldiers think much about causes. That's one thing that worries me about this war."

Nicolo said: "That's what worries me, too. Giorgio was an exception."

Major Joppolo said: "That's true, he was. He would have been an exception on our side, too."

Captain Purvis said: "Look at that sonofabitch holding hands with your girl, Major, you ought to root him in the tail and teach him a lesson."

Major Joppolo took Tina home and spent the afternoon with her. He was wonderfully gentle with her. His sympathy seemed to help her, and quite often she looked up into his face in a way which gave him a feeling in the chest.

Finally he said to her: "Tina, I don't know whether it's fair to say this now, this afternoon, but I'm going to say it anyhow. Tina, I — well, maybe I'd better wait and tell you another time."

She looked up into his face in a way that made him think she was disappointed, but she said very softly: "Maybe you'd better."

He said: "I'll tell you at the party on Friday."

She repeated softly: "On Friday." And then she looked away and said: "You know, it's very strange, but I never knew whether I loved Giorgio. I admired him and sometimes I was afraid of him, and he meant very much to me in ways. But his flesh was very cold. His mind was very stubborn. I still don't know. . . ."

She started crying again.

Chapter 32

In Lojacono's studio — if a single room with small windows could be called a painter's studio — a delegation of town officials stood around and criticized as the white-haired artist tried to work.

The old man stood before two easels. One held his unfinished painting, the other his subject: the photograph of Major Joppolo made by the crazy Spataforo. The photograph was an excellent likeness, and the portrait was already a fair one.

Gargano the Two-Hands made two circles with his thumbs and forefingers and put the circles up to his eyes and peered through them at the picture. He said: "The eyes. On the whole, the face is good, but the eyes: it seems to me the eyes are not quite the eyes of the Mister Major."

Old Lojacono said: "The portrait is not yet finished."

D'Arpa the Vice Mayor said in his little weasel's voice: "Should the nose seem to recline on the mustache in such comfort? I think that nose is asleep."

The old painter said: "It is not finished."

Saitta, the clean one, the man concerned with keeping the town fresh, held his white suit close to him so as not to get any driblets of paint on it and said: "Could not the background be cleaned up a little?"

The white-haired painter turned on his critics and said: "It is not finished. It is not finished. It is not finished. Can you get that through your thick official skulls?"

D'Arpa, in his capacity as senior official on the spot, took it upon himself to say: "We are not deaf, Lojacono. We are here on behalf of the town of Adano to see that you finish this portrait well and make it good enough for its purpose."

Gargano lifted his shoulders and stretched his hands out, palms up, as if to say what he did say: "We mean no offense, old man." Then he made motions of painting and said: "Go ahead, old man."

Lojacono went back to his work. He grumbled as he dabbed. "Now for the first time in months," he said, "I have a subject of which I wish to make a superior painting. What happens? I get into my work, I begin to love it, my brush seems deft in my hand. Then what happens? Officials visit me, men who know less about art than I do about cleaning streets" — he said this with great contempt and Saitta the street-cleaner drew his white suit a little closer around him, as if he suspected that the angry old man might flick a blob of pigment at him — "and they criticize my work, though it is not finished."

Gargano made the two circles again and said: "I merely pointed out that the eyes are not yet those of the Mister Major."

D'Arpa said: "I simply said that the nose looks comfortable, perhaps a trifle too comfortable, perhaps even asleep."

Saitta said: "To suggest that the background might be cleaned up a little is not to criticize the likeness."

Lojacono said: "I told you that the painting is not finished. When it is done, I promise that you will like it."

D'Arpa said in his high voice: "It is more important that the Mister Major should like it."

The old painter said: "He will, I promise it."

Gargano placed both hands over his heart and said: "He must, old man, or else the whole point of our presenting it to him will be destroyed. Do you know why we are giving it to him?"

Lojacono said wearily: "Yes, I know why you are giving it to him."

Gargano had not expected the old man to answer his rhetorical question. He took his hands off his heart and said: "Well then . . ."

The white-haired painter turned again toward the three men. "Well then," he said, "why don't you leave me alone so that I can put into the painting what you feel toward this man?"

Gargano started to make the circles and said doubtfully: "The eyes —"

The painter said: "The eyes are not finished. Neither is the tired nose. Neither is the dirty background. I might explain to you, street-cleaner, that I use the background as the place to test my colors. Do I come to you with suggestions as to how to remove horse-manure from the streets?"

Saitta tugged on his suit and said grudgingly: "No-o-o."

Lojacono said again: "Well then," and turned to his painting.

And then the old man said, as if to the face in the photograph: "This is a portrait I wish to make as nearly good as my talents will allow. There are many things I hope this painting will have — when it is finished." He said this last grimly, for the benefit of his critics.

He went on to tell what he was trying to achieve in this painting, and in so doing he fulfilled the purpose of the criticism: he told the critics what was in his mind, so that when the picture was finished they could point out what was there to be seen if you looked for it.

"The main thing I hope this painting will have," the old man said, "is the life and breath of the Mister Major. In the eyes I hope there will be a slight look of mischief which I have seen there, something which I think shows that he is rather fond of young ladies." He turned on Gargano severely: "But that is not all that I intend to have in the eyes."

He went on: "In the way the mustache is trimmed,

there will be a little vanity, not much, just enough to make a man dress neatly and look once, not twice, in every mirror he passes."

D'Arpa said in a high voice: "These are ridiculous little things, what about the big things?"

Lojacono said: "Sometimes I think you are a ridiculous little man. The big things come from the little things. I am not finished. There is something about officials that makes them poke their noses, which are usually asleep on their faces, into unfinished matters."

D'Arpa said: "Go on, old man."

"In the chin, there will be strength, in the ears, alertness, in the fix of the hair, neatness, in the cheeks, a sympathetic warmth. You will like it," the old man said. "So will he."

D'Arpa said again: "But the big things, what about the big things?"

The painter said: "You will not see the big things until you have seen the portrait for some time, just as you did not recognize them in the man until you got to know him. Why list them? You know what they are as well as I do."

But D'Arpa said: "What do you think they are, Lojacono?" The critics did not really come to criticize. They came to find out what to look for.

The old man said: "There is only one big thing, really. All the others are tied up in it. It is the wish, which is visible in this man's face, that each person in this town should be happy. That is a very big thing. If that were visible in every official's face, well, painters would not be criticized before they were finished."

Gargano squinted at the portrait and said: "I think the eyes will be all right."

D'Arpa said: "There is obviously something unfinished about that sleeping nose. It will be all right when it is finished."

Saitta said: "I am glad you explained to me about the background, painter. Have you any suggestions about the manure?"

Lojacono said: "I only suggest that you leave me alone until I have finished. When is it that you want the painting?"

D'Arpa said: "We thought we would give it to him next Friday, on the afternoon before the party which is in his honor. We thought we would make it entirely his day."

The white-haired painter said: "It will be finished, and you will like the face, I promise you."

Chapter 33

GENERAL MARVIN believed in what he called "keeping in touch." He liked to know what was going on, both in the world and in the Army.

Accordingly he had his aide Lieutenant Byrd read to him for about an hour each morning. On Monday, Wednesday and Friday mornings, when the courier pouches arrived from Algiers, he had the Lieutenant read him various things from the pouch.

That Monday morning, the Lieutenant read him Ernie Pyle's column and Pup Tent Poets from the *Stars & Stripes*, an article on Teller mines and S-mines in the *Infantry Journal*, a condensation of birth control in the *Reader's Digest*, three situation reports from A.F.H.Q., a handful of fan letters arising from an article about the General in some magazine, and a letter of commendation of the General from Secretary Stimson, referring to a battle in Tunisia. This last had arrived several days before, and without being told, Lieutenant Byrd had had the sense to read it to the General every morning.

By the time these things were finished, the General was in an excellent mood. But as always seemed to be the case, when Lieutenant Byrd started in on the memoranda from various officers, the old man gradually got angry.

Memoranda always seemed to be written about things that had gone wrong. This morning there was one about how some signal corps telephone wire had been lost on an LST, so that one unit was very badly off for communications; there was another about the need for gasoline dumps to be established closer behind a certain division so that trucks would not have to run so far for fuel; a third about the way close air support was occasionally attacking friendly troops . . . and so they went.

After some of the memoranda, the General would bellow directions to Colonel Middleton, sitting in the next room. After others he would roar: "The hell with 'em. They're no worse off than all the others. The answer is no."

Lieutenant Byrd picked up one of the memoranda and read: "To General Marvin for information etcetera etcetera, routing address, and so forth. Subject: mule carts, town of Adano."

The General rumbled: "Goddam mule carts."

Lieutenant Byrd read: "On July 19, orders were received from General Marvin, 49th Division, to keep all mule carts out of the town of Adano. Guards were posted at the bridge over Rosso River and at Cacopardo Sulphur Refinery. Order carried out . . ."

The General said: "Goddam right, stop the goddam carts. Lousy Italians trying to hold up the whole goddam invasion. They better carry out the goddam order."

Lieutenant Byrd droned on, hardly noticing what he read: "On July 20, guards were removed on order of Major —"

Lieutenant Byrd suddenly realized what he was reading. He put the memorandum down and picked up the next.

But the General roared: "Finish it, goddamit, finish it."

The Lieutenant read: "— were removed on order of Major Victor Joppolo, Civil Affairs Officer, town of Adano, because carts were essential to town and town was —"

Now the General had forgotten about finishing the memorandum. "Joppolo," he shouted, and his face was the color of distant mountains. "Joppolo."

General Marvin's memory worked in a peculiar fashion. "Middleton!" he shouted. "Come in here, Middleton."

The Colonel came in.

"Middleton, remember the name of Joppolo, a lousy sonofabitching little wop named Joppolo?"

Colonel Middleton said, with a tired face: "Yes, sir. The carts."

General Marvin bellowed: "I just remembered something. That goddam wop was out of uniform that day. You remember? He had on pinks and a goddam khaki shirt. You remember that, Middleton?"

Colonel Middleton said: "No sir, I had forgotten that."

The General shouted: "Well, I remember it. I've had enough of that goddam little upstart. You know what he's done now, Middleton?"

Colonel Middleton said with a tired voice: "No sir."

"Goddam him, he had the nerve to let the carts back in that town, what the hell was the name of that —"

Lieutenant Byrd said: "Adano, sir."

"Adano. Goddam upstart."

Colonel Middleton said: "Perhaps there was some reason why he had to —"

"Goddam you, Middleton, you're getting too goddam independent minded."

Colonel Middleton said: "Yes sir."

Lieutenant Byrd said: "It goes on to say here, sir: 'carts were essential to town and town was in bad shape without same.'"

The General stood up: "Goddamit," he said. "I've had enough of that little wop. Middleton."

"Yes sir," the tired voice said.

"Make out an order recalling that Italian wop from that town, goddamit, what's the name —"

Lieutenant Byrd said: "Adano, sir."

"Order him to report back to Algiers for reassignment. Make out a separate report to Algiers explaining why. I'll fix that little bastard. Get it off today, too, goddamit, none of your goddam delays, Middleton."

"Yes sir," the tired voice said.

Chapter 34

THE DAY before the party, the fisherman named Agnello and his men talked about it as they fished.

"Are you going, Merendino?" Agnello asked.

Merendino, who was not one to commit himself too far, said: "I have been invited."

Sconzo, the youngest of Adano's fishermen, said: "I am going. You'd better go, Merendino. I hear that we fishermen are lucky. Mostly the guests will be officials and big people, but because of Tomasino —"

Agnello said: "And perhaps because the daughters of Tomasino are not pock-faced."

Sconzo said: "Perhaps," and laughed.

The men hauled in their net. They spilled the shining,

flopping fish into the bins. They were good fish, mostly of the four- and five-lira grades.

Sconzo said: "It is a rare chance for us fishermen, Merendino. You'd better go."

Merendino said: "I will think about it."

They let the net over the side again, and Merendino took the wheel as the boat moved away from the net. As they slowly pulled away, Sconzo lay down at the very bow, with his cheek on the hawser eye, and he watched the forefoot cutting the water and the reflection of the upper parts of the bow moving across the glassy water. It was one of those rare Mediterranean days with not a breath of air on the deep blue water.

Sconzo watched the image of old Lojacono's painting of the Mister Major riding a porpoise. It skimmed along on the water and sometimes actually seemed to be a man riding a fish along the surface.

Sconzo said: "Do you think the Mister Major is in love with the blonde one? I heard he had his arm around her when the prisoners came back without her Giorgio the other day."

Merendino said: "It is none of my business."

Agnello said: "I think he is."

Sconzo said: "We will see tomorrow night at the party."

Agnello said: "Merendino, don't you think perhaps we are getting too far inshore?"

Merendino said: "I will look at the chart."

Sconzo said: "He's just trying to get away from Tomasino's boat. Old Tomasino splashes his net so much that he scares the fish away. Tomasino has such a bad temper, he's probably angry with the fish and that's why he splashes the net. Merendino's just trying to work the boat away from Tomasino's, aren't you, Merendino?"

Merendino said: "I do not think Tomasino is angry at the fish."

Agnello said: "We'd better not get in too far. We were warned about what would happen if we went out of the zone which they marked for us on the chart."

Merendino looked at the chart and then at the headlands up and down the coast and he said: "Perhaps we are a little far inshore." And he put the wheel over and headed out, but diagonally away from Tomasino's boat.

Sconzo said: "Personally I like the younger daughter of Tomasino better than the blonde. I like honesty in the color of hair."

Agnello said: "Not that either of Tomasino's daughters would pay any attention to you, Sconzo."

Sconzo said: "Oh, I think I could make an impression if I wanted to."

Agnello mimicked Sconzo: "'If I wanted to.'" And then he said: "What makes you think you could? Your nose is too big."

Sconzo said: "What makes you think the daughters of Tomasino are so hard to impress? What do you think, Merendino?"

Merendino said: "I think that people with big noses who are fishermen are apt to retain a smell of fish in their nostrils after working hours, and sometimes they attribute the smell of fish to the young ladies they are with. I think it is time to pull the net in."

The three men stood and began to tug at the net.

"We have a good catch this time," Sconzo said. "Feel that load."

They pulled some more, then Agnello said: "It feels sluggish. It does not have the lively feeling of a good haul of small fish. Don't you agree, Merendino?"

Merendino said: "I never divide the fishes into grades until they are in the bins."

But as the net came in it became more and more obvious that the net had something besides little fish in it.

Sconzo said: "Maybe Lojacono's painting has at-

tracted a porpoise. Maybe Lojacono painted a she-por-
poise and maybe it is the mating season among porpoises."

Agnello said: "It doesn't feel right. It feels like the
time we pulled in the hogshead of nafta."

Merendino made a positive statement: "It feels like
something we do not usually catch."

The boat had come around as the men hauled at the
net. They were pulling the dripping net in over the star-
board bow by this time.

When the net was almost in, Sconzo said: "Wait a
second, let me look and perhaps I can see what we have
before we haul it aboard."

He lay down at the bow again, and put his cheek on
the hawser eye again, and looked. What he saw was the
last he ever saw.

He saw the smooth blue water. He saw the reflection
of the Mister Major riding the porpoise. He saw the little
ripples at the forefoot. He saw the net, dripping above
the water and bent by refraction under it. He saw a large
number of fish, bewildered that their school had become
so tangled and confined, trying to twist away. And then,
cradled at the extremity of the net, he saw a round metal
thing with spikes on it.

"Stop!" he shouted. "Stop hauling!"

But it was too late. The slow forward motion of the
boat and the slow reactions of the heaving fishermen
drove the bow onto the mine.

The explosion could be heard easily in the town. The
wives of farmers and land laborers thought it was just
some blasting by engineers. But the wives of fishermen
ran down to the harbor and looked out over the water.

There they saw unusual activity among the fishing
boats. They were all clustered together, and there were
one, two — only five!

At the moment of the explosion, Tomasino turned toward the point where Agnello's boat had been. Fortunately Tomasino had his net in and could move fairly quickly.

When they reached the place they found only splinters of wood, many dead fish floating, dead Agnello floating, dead Merendino, and some pieces of Sconzo.

Tomasino and his men hauled the two whole bodies aboard as the other fishing boats came up.

Tomasino shouted to the others: "Continue to fish. Move farther offshore. I will take Agnello and Merendino in."

Someone from another boat shouted: "And Sconzo?"

"Sconzo," said Tomasino, not looking at the small pieces of Sconzo floating in the water, "is missing."

Tomasino was careful to take bearings on the headlands with his compass before he started in.

One of his men said, "It is too bad about Sconzo. He wanted very much to go to the party tomorrow night. He has talked of nothing else for three days."

Another of Tomasino's helpers said: "Sconzo liked parties. Except for his nose he was handsome."

Agnello and Merendino were just as dead as Sconzo, but their deaths seemed less terrible since they were not missing, as Tomasino put it. That is why the men talked about Sconzo as they went in, and not about the other two.

As soon as they tied up, Tomasino jumped ashore and walked quickly uptown to the Palazzo. He was the first to bring the news to the Major.

"Good afternoon, Tomasino," the Major said cheerfully. "I'm looking forward to the party tomorrow night. I hear you are one of the hosts."

Tomasino's face was black with misery, but the Major had not thought that unusual.

"I cannot go," Tomasino said.

"Why not, Tomasino? It wouldn't be the same without you."

Tomasino said grimly: "I came to talk about the explosion. Did you hear the explosion?"

Major Joppolo said: "I did hear an explosion. About half an hour ago, was it?"

Tomasino said: "About half an hour ago."

"What was it?"

"One of my ships. A mine, I suppose, just as you warned."

The Major stood up. His face had gone white as soon as Tomasino started talking about the explosion. He went around his desk to Tomasino and put a hand on his arm.

"It is my fault, Tomasino, not yours," he said.

"It was Agnello's fault," Tomasino said. "He was too far in. I took bearings, and I know that he was outside the fishing zone."

"I am sorry," the Major said.

Tomasino said: "Why are you sorry? I thought you would be angry."

"I feel as if I had killed your men, Tomasino."

"Accidents happened here before you came, Mister Major. Men have died here before."

And so it happened that before he left, Tomasino was consoling the Major instead of being berated by him for allowing carelessness in the fishing fleet.

As Tomasino started to go, the Major said: "You will continue to fish?"

Tomasino said: "Of course. Four of the boats are still out."

The Major said: "Good, Tomasino." Then he said: "I'm sorry about tomorrow night."

Tomasino said: "I am sorry too. But it would not be decent. I am supposed to be the head of the fishermen."

Major Joppolo hesitated. Then he said, trying to sound delicate about it: "Do you feel that your family should stay away as well?"

Tomasino looked at Major Joppolo's face. Tomasino looked no less sad as he said: "No, I think Tina should go."

Chapter 35

AT a little before seven that evening, Major Joppolo, who was still working so as to be ahead for the next day, heard a commotion outside the door of his office. He heard a woman crying and shouting, and Zito the usher arguing with her, evidently trying to keep her out.

The Major went to the door, opened it, and told the woman to come in. She had a child in her arms.

As he went back to his desk the Major thought, without giving the thought much importance, that the child was quite a big one to be carried. The sound of the woman's wails followed him to his desk. She held the child across her body, with its head turned toward her breast.

When the Major was seated, the woman burst into a swift hysterical flood: "He almost died of the malaria, but God saved him, oh heart of Jesus, when he had the pox Father Pensovecchio prayed over him and he was spared, oh Lord Jesus he had such beautiful little eyes the eyes of his father, oh my child, my child, I have brought him through so much and I love him so much, what shall I do?"

The woman gently laid the child down on the Major's broad desk, and the Major saw that the child was dead.

She babbled on with her hysterical, lonely talk. Major

Joppolo called Zito and asked him to get Gargano.

While he was waiting for Gargano, the Major tried to get the woman to tell him what had happened, but all he could get out of her, besides sobs, was more of her heartbroken babbling. Once or twice she did mention the word "truck."

When Gargano came in, the Major asked him what had happened. Gargano did not know and went out to find out. He came back soon holding another child by the hand.

From Gargano and the boy he brought in, Major Joppolo learned that the child had been struck and killed by an American military truck, which had driven on without stopping.

The boy had been shouting for caramels along with all the other children. He and two or three others had noticed that the ones who always got the candies, when the American soldiers threw them, were the ones who were out in front. The ones who noticed this were a little bigger than the others, so they banded together into a team: one scrambled for the candies while the others joined hands and held the other children back. The others saw they were being cheated by the superior wits and strength of the team, so they in turn banded together to break through the cordon. The very first time they tried to break through, with a squealing rush, they succeeded. Their momentum threw two children against this boy, who was out in front picking up the candies, and the blow threw him in front of the next truck. The bumper of the truck hit him in the forehead.

Major Joppolo did what he could to comfort the mother. He told her that she would be paid some money and that the town would try to look out for her. He sent for Signora Carmelina Spinnato, the big health officer, and asked her to take care of the woman, and to see that the child got a decent burial.

Then he turned to the woman and said: "I hope you will not hate the Americans because of this thing. Please try to remember in your grief that the reason the children were out there, running into danger, was that the Americans have been generous with them, too generous. If the Americans did not throw candies to them, they would not keep on running beside the trucks and begging. Sometimes generosity is a fault with Americans, sometimes it does harm. It has brought high prices here, and it has brought you misery. But it is the best thing we Americans can bring with us to Europe. So please do not hate the Americans."

The woman just sobbed. Signora Carmelina Spinnato took her out.

"Gargano," the Major said, "I've been afraid this would happen. It will make the children unhappy, but we are going to have to stop them from running after the candies."

"What can we do?" Gargano said, raising his hands, palms up.

The Major said: "Tomorrow evening I want you to go out with Rotondo and two or three others with your truck, and I want you to round up all the children who are on the street shouting for caramels. Take them to the police station and keep them there till it is dark. Then call their mothers in and let them take them home. It's the only thing we can do — teach them a lesson."

Gargano's face fell. "But Mister Major," he said, placing his hands together in the attitude of prayer, "tomorrow night is the party. I would be bitter if I had to miss the party."

The Major said: "Gargano, the children of Adano are much more important than any party."

Gargano raised his hands in resignation. "Yes, Mister Major," he said.

Chapter 36

THE DAY of the party came, and many things happened.

At about 9:30 in the morning, a U.S. Navy truck pulled up in front of the Palazzo. A Chief Petty Officer and five men unloaded a crate from it onto the sidewalk, and the Chief went inside and delivered a note for Major Victor Joppolo.

Major Joppolo was busy at his desk, and had not noticed the truck. He opened the note and read:

"Dear Major:

"The U.S. Navy is delighted to be able to do the U.S. Army a favor. Here is your bell. . . ."

The Major jumped up and shouted: "Where is it?"

Zito the usher said: "Where is what, Mister Major?"

The Major said: "The bell! The bell! They have brought us our bell." And he ran out on the balcony just in time to see the Navy truck pull away. He saw the crate sitting there on the sidewalk.

Major Joppolo shouted down to an M.P. in front of the Palazzo. "Hey, stand guard over that box, don't let anybody walk off with that."

The M.P. grumbled out loud, but not loud enough for Major Joppolo to hear: "From the way them sailors was gruntin' and groanin', don't strike me that nobody's goin' to strut off with that thing."

The Major hurried back inside, and he said to Zito: "How long did you say it took them to take the old bell down, Zito?"

Zito said: "They had to use six sets of block and tackle. It took them two days to get it down. Then one day to crate it."

The Major said: "I can't wait that long."

He went to the phone and called up the Engineers.

"Major Harvey, please. . . . Major? This is Joppolo. Say, I wonder if you could arrange to do this town a big favor. We've got a delicate job to do, and I'm afraid the workmen we could round up to do it would take ages and maybe hack it. The job is raising a new bell on the clock tower of the Town Hall here. I guess it would take about eight men, and if you've got a good strong block and tackle, and maybe a tow truck to haul out the tackle and raise the bell. . . . You can? That's swell. Can they start right in? What time you think they could get here? Okay, I'll be on hand at eleven thirty to tell them what to do. Don't know how to thank you, Major."

Major Joppolo was excited. He called up Lieutenant Livingston and thanked him for his part in getting the bell. "Why hell," he said, "it ought to be up this afternoon. Maybe we can ring it for the party tonight. You're coming, aren't you?"

"Wouldn't miss it, Major."

"Well, see you there, Captain. Thanks a hell of a lot."

"Don't mention it. Say, there's just one thing, Major."

"What's that?"

"I'm a Lieutenant. It takes a long time to get to be a Captain in the Navy."

"Is that a fact?" the Major said. "Well, you ought to be a Captain soon," and he hung up.

He picked up the note and finished it:

"Thought you might be interested to know a little more about Corelli and the background of the bell. Toot Dowling, who, by the way, was very generous to give up his bell — I don't think it would hurt to write him a letter about it (U.S.S. Corelli, care Postmaster, New York) — Toot told me a little about Corelli. He said his full name was Vincent Corelli and he had a destroyer in

*the last war. I had it a bit wrong the other day. What
happened was that Corelli was on escort duty in the
North Atlantic, and this Italian freighter got in a hell of
a storm and broke down. Corelli left his station with a
convoy and he went and took off all the Italians with
breeches buoy although I don't know how much you
know about navigation, it was very dangerous to close
with the freighter in that kind of a storm. That was on
November 12, 1917, Toot says. Of course Toot is an old
classmate of mine and a lousy football player and I
never know what to believe when he says it. But I think
this dope is correct and hope you enjoy the noise it
makes.*

*"If you ever get in any trouble, just come around to
the Navy, and I'm sure they'll be able to fix you up.*

"Yours for collaboration between the services,

"Rock Robertson (Lt. Comdr., usn)."

Zito moved near to the desk while the Major read, and
when he was finished, the usher said: "We have a new
bell, Mister Major?"

"We have a new bell, Zito."

"Is the tone good enough?"

"I hope so, Zito. I think so."

"Is there some history to it?"

"Yes, Zito, I'll tell you about it when the bell is up.
Do you think I ought to make a little speech explaining
the bell to the people here?"

"Oh yes, you should, Mister Major. The people of
Adano will be curious about the bell."

"Zito, do you think they will understand all that the
bell means? I mean that it stands for the things that
I believe in? Do you think I could explain that to
them?"

"I think so, Mister Major. I understand what you
mean, and Zito is not very clever."

A few minutes before eleven o'clock the funeral procession of the three fishermen who had been killed in
the explosion went through the Piazza. Major Joppolo
went out onto the balcony to watch it. At the head of the
procession there were three carts. The first two carried
the bodies of Agnello and Merendino. Their coffins were
small dinghies such as the fishermen used to get out to
their boats, with the tops planked over. The third cart,
which was for Sconzo, carried a dinghy which was not
planked over, but was filled with flowers.

Long before eleven thirty, Major Joppolo was out on
the sidewalk beside the crated bell, waiting for the Engineers to come. He poked and shoved at the crate af-
fectionately, as if there were something delicious to eat
inside it.

The gang from the Engineer battalion was surprisingly on time. The Major explained the job, pointing to
the top of the clock tower.

"How long do you think it will take?" he asked the old
buck sergeant in charge.

"Well," the sergeant said, "some days the boys gets
cramps in their stomachs and they claim they shouldn't
ought to hurry when they has the cramps. Other days
they don't get no cramps. It all depends."

"How long do you guess?"

"We'll have it for you today or tomorrow. It all depends."

"Try to finish today, will you?"

"It all depends," the sergeant said, and he turned furi-
ously on his men, who slowly gathered themselves for
work.

Major Joppolo went to lunch at noon. Sergeant Borth
was already in the Albergo dei Pescatori when the Major arrived. The Major sat down with Borth, as he often
did, in spite of his rank.

He told Borth about the bell, and his excitement about it gave Borth something to tease.

"You're worse than the first day we came here," the Sergeant said.

"How am I worse?" the Major said.

"You're so damn sentimental."

"Oh, cut it out, Borth."

Borth's teasing cut a little deep. "No, I'm serious," he said. "There's a war going on. Fishermen get blown up in the harbor here. Children get run over in the streets. There's one case of malaria in every six people. And you can't think about anything but tinkling a bell."

Major Joppolo said: "I'm worried about those fishermen, Borth. I could get in trouble over that. Do you think I was guilty of carelessness about it? You know I forced the Navy to let them go out."

Purely by way of teasing, Borth said something he had cause to regret later: "Sure," he said, "you could catch hell for that. You could get sent back to the States."

And Major Joppolo said: "They wouldn't do that, they couldn't."

Borth said: "Why the hell couldn't they? I heard about a fellow in airborne who got sent home just for getting drunk."

Major Joppolo said: "They couldn't, Borth, there's so much to do here. Think if they got somebody bad in this town. Think if they got a dope like that fellow up at Pontebasso."

Borth said: "You don't like yourself much, do you?"

Major Joppolo said: "Oh lay off, Borth, sometimes you aren't funny."

At 12:25 Zito came running down to the Albergo dei Pescatori to tell the Major that the bell was uncrated. "It looks nice," he said.

The Major tried to get Borth to go up with him to look

at the bell, but Borth said: "This eggplant is so good, I don't see how I could leave it."

So the Major went up with Zito. On the way the usher said: "Before I forget it, Mister Major, the officials are very anxious to meet with you at four o'clock. They said it was important."

A moment of worry showed itself on the Major's face. "Is it about the fishermen, Zito?"

Zito said: "I am the usher, Mister Major, the officials do not tell me what is on their minds." Then Zito seemed to think better of what he had said, and he added: "No, it is not about the fishermen."

The Major said: "Oh, so the usher has ways of finding out what is on the officials' minds?"

Zito just smiled.

There were quite a few people standing around watching the Engineers working on the bell. One of them was the ancient Cacopardo. Because he had spoken to the Major about the bell on the very first day of the invasion, he had appointed himself a kind of supervisor of the work, although none of the Engineers could speak Italian.

As soon as the Major came up, Cacopardo said: "I have sent for Guzzo, the bell-ringer at the Church of San Angelo. He will be able to tell just by looking at it whether it is a good bell. If it is not, you will of course have to send it back."

The bell stood on the sidewalk just where the Navy men had put it down. The crate had been peeled down from around it.

It was bronze, and the men of the *Corelli* had taken the trouble to polish it, so that it was like gold in the midday sun. On one side there was this inscription:

U.S.S. CORELLI
America ed Italia.

When Cacopardo saw the Major reading the inscription, he asked: "Who is this man *Corelli,* and how does he happen to get his name on the bell of Adano?"

The Major said: "I will tell you later, when the bell is hung." Then he got a little stone out of the street and tapped it against the side, but of course there was only a dead sound, since the bell was sitting on wood. "I wonder how the tone is," the Major said.

"Guzzo will know," Cacopardo said.

In time the bell-ringer came. He was almost as old as Cacopardo. His hands and forearms looked very strong, but the rest of him looked as if it were long overdue.

Cacopardo called him to the center of the crowd and told him to examine the bell. The old bell-ringer walked round and round the bell, looking at it. Then he leaned over and ran the flat of his hand from top to bottom. Then he stood up and seemed to read the inscription over and over. He looked once up at the top of the clock tower, where some engineers were rigging a hoist. He asked that the bell be turned over and when some of the engineers had turned it up on its side, he looked inside.

He stood up finally and shrugged his shoulders and said: "It is all right."

Cacopardo was delighted. He said to the Major: "I know old Guzzo. He does not exaggerate. When he says something is fair, he means it is perfect. The bell will be very good."

"I'm glad," the Major said.

At a few minutes past one o'clock, Major Joppolo went home to his villa to take a nap. He wanted to save up some strength for the party — but he also wanted to think a little about his speech about the bell.

He lay down on his bed. At first his thoughts were confused, because he was excited. But gradually the thoughts began to sort themselves out, and everything came very straight to Major Joppolo.

He would say a few words, he thought, about the removal of the old bell. Then he would tell about how the people of Adano had interested him in trying to get a new one. Then a few words about Corelli, and what he had done for Italians in the last war, and then the meaning today of the inscription on the bell, *America ed Italia*, America and Italy, and then perhaps something about the Americans' Liberty Bell. After talking about it that day, the Major had been curious about the Liberty Bell, and he had written a letter back to Amgot headquarters inquiring about it, and now he would be able to explain the crack, and he would tell the people of Adano the inscription on that bell, the words from Leviticus: "Proclaim liberty throughout the land and to all the inhabitants thereof."

And then everything was wonderfully clear in the mind of Victor Joppolo. He knew exactly what he would say. Words came to him which were beautiful and were the truth about the new bell and its meaning for Adano, and about what he, Victor Joppolo, wanted for the people of Adano. The words were as clear as anything can be, and as true.

At about two o'clock the courier came by motorcycle from Vicinamare. From his office Sergeant Borth saw him throw the pouch onto the sidewalk in front of the Palazzo. Mail, even official mail, was enough of an event so that Sergeant Borth got up and went across to the Palazzo and up to Major Joppolo's office to see what there was.

There was nothing for Sergeant Borth, but as long as Major Joppolo was out, Sergeant Borth decided to riffle through what there was.

A BELL FOR ADANO

In time he came on a paper addressed to Major Joppolo. He read it:

"1. *You are authorized to proceed by first available transportation to A.F.H.Q., Algiers, via port of Vicinamare.*

"2. *Reassignment of station will be made by A.F.H.Q.*

"3. *Reason for this order is that reference (1) did wilfully and without consultation countermand orders issued by General Marvin, 49th Division, re entry of mule carts into town of Adano.*"

And the order was signed by General Marvin.

Sergeant Borth folded the order, put it in his pocket, and left the building. He went directly to the M.P. command post in the Fascio.

He said to Captain Purvis: "The Major's been relieved."

Captain Purvis said: "What the hell do you mean?"

"Just what I said: he's been ordered back to Algiers for reassignment."

"What the hell for?"

"Insubordination. Countermanding an order by Marvin about mule carts. I guess it was after that affair of the mule the General shot outside town."

Captain Purvis had forgotten all about the report he had sent to Division. Now that he remembered he didn't have the courage to say anything about it. All he said was: "What a hell of a note."

Borth said: "I'll say it's a hell of a note. The Major's just begun to accomplish things in this town."

Captain Purvis said: "Yeah, I guess he has." A suspicion crossed his mind: this fellow Borth had a way of knowing too much. "How did you know he was ordered out?"

Borth said: "I saw the order up in the Major's office."

254

"Does the Major know about it, then?"

"No, the Major's out. I have the order in my pocket. I took it. I'm not going to tell him about it until after the party tonight."

The Major got back to his office at about a quarter to four. He went through the courier mail and worked for a few minutes on a report to Colonel Sartorius. Promptly at four Zito came in and said: "Will you see the officials now?"

"Yes, Zito."

Now when the officials came in — old Bellanca first as usual, then the others, Gargano, Saitta, D'Arpa, Rotondo, Signora Carmelina Spinnato, and Tagliavia — Major Joppolo could see by their cheerful expressions that there was to be no unpleasantness in this interview.

Old Bellanca spoke: "We have something we wish to give the Mister Major."

D'Arpa could not resist saying in his high voice: "We wish to give the Mister Major a Mister Major." The others snickered.

Bellanca said: "Please get it, Zito." Zito went out.

First the usher came back carrying an easel. He went out again. Then he brought in Lojacono's portrait of the Major.

It was really good. When the Major saw it, he stood up in delight. He said: "So that is why you wanted my picture taken!"

Gargano posed as if with one hand on a camera and the other squeezing a shutter bulb and tried to imitate the cracked voice of old Spataforo: "Young man, you are vain. All you want is to look at your face."

This time when all laughed, the Major laughed with them.

Old Bellanca cleared his throat. The group were silent, as if they had been called to order. The Mayor said: "I was for so many years just a Notary here in Adano, I never made speeches, I do not intend to begin now. But these others have asked me merely to tell you, Mister Major, that this picture may not be the best picture that was ever painted, although it is very good for Lojacono, but even if it were very bad, we would still give it to you, because we wished to show you that — "

Old Bellanca was very embarrassed. He cleared his throat again and said: "What these others asked me to tell you was that this portrait — "

The old Mayor looked at the others in despair. Gargano stepped forward and said: "What the Mister Mayor wishes to say is that the eyes" — Gargano made those circles with his thumbs and forefingers and put them up to his own eyes — "the eyes of the portrait are honest."

D'Arpa said, pointing at the picture: "In the chin there is strength."

Gargano grabbed one of his own ears with one hand and pointed at an ear in the picture with the other: "In the ears there is alertness."

Saitta the street-cleaner said approvingly: "In the fix of the hair there is neatness."

And finally old Bellanca remembered enough of his coaching to say. "In the cheeks there is a sympathetic warmth."

Then Gargano said, and this time his hands stayed still by his sides, in proof of his absolute sincerity: "And you can see in the picture that that man wishes that each person in the town of Adano should be happy. That is a very big thing in a face."

Old Bellanca said: "Lojacono has painted a good picture. We wanted you to have it."

"Thank you," Major Joppolo said. That was all he had time to say, for the officials of Adano left the room quickly. In any case, it was all the Major was able to say.

A little before five the sergeant in charge of the Engineers working on the bell came in and said: "We run into a snag, sir."

"What's that?"

"The rod the bell's supposed to hang by, it's too big for this here bell, we got to get another."

"Will you be able to find another?"

"Sure. But it's going to slow us up some."

"How much?"

"It's all according to how long it takes us to find this new rod. I don't know how much work we got to do to put it up when we find it. It all depends."

"Can you finish this afternoon, do you think?"

"Not hardly, sir. But we can have it for you easy by morning."

A little after seven o'clock, Gargano went out to round up the children who were shouting for caramels.

He took Rotondo and two other carabinieri and the police truck. They drove down the Via Umberto the First, and there they found the children out in force, shouting: *"Caramelle! Caramelle!"* at every vehicle that passed.

Even when the police truck passed, going down the street to turn around at the Via Favemi, the children shouted: *"Caramelle! Caramelle!"*

Their shouting at the police truck gave Gargano an idea.

When the truck had turned around and came up the street on the side where the children were and stopped there, Gargano told the others to open the back and let down the little ladder there. And he stood up near the back of the truck and shouted: "Come little children and get your caramels!"

At first the children were frightened by the police truck and drew back. But Gargano beckoned with both hands and shouted: "Come, children, we will have a regular picnic of caramels. First come, first served. Come with Gargano for the feast of caramels!"

The children wavered. They looked at each other and wondered.

Gargano made motions of putting things in his mouth. "Huge piles of caramels! Come little children to the picnic. No shouting. No scrambling. Just eating! Come with Gargano."

It was the son of an official, the clean little Saitta boy, who allowed himself to be persuaded first. He said to the children nearest him: "I am going. Gargano is a friend of my father. He will give us caramels without any work." And he ran toward the police truck.

"Good little boy!" Gargano shouted. "Neat little boy! Clever little boy! You will have the most caramels because you were first."

Now there began a general rush for the truck. As the children fought for positions at the ladder, they squealed: *Caramelle! Caramelle!*

Then one of the children shouted: "Think of our friends who are not here tonight, they would hate to miss this."

Another said: "We are selfish not to call them."

One said: "Antonino the son of Ugo is not here. I'll get him," and the child ran off.

Another said: "Wait for me. I'm going to get Romano."

Another said: "Where is the red-head Occhipinti? Wait while I get him."

Little Erba, who was just as stupid as his father, said: "Someone is not here who ought to be. Who is it? Who is it?"

As the children ran off for their friends, Gargano said: "Hurry! Hurry! We haven't much time. There is a party for grownups as well as for children tonight. Gargano hasn't much time for the caramels. Hurry!"

Little Erba said: "Who is the one I am thinking of? Who is the one who wears a blue suit?"

The ones who had run off began to trickle back with their friends. All the children in the truck still squealed: *"Caramelle! Caramelle!"*

But little Erba kept muttering about the one who was left behind. Just as the last of the ones who had run off came back, he shouted: "Cac, Cac, it is something, it is Cacopardo!" He hurried down the ladder and said: "Wait for me! The Cacopardo who wears blue! He holds my hand! I must get him. Wait!" And little Erba ran off.

Gargano got impatient. It was already seven twenty, and the party was scheduled to begin at seven thirty, and already couples were walking down the street toward Quattrocchi's house.

Little Erba ran two blocks and then realized that he had no idea where Cacopardo lived. He shouted the name, but no one answered. He looked for someone to ask, but there was no one in sight. So he started home to ask his father.

Gargano could wait no longer. He ordered the truck to go.

Now the children were shouting in unison: *"Caramelle! Caramelle!"*

The truck drove off toward the police station, where there was not a single piece of candy.

The committee of hosts stood waiting in the entrance hall of Quattrocchi's house. Old Bellanca was there, ex officio, and Cacopardo, the only resident of Adano who owned a swallow-tail coat and the only one who would wear one if he had it, and the fat Craxi, who appeared to have exceeded his limit of three bottles of wine for dinner, and Signora Carmelina Spinnato, representing as well as she could the fair sex, and the white-haired Lojacono, who was included because he had done such a good picture. The ones of the committee who were absent were Tomasino, out of respect for the dead fishermen, and Gargano, who was otherwise engaged.

It was ten minutes after starting time, and the guest of honor had not arrived. Giuseppe, who had arranged the whole thing, hovered in the background, saying over and over: "The Mister Major will be here any minute now."

The Mister Major was at that minute calling for Tina, and Tina, in the way of all women, either was not ready or was not willing to admit that she was ready.

Finally, at a quarter to eight, Tina came out of her room. She was dressed in a flimsy white blouse and a huge red taffeta skirt.

Major Joppolo's slight annoyance at being kept waiting dissolved at once. "This was worth waiting all night for," he said.

Tina curtsied gravely. She gathered some of her skirt on her left arm and reached with her right hand for Major Joppolo's arm. He offered it to her and the couple left, shouting good-byes to Tomasino and Rosa, who was beady with perspiration from helping her daughters get ready.

On their way down the Via Umberto the First the couple heard two small children crying. In the darkening evening they could just make out two little figures huddled on the curb on the other side of the street. They crossed.

They found the ragged little son of Erba and the well-dressed grandson of Cacopardo sitting with their arms around each other crying hard.

Major Joppolo crouched down and patted the boys'
backs and asked what the matter was.

Between sobs, little Erba managed to say: "We were
too late — for the feast — of the caramels."

Little Cacopardo said: "Too late."

"For the what?"

Little Erba said: "For the picnic of caramels. We —
we — are the only ones — who were left behind."

Little Cacopardo said: "All the other children."

Major Joppolo remembered what he had told Gargano to do, and he said: "Well, never mind, we'll take
you instead to a grownup party. Come with us."

So the Major and Tina walked on toward Quattrocchi's house, each holding a little child by the hand.

When they entered the house, the fat Craxi, who had
a little too much wine in his belly, rushed forward in
amazement. "Son of Mary!" he exclaimed. "He has a
family! Two fine little boys" — he patted the youngsters
on the head — "and a beautiful — "

He gulped when he saw that the "wife" was Tina.

"Mister Major," he said, "why did you not tell us?"

But by this time the rest of the committee had come
forward, and the confusion of their greetings over-
whelmed Craxi's confusion. Old Cacopardo took both
his well-dressed little grandson and the ragged little
Erba by their hands, and kept them with him all evening.

The party started out to be a success from everyone's
point of view. The people of the town were immensely
happy: they had not had such a time for years. Giuseppe, the organizer, basked in constant congratulations.
There was enough champagne to suit Captain Purvis
and too much to permit him to molest any pretty girls.
Craxi perpetuated his happy glow. The lazy Fatta had
three drinks and then went into an empty room and fell
asleep. Afronti Pietro, the loud-voiced cartman, was en-

couraged to shout a song for the entertainment of the guests. The maidenly Laura Sofia got Captain Purvis aside after he was fairly far along and smothered him with kisses. Nicolo and his sweetheart danced together. Sergeant Borth, who seemed to be in a terrible mood at the beginning of the party, did not move from the wine bowl, and gradually he mellowed and attached himself to the glowing Craxi.

And Major Joppolo and Tina managed quite early in the evening to slip out onto a balcony.

Tina said: "Are you happy?"

Major Joppolo said: "You asked me that the last time we were on a balcony together."

Tina said: "I was just making conversation then."

"What are you doing now?"

"I'm asking you: are you happy?" The light place in the night that was Tina's face turned up toward the Major's.

"Of all the happy days I've had in Adano," the Major said, "this has been — and still is — the nicest."

"Then tell me what you promised the other day you would tell me."

"Tell me first: have you decided what you felt about Giorgio?"

Tina said: "No." Major Joppolo thought he detected a coquettish note in the way she said it, but then she added: "I'll never know now."

He said: "Why not?"

She drew away a little and said in a very small voice: "Because I know how I feel about you."

He went to her and without touching her said: "That was all I wanted to tell you, Tina. I know how I feel, too. I am very fond of you. I am only really happy when I am near you."

He wanted to kiss her, but she said: "What's that?"

He said: "What's what?"

She said: "That noise, can't you hear it?"

There was a murmur on the air. It had been there for some time, but the murmur of the party inside had swallowed it. Now the murmur outside seemed to be growing.

"What do you suppose it is?" he said.

"I've never heard anything like it," she said.

He pointed off to the left and said: "It's over there. What's over in that direction?"

"Well," she said, "there's the Church of the Orphanage, and the house of Cacopardo, and Zapulla's bakery, and the police station —"

"The police station!" Major Joppolo took Tina's hand, and said: "Come with me."

They walked to the police station, and all the way the murmur seemed to grow on the night air. By the time they got close, it had clarified into the wailing and shrieking of many children.

When the Major and Tina went in, they saw all the children weeping and shouting angrily at Gargano. He stood on the stairs to the second floor. His face was covered with sweat. He was trying, with gestures and at the top of his voice, to explain to them why there were no caramels in the police station. But the terrible guilt of his lies would not be forgiven by the children.

Major Joppolo pushed his way through the crowd of children and went up three or four stairs. When the children saw the Mister Major, they started stamping and shouting in unison: *"Caramelle! Caramelle!"*

The Major held his hand up. Gradually the noise subsided. He waited until there was silence, all except for the catching of breath that children do when they have been crying.

And now the Major made the last public speech he would ever make in Adano. He didn't know that it would be his last, but he made it simple and right, and if he had planned a farewell speech, he couldn't have done better.

"Children of Adano," he said, "I am sorry to have to tell you that there are no caramels here." There was a brief wail of protest.

"I'm afraid that you have been misled. But I'm sure that Gargano didn't mean any harm when he told you that there would be caramels here. He told you that so as to be sure that you would come, because he had something very important to tell you.

"Gargano, may I tell them?" Gargano nodded.

"Children, you know the little Calvi boy who was hit by the truck last night? Do you know why he was hit? Pasquale son of Gigante do you know why he was hit?"

Pasquale son of Gigante was one of the larger boys who had teamed up to outwit the others. He shook his head.

"Massimo son of Zupi, do you know why?"

This boy, another of the team, also shook his head.

"I know," a small voice said, and a small hand went up.

"Why, Marco?"

Marco son of Manifattura, one of the smaller ones who had been cheated, said: "Because he was selfish."

"Marco is right. Marco says that the Calvi boy was killed because he was selfish. Marco, you are exactly right. That is what Gargano wanted to tell you, isn't it, Gargano?"

That was not just what Gargano had in mind, but he nodded absently.

"The Calvi boy would never have been killed if he and Pasquale and Massimo and the other big ones had not been selfish. If they had not tried to get everything for themselves, no one would have been hurt, and all would have had some candies.

"Now we don't want any more children killed in this

town. You don't want any more of your friends to be killed, I'm sure. So from now on this is how we will handle the candies. I am going to appoint a committee, and the committee will take down the names of all the children who want caramels, and they will appoint two children to collect the candies carefully each evening as the trucks go through town. The American soldiers will go on throwing candies, of that I'm certain. The two collectors will put the candy in a box, and the committee will give out the candies in order, according to the names on the list. That means that everyone will have some, and no one will be hurt.

"For the committee I want Marco and Pasquale —"

A voice shouted: "Pasquale will be selfish, he will put some of the candies in his pocket instead of in the box."

The Major said: "I don't think he will. Pasquale and Massimo and Eliodoro and Elisabetta."

And then the Major added: "I want you to be happy together. I want all of you to have as much as you can of what you want, without hurting anyone else. That is what I want in Adano."

The Major left and Gargano took the children home.

On the way back to the party, Tina said: "Now I know why I love you."

Major Joppolo said: "Why?"

"Because of what you want for Adano. That's why everyone here loves you. There is no one here who will say a bad word about you, and that's a rare thing in Adano."

The Major said: "And I know why I like you."

"Why?"

"For a very selfish reason: because you make me feel as if I were almost important."

"Oh, you are," Tina said, with just enough mockery in her voice.

When the Major and Tina got back to the party. Giuseppe met them, wringing his hands and making desperate faces. "Mister Major, where have you been? I have been looking for you on all the balconies and in all the bedrooms."

"That was hardly necessary, Giuseppe," the Major said. "What did you want?"

"Fat Craxi and your Sergeant, they are misbehaving. I can't do anything with them."

The Major said to Tina: "Wait here," and he went off with Giuseppe to find Craxi and Borth.

They were in the library. If there had been other guests in the room, they had left. Craxi and Borth were alone, and quite drunk.

When the fat Craxi saw the Major, he said to Borth: "Shall we relieve nature on the leg of the Mister Major?"

Borth said: "Have you any left?"

Craxi said boastfully, beating himself on the chest: "If I wanted, I could relieve myself for two hours, and then I would still be able to pass wind for fifteen minutes. Shall we do it on the leg of the Mister Major?"

Borth said: "No, only on the enemies of Adano. He is a friend." Suddenly Borth began to cry.

Major Joppolo said sharply: "Borth, behave yourself."

When the Major spoke so angrily, fat Craxi tiptoed out of the room, and Giuseppe followed him to keep an eye on him.

The Major and Borth were alone. The Major spoke again: "Behave yourself or go home."

Borth was drunk because of the Major. He had never been drunk in uniform before. But when the Major spoke so angrily, that streak of contrariness in Borth which made him tease people so much, which made him always laugh at serious people and deflate pompous ones, came out in him. He said thickly: "You can't boss me around."

"Sergeant Borth," the Major said, with obvious emphasis on the word Sergeant.

"Don't Sergeant me," Borth said; "you have no 'thority to boss me."

"I have just as much authority as I ever had, and if you don't behave — "

"Oh no you haven't," Borth said. "You can't boss *anybody*, not in Adano."

"Borth, you're drunk. Now behave."

"Joppolo, you're fired. You been relieved. You're nobody round here." And Borth began to cry again.

"Borth, I don't know what you're talking about, but I — "

The Major broke off and went over to Borth and took him by the arm, to try to lead him out.

"Take your hands off me," Borth said. He reached in his pocket and said: "Here, read that."

Major Joppolo read the order recalling him from Adano.

"Where did you get this?" he asked.

Borth was crying again. "Your desk. I wanted to keep you from seeing it until after the party."

The Major walked out of the room.

Victor Joppolo put up a beautiful front for the rest of the evening, until the very moment when he was saying good night to Tina just inside her front door. Then he put his arms around her and said miserably: "I'm so unhappy."

Tina pushed back and looked at his face. She put her hands on his shoulders and said: "But I thought you were so happy?"

The Major was in control of himself again. "I am," he said, "I'm sorry."

"Is it because of your wife?" Tina asked.

"No, Tina, it's nothing." Then, in the shadow of the

stairway of her house, he kissed her tenderly and said: "Till I see you again."

She was frightened and she said: "What is the matter? Why did you say good-bye instead of good night? What is the matter?"

"Nothing, Tina. Good night, Tina."

Chapter 37

It was the middle of the morning before Major Joppolo could get his papers straightened up and his last-minute directions given. Sergeant Borth was the one who helped him get everything arranged. Captain Purvis did not have the courage to show himself all morning.

The Major called the motor pool and asked for a jeep to take him to Vicinamare.

Then he told Borth: "I don't want to say good-bye to anyone, Borth. I don't know whether I could."

Borth did not mock this morning. He said: "I am sorry about last night, Major. My intentions were good. I wanted you to have a good time at the party."

"I know."

The Major thought a minute and then said: "Borth, try to help whoever takes my place to try to do a good job in Adano."

Borth said: "I'm afraid it will be that awful dope from Pontebasso."

The Major said: "I hope not. Adano needs an understanding man."

Borth said. "Adano needs you, Major."

The Major said: "Too late to talk about that. I wonder how Marvin ever found out about the carts."

Borth suspected Captain Purvis, but he said: "One of his staff must have driven through or something."

The Major said: "Yes, I guess so."

The jeep came. So as not to arouse suspicion, Borth went with the driver to the Major's house and got his baggage. His entire possessions consisted of a bedroll, with his clothes rolled into it.

When the jeep got back to the Palazzo, Major Joppolo took his portrait under his arm and went downstairs and got in.

He shook Borth's hand but he did not say good-bye.

The lazy Fatta, standing on the sidewalk, said by way of making conversation: "Going somewhere?"

Major Joppolo tried to sound cheerful as he said: "Not far. How is Carmelina this morning?"

The lazy Fatta said: "She is making a rabbit stew."

The driver said: "Where to, Major?"

The Major did not want to say Vicinamare so that Fatta or anyone else could hear it. Perhaps he could not say it. Anyhow, he just said: "This way," and he pointed out the Corso Vittorio Emanuele.

About four miles outside the town the Major said to the driver: "Stop a minute, would you, please?"

The driver stopped the jeep.

"Listen," the Major said. "Do you hear something?"

It was a fine sound on the summer air. The tone was good and it must have been loud to hear it as far as this.

"Just a bell," the driver said. "Must be eleven o'clock."

"Yes," the Major said. He looked over the hills across the sea, and the day was as clear as the sound of the bell itself, but the Major could not see or think very clearly.

"Yes," he said, "eleven o'clock."